LOST THROUGH TIME

Jessica Tornese

Dedication
To Melanie, Mark, and Brett.
May our family stories live on through you.
I love you forever and always!

Advance review

"*Lost Through Time* is a science fiction time travel novel that you won't be able to put down. Tornese's cinema graphic descriptions and action scenes brings readers into the lives of early 20th Century Minnesota settlers during the time of the devastating 1910 Baudette Fire. Kate, a spoiled 21st Century teen takes over the body of her great Aunt Vickie. With the help of Viv, Vickie's identical twin sister, Kate quickly learns to attend to the needs of her six children and overworked husband. Kate also knows the family history. Sometime in October Vickie and her daughter, Mary, will die in the horrendous prairie fires that destroyed Baudette. Kate can only hope to change the course of history if she can only survive the daily trials of prairie life."
-Michael Thal, author of *The Legend of Koolura*

ALL RIGHTS RESERVED
No part of this book may be reproduced or transmitted in any form or by any means, electronic or mechanical, including photocopying, recording, or by any information storage and retrieval system, without permission in writing from the author, except in the case of brief quotations embodied in reviews.

Editor in Chief: Nik Morton

Cover Art:
Select-O-Grafix, LLC. www.selectografix.com

Publisher's Note:
This is a work of fiction. All names, characters, places, and events are the work of the author's imagination. Any resemblance to real persons, places, or events is coincidental.

Solstice Publishing - www.solsticepublishing.com

Copyright 2012 Jessica Tornese

Chapter 1
It's in the Genes

The first drops of rain on the tin roof above scarcely masked the pounding of my heart. How could Gran sit there across from me and mention time travel like we were talking about something as trivial as baking banana bread?

It had been a long, torturous climb back to reality in the past month since I had returned from the year 1960 with the knowledge my Aunt Sarah had been murdered. My body had healed but my mind was a fractured, tormented mess, resembling something of a windowpane after a brick has gone through its very center. And now, Gran sat across from me casually throwing out the fact that she, too, had gone back in time. Like it was normal.

What did it all mean? Did I have some sort of freaky genetic trait passed down in my DNA? Or was it something more sci-fi, like Gran had been bitten by a radioactive spider kind of thing? There was a fleeting moment where I had been afraid no one would believe my outlandish story, and now I had the sinking feeling I was going to be sorry that anyone found out at all. I had a million questions, but wasn't sure I wanted to hear the answers.

The third stair squeaked loudly, giving away Dad's presence in the stairwell. He had disappeared moments before to investigate a loud squeal and crash coming from the kitchen downstairs.

Sitting across from me, Gran's eyes widened and she touched the hourglass shaped birthmark by her eye with one hand and held a single finger to her lips to silence my already gaping mouth. So this was supposed to be some sort of secret now? A clandestine club that only she and I were privy to? But Dad knew my story. He even believed it. Maybe.

Gran sent me a look that spoke volumes. Her blue eyes, wise with age and crinkled in the corners with a cobweb of numerous lines, held a deep understanding beyond my simple tale. We weren't finished talking, not by far. But whatever she had to say was for my ears only. No genetically normal humans allowed.

I closed my mouth and relaxed the death grip I had on the worn, faded quilt. Dad appeared in the doorway, eyes tired beneath the smile.

"Ready for some rhubarb cobbler?" he said with a sigh.

"Cobbler?" Gran piped up. "I made a pie this morning!"

Dad grinned and lifted his shoulders in an apologetic shrug. "When you have a seven year old boy in the house, pie can easily be turned into cobbler."

I rolled my eyes and flopped back into the cushy mattress, sending the springs into a noisy symphony of dissent. So that explained the crash from the kitchen.

"I'll be down in a minute," I offered up. "I need to put away some of my clothes." I indicated the large, teetering pile of freshly laundered clothes Gran had pulled in from the line outside. Thankfully, some things never changed, even with technology. Like the brilliance of sun dried clothes and the taste of home cooking.

I stood and stretched, lifting the first piece of clothing to cross my path. I breathed in the warm scent of sunshine and closed my eyes. A brief image of Travis flitted across my closed lids and I gasped. He had floated in and out amongst my harried thoughts for days and I could not deny the ache and sorrow I felt at his absence. How easily I had lost my first real love. He had been more than a girl could hope for, and I knew no one else like him. It made the future look bleak for romance. Could I feel that way about someone else?

My heart moved into my throat and I swallowed hard. Would I ever forget him? Could you count what we had as real? And the hardest part, the part I would try and convince myself to believe forever, was that Travis had loved me. Not Sarah. Me.

I dropped the clothes back onto the pile with a sigh of frustration. I had to be stronger than this. I had to move on. What was the point? I couldn't get Travis back. I had to treat it all like a dream. One so real that it had changed me to the core.

Thinking of my former self, the Kate that lived before going back four decades, made me shake my head with a snort of incredulity. My transformation might as well have been from caterpillar to butterfly, I was that different now. Who would have believed it?

***

Gran spent most of the next day volunteering at church. I had developed an almost physical ache wanting to find out what she had to say, but there was never a time when we were alone. Thoughts about travelling consumed me and I found myself relentlessly examining the hourglass birthmark above my eye in the mirror, as though it held all the answers. Time was running out; our vacation almost over. It was hard to imagine returning to my normal life after everything I had gone through. It felt like years since I had set foot in a Starbucks instead of weeks. I couldn't even name the current songs on the radio or tell what movies were playing in the theater. That's how remote and out of touch I felt with the world.

Weirdly enough, it didn't really bother me that much. Spending time in the past had given me a glimpse of everything that was real...everything that mattered. It had saved my relationship with my father and given me a new appreciation for life. I learned what it meant to work...and work hard. I could feel the blisters I'd had even though I couldn't see them. Scars from another time.

Seeing as how I wouldn't get to talk to Gran, I wanted to go somewhere I could think, somewhere I could be alone. That afternoon, I waited until Dad and Corey went fishing on the back forty acres before heading out to the rapids.

Despite the evil that had happened to me there *twice*, morbid curiosity won out in the end. The rapids seemed to beckon through the roaring of the water. The unforgiving pounding of the waves drowned out any wayward thoughts and the roiling, rolling water hypnotized me in its hostile takeover of the rocky channel. It reminded me of the ocean on a stormy day, when the waves crashed to shore in massive sets, swallowing and upsetting everything in their path. The ocean had always been a good thinking place for me, and with the threat of Dave gone, I figured the rapids would be just as cathartic. A little closure with the place that had almost taken my life would be a good thing before I left. I wanted to remember Baudette for all the good that had happened and leave behind the tainted memories.

I decided to walk to the rapids, crossing the field of the deranged black bull encounter, the rusty manure spreader where I'd taken shelter still living out its days baking in the sun. Crawling between the twisted strands of barbed wire fencing separating the field from the highway, I headed toward the leaning remains of Slater's farm store, the ramshackle boards broken and hanging like loose teeth.

I came up out of the ditch on all fours just in time to have a truck roar by spraying a cloud of dust into my face. I flinched and coughed into my shirt, hiding my eyes from the rest of the fine grit. "Jerk," I muttered, perfectly aware it was my fault for being in the ditch, not the driver's. The truck had already begun to slow, its brake lights brightening and flashing as the driver switched gears and rolled to a stop in the entrance of Gran's driveway. I held a hand up to my eyes. Did I know this truck? The body was a hunter green with patches of rust around the tires and underbelly of the frame. The bed was empty save for a lone fishing pole poking out behind the driver's rear window. The driver did a quick check before pulling back on to the highway.

Annoyed, I stood with my hands on my hips and waited for the stranger to approach. If they were going to offer anything other than an apology, I was ready to offer a few choice words of my own- right after I had jumped back into the ditch and jumped the fence.

But it was T.J., Travis Kochevar's son. I recognized his face the moment he stopped beside me, his goofy grin stretched from ear to ear. My heart did a small flip flop patter of pleasure before plummeting into a massive belly flop in the pit of my stomach. T.J. looked so much like Travis it was painful. My first inclination was to lean over and kiss him, but luckily my brain kicked in and kept me from completely embarrassing myself.

"I have to know how you did it," he said.
"Did what?" I said, stupidly.

"Piss off my Dad. You left him in quite a state," he shook his head. "I haven't seen that much emotion from him my entire life."

Pleased he remembered me, but not for the right reasons, I shrugged. If T.J. didn't know, I wasn't about to enlighten him. "I knew something he didn't want to hear," I said, refusing to elaborate.

T.J. didn't seem to mind. "How long are you up for?" He grinned wider, which I had thought impossible. "Since you're not my long lost sister or anything, I thought maybe you'd want to hang out sometime. I drive by here twice every day hoping I'll run into you."

A pang of disappointment went through my mind and I winced. Any other time, T.J. would have been the perfect distraction, maybe the perfect summer fling. But as Jerry Springer shows go, this triangle was one for the books. How would T.J. react if he knew I'd almost slept with his Dad? *Forty years ago*. The summer had been one episode after another of horrible timing.

I hated to see his feelings hurt, so instead of going full-on dismissal, I went for the elusive, keep 'em hanging approach. "Maybe," I said, flashing him a flirtatious smile. I would be on my way home before I ever saw him again. "I'll be around for a few more days."

He nodded. "I'll call you. Your Gran's in the phone book," he said before I could offer the number. He winked and then slammed on the gas, squealing his tires in celebration. The truck rumbled down the road and did another careening U-turn to head back toward town. I felt myself grinning like a fool, watching T.J. show off for me. The two of us could never happen, but it was fun to feel normal again, butterfly flirtations and all. At least I knew I wasn't completely damaged goods. Love was still a possibility in my future. The distant future.

I skipped along the highway all the way to the gravel lot next to the Rapid River. The sweet sense of security and content disappeared the moment my foot touched the edge of the forest floor. Anxiety shivered up my spine and took hold of my throat once I entered the perimeter of pines by the gravel parking lot. I fought back the images of Dave's arm snaking through the limbs, his evil snarl as he grabbed my hair and forced me to the ground. I spent minutes frozen in the ring of trees forgetting how to draw a single breath. My heart pounded in triple time and my palms grew hot and swollen with heat.

"Dave is dead," I said in a whisper that lacked any measure of confidence. Above the tree line, I caught sight of the old bridge, its arc stark white against the heavy green of the summer pines and poplars. An icy chill fought with the perspiration trickling down my sides. How was it possible to feel cold and hot at the same time?

Pushing through the trees, I burst onto the shoreline, stopping at the rocky outcropping of boulders that led to the rapid's channel. Gulping huge breaths of relief, I basked in the open sunlight. I didn't anticipate it to be this hard, never expected the crippling fear. I thought it was gone…the situation remedied with Dave's death. Apparently, my mind and body did not agree.

Three times I had to attempt the rocky climb before my shaky legs would hold my weight. Crawling on my hands and knees, I collapsed in a heap of nervous exhaustion once I had cleared the edge. Raising my head, my eyes traveled the foaming, white rapids from beneath the bridge down to where the water converged with the swift current of the Rainy River.

Stunned, I barely kept from crying out when I spied Gran's ancient body sitting near the channel, her toes inches from the onslaught of the thrashing waves.

"Gran!" I screamed, nerves taught and tingling. *What was she doing here?* Forgetting my own fears, I crept along the cracked and creviced shelf until I was only a few feet away. The roaring of the water silenced my approach; she remained still, head tilted to the sky, eyes closed- brow furrowed in concentration.

Afraid of startling her and possibly sending her tumbling into the rapids, I approached her from the side, hoping she would catch me in her peripheral vision.

"Gran?" I tried again, shuffling my feet in tentative steps.

Gran turned, saw she had been discovered, and quickly pulled back her feet from the water.

Squatting down, I grabbed hold of her shoulder and wagged my finger in her direction. "What are you doing here? You were supposed to be at the church!" Puzzled by her bizarre behavior, I could only sit and wait for her to explain herself.

"There was never a body, you know," Gran said over the crash of the waves. Gray wisps of hair blew gently across the mask of serenity covering her face looking as though she had just awakened from a dream. Her floral print dress fluttered in the breeze; the hem stained with dark splotches of water.

Baffled, I fell back a step, throwing my body out of balance and almost keeling over if it weren't for the surprisingly steely grip of Gran's hand on my arm. Certain she had gone crazy, or maybe into the first stages of a debilitating brain disease, I gripped her arm back and tried to pull her away from the river. The mysteries surrounding Gran just got bigger and bigger.

"Gran, let's go somewhere safe. Maybe not so close to the water," I urged. Gran's eyes lost their dreamy stare and locked on mine, penetrating my anxiety like a knife. She wasn't going crazy; the sharp, clarity of her gaze stopped me in my tracks. She was all there, coherent and calculating.

Her words sank past the barriers of my frazzled brain. *"There was never a body, you know."*

Kicking off my shoes, I changed tactics and sat down next to Gran, my stomach flip flopping in time with the churning river. "What do you mean, Gran, 'there was never a body'?"

"Sarah's body. They never found it." She stared into the water, as though waiting for Sarah's remains to appear. "Oh, we carried on and had a funeral and such, for appearances. But I always had hope."

"Gran, I don't understand. What are you trying to say? Is this what you were trying to tell me last night?" My mind spun trying to recall all the questions I had wanted to ask and listen at the same time.

"Sarah was presumed to have drowned. The only evidence to her disappearance washed up on shore two days after she disappeared. Well, that and her sweater left behind in those trees back there." She nodded her head toward the very trees Travis and I had gone to complete our date night- the same place Dave had hidden, waiting to kill me.

I opened my mouth to protest. "But Dave kil-"

Gran held up her hand. "I'm not saying he didn't try to kill her. And I am sure he *thought* he killed her; his poor, troubled soul," Gran sighed, looking out over the foam topped, root beer colored river. "He certainly had us all fooled."

Rolling my eyes, I waved my hand as though to speed her up. "I still don't get what you're saying. What does this have to do with time travel? And our birthmark? We know what happened to Sarah!" Frustrated at her lack of sense, I dug out a loose stone from a shallow crevice and threw it into the water.

"Kate," Gran said, "have you forgotten Sarah carried the same birthmark above her right eye as you and I have?"

She waited silently as I mulled over her random hints in my head. Like the pieces of an intricate puzzle, the satisfying yet sickening feeling arrived as I put the final piece in place. My eyes widened, and my mouth hung open in disbelief.

"Are you trying to say you think Sarah didn't die that night? That she disappeared and traveled to another time?" Incredulous, my voice rose an octave with each word I uttered. "You think Sarah went back in time?" I repeated, more as if to convince myself than to hear Gran affirm her outlandish theory.

Gran's eyes twinkled. "I know she did."

"No way. I hate to burst your bubble, but I was there. I lived through Sarah's death," I said, goose bumps popping up on my arm as I envisioned the ghost of my body spiraling down from the bridge and into the frigid water. "Sarah died, Gran. Dave killed her."

"That's where you're wrong, Kate. It took you to remind me that it was possible. That it could have happened…that it *did* happen." She stumbled over her words, seeming to have trouble putting order to her thoughts. "Kate, I…"

The river picked up in intensity matching the suspense of the moment when the words Gran had wanted to share with me, and only me, would be revealed.

I flinched as the fingers of a wave slid up the rocks and reached for my feet, as though trying to pull me in. I slid backward an inch and pulled my legs up beneath me. Despite the sun, I shivered.

Gran's fingers encircled my arm and squeezed tightly. Her watery eyes grew round and luminous, the blue shining like the crystal clear surface of the ocean. Without even noticing, I held my breath.

Gran leaned in close enough for me to feel her breath upon my face. "I want to bring her back, Kate. I want you to help me bring her back."

Chapter 2
Only a Theory

"You can't be serious," I said, stumbling over my feet as I crossed the rocky terrain back to the gravel lot. "That's the craziest thing I've ever heard." I kept talking to Gran's back as we scaled the concrete underpass beneath the bridge to the highway above.

"Just because you and I traveled in time, doesn't mean Sarah could, too. Besides, how would I ever find her? How do we know she's even alive? What makes you think I could control the outcome?" I threw out questions faster than my brain could process the rationality of them.

We reached the top of the bridge breathless and panting. At eighty years old, Gran's ability to keep up with me was almost embarrassing. Her aging frame was a ruse; the farm life had kept her strong and sturdy. She was a force to be reckoned with.

As though she never heard a word I said, Gran began the tale that fueled the theory she had come to believe.

"I thought there was only one kind of time travel. But then you came along and proved there's another. It got me to thinking. If Sarah traveled the same as you, she's stuck. Stuck in the past."

"Stuck?" I stumbled on the loose highway gravel and sprawled face first into the prickers and thorns growing at the edge of the ditch. "Son of a-!" I bit my tongue to keep from finishing. The fresh, hot burns singing inside the abrasions of my knee made it certain I wasn't dreaming.

Gran knelt down to help me up. "Let's just say there are two types of time travel now. Suspended and sustained. In one instance, suspended time travel, the one you experienced, the traveler goes back in time but returns without any time passing. Sort of a glimpse or a dream state of the past. In the instance of sustained time travel, what I experienced, the traveler goes back in time while the present world continues to exist; a sort of parallel world. I'm not sure why you would travel one way than the other, but I think Sarah is stuck in a suspended sort of time travel, lost in the past for over four decades. You both went through a portal in the rapids...it makes perfect sense."

"I don't think so, Gran. Time has passed. We've all aged. Plus, I went through the barn portal first. It doesn't fit your theory." I quit walking. Gran was throwing information at me like it was supposed to be normal. Like everyone had these thoughts all the time and we should both be on the same page. But I was far from comprehending. In fact, I had a hard time remembering what the word sustained meant.

"Well, I still think she's stuck. She needs help," Gran insisted. "Maybe she doesn't understand how the portals open. Maybe she's been waiting for someone to find her."

"Gran, this is too much. My head's going to explode." I knelt to the ground next to a patch of cattails letting the gravel dig its way into my skin. The thorns and thistles had been a good distraction, a brush of normalcy. I wanted to feel anything against the numbing sensation of this mind blowing information.

Nausea swirled and dipped in the pit of my stomach like a top. Had Gran actually asked me to help her bring Sarah back? The debilitating brain disease theory came back to mind as I stared at her from the ground. Maybe losing a child made you irrational. What if you always held onto the idea of getting them back? Maybe without a body to bury, Gran never had closure.

After a few moments, I was able to walk again; the roaring in my brain had quieted and the swirling in my stomach had settled to a simple rolling. Gran turned her thoughts inward, making the walk back to the farm strange and uncomfortable. I could see her gesturing with her hands, her movements methodical and rigid as she fought the battles in her mind.

Once we made it to the house, the screen door screeching our arrival, Gran left me alone in the kitchen and padded to her bedroom, disappearing behind the door. For once, I wished Corey or Dad to be there for a distraction. Even Grandpa. At least she couldn't pass off her wild tales on me with them around.

I chose to dig into the peanut butter cookies left from the day before; nothing cured an upset stomach and brain drain like a handful of cookies and a tall glass of milk. I sat down with a heavy sigh, dragging the peanut butter cookies and carton of milk right in front of me. The milk had traces of ice clinging to the sides; the same boxy refrigerator from 1960 still inhabited the same spot in the kitchen and it kept everything to arctic conditions.

Gran appeared with a shoe box. She set it on the table with an ominous thump; the lid popped free and slid off kilter, exposing black and white photographs and yellowed newspaper clippings.

"The pictures don't go back very far. Too much was lost in the fire," Gran said, as though I was supposed to know what she was talking about. "As far as I can tell, the birthmark goes back as far as my Mother, Vivie, and her twin, Vickie." She rifled through the shoebox and pulled out a photo, its corners bent and stained with brown.

"Mark? Fire?" I flopped down into a chair before my knees gave out. Gran had gone off the deep end. I couldn't help but slide my eyes to the pictures on the table, one a stark black and white photo of two identical young women, straight faced and grim, shepherding several young children at their skirts. The background didn't offer much, just a simple clapboard home with hardly any windows and a crooked door.

Upon closer examination, I stifled a gasp. Dark and distinct, I saw the tell-tale hourglass birthmarks right away. Both women had it, and so did one of the smaller girls, who couldn't be more than seven.

"Gran, who else knows about traveling? Are these women like us?" I found myself asking. Again with the morbid curiosity.

Gran finally took a chair after sorting through numerous clippings, random notes written in perfect script, and the occasional photo.

"Kate, there is so much to tell you. And so little time. The northern lights will be out soon, and that is the last we will be able to see them for a while."

I tried to keep from groaning aloud. She had switched topics *again*. Slamming my hands on the table, I watched as the papers jumped and the table slid to my right; the clock on the wall rattled against the bead board.

"Enough!" I barked out in my firmest voice.

Gran jumped, made a pawing motion at her heart, and then sat back with a huff. "What's got into you, Kate?" she accused. "You scared the wits out of me!" She had the nerve to sound hurt.

"I'm scaring you?" I repeated incredulous. "Gran, you're scaring more than the wits out of me. The last thing I coherently heard and understood was that you thought Sarah was alive. After that, I just figured you went crazy."

Her face wrinkled and puckered, resembling a pale raisin.

"Kate, I am not crazy. I apologize. I have been thinking and dreaming about the possibilities for years. Of course you are confused! I had lost sight of my dream long ago, and ever since you came back from your time travel experience, the little box I kept locked up in the back of my brain has resurfaced, bringing years of research and theories back to light. I thought the line had ended with Sarah...and then you came along!"

Was I supposed to be thrilled? Complimented? I only felt queasy. Sighing, I grabbed the picture from the table. "I still don't understand what you're getting at. Why don't you start from the beginning, Gran. In order. So I can follow."

Shuffling the papers, Gran slid over as close to me as possible without actually touching. "It all started after I first went back in time. I was confused, upset. I didn't know what was going on. I not only went back, but I took on the body of someone else- my brain but an older woman's body. I kept to myself, stayed close to where I had come through the portal, and survived by sheer luck. I thought I was dreaming for most of it. But when I came back, time had passed without me. My parents were angry and accused me of all sorts of things. Things I had no idea what they were talking about. I spent most of the next year hiding at home afraid to go outside. I didn't know what had happened to me, but I knew I didn't want it to happen again."

Gran took a deep breath and continued. "I started a journal to catalogue everything I remembered from before, during, and after the episode. I went to the library and read books about time traveling, though they were mostly fiction. I figured if people wrote about it, maybe it actually happened." Gran grabbed a cookie from my plate and took a healthy bite. She chewed patiently, methodically. I counted the beats of my heart until she spoke again, the waiting as unnerving as the ring of the phone in the dead of night.

"And then, when Sarah disappeared, everyone thought it was suicide, or an accident, but when they never found a body I began to wonder if she had met the same fate, but couldn't find a way to get back. I wrote down everything I could remember about those days as well. I should have known when you came and I saw the birthmark, to watch for the signs, but I wasn't paying attention. I thought the time travel link had been broken when Sarah disappeared, because it died off on the other side of the family when my cousin Mary and Aunt Vickie died in the fire."

"Ok," I hedged still confused at all the information she was throwing at me, "so what did you find out? Is it something we can control? How long does it last?" *Who were Mary and Vickie? What fire?*

Gran looked down her nose at me. "I thought you wanted me to go in order."

Sheepish, I relaxed the grip I had on the edge of the table. Something about the black and white pictures before me left me uneasy. From the moment I had found Gran, the day had taken on a fuzzy, surreal quality. How was this possible?

"When I went back, almost a century, I took the place of one of my ancestors so deep into the family tree; there was little record of her. I do know I traveled to someone's body and they to mine, because of all the confusion when I returned. Somehow, we switched places in the portal and lived out each other's lives. Whoever played me did a rather poor job at that, which is why my parents were so furious with me...er, her. Of course, it's understandable thinking of the circumstances. I barely survived myself."

I rolled my eyes. I was in one hot mess.

Gran kept going despite my obvious discomfort. "What I can't quite figure out is that when you traveled you lived Sarah's life but had little control over the outcome, like in a dream. When I traveled, I actually became this ancestor of ours, taking over her body, her fate. That's the only difference I think, between the two kinds of traveling."

I made an attempt to interrupt, but Gran waved me quiet.

"As I was saying, I went back for two weeks' time. I managed to survive in the wilderness, living off of fish and berries. I didn't dare try to find someone to help. Eventually, by the end of the second week, a storm came up suddenly while I was bathing in the river. I went through the portal and came back to my real time. I never told a soul what had happened." Her eyebrows went up a notch and she whispered, "It took a few weeks to convince myself I wasn't crazy!"

I shook my head. "Who do you think you were, Gran? You said you had a different body?"

"I don't know, Kate. I went back too far. There were no records to survive that time."

How could Gran talk about this so easily? She had become another person. In another time. It was the stuff of mental wards and padded rooms. "So you think Sarah went back in time? To another world?" I had to shove a cookie in my mouth to stop the sarcasm from getting through.

"Sarah *must* have had the same thing happen to her. You say she can't be suspended because time has passed, so maybe she traveled like me? She is in the sustained or parallel time travel state- where time passes in both worlds, and she has never figured out how to travel back. She might even inhabit someone else's body, like I did." Gran eyed me suspiciously, as though I was hiding something. "Somehow, you traveled a completely different way. You could see Sarah's life as though you were Sarah, but it wasn't real."

I coughed. "It felt pretty darn real to me," I said, not wanting my experiences to be slighted in the least. Gran's theories didn't pan out in my mind. There had to be a different reason.

Gran snorted and stared at the ceiling. "It had to have been pure luck that you were fifteen and Sarah was fifteen. The two of you look so much alike, it would be hard to know if you kept your own body or not. I don't know." She shook her head, puzzled. "I can't explain it all. It's a tricky business, this time traveling. Maybe you're linked to Sarah in some way. Or maybe you witnessed her time travel so that you could prove what happened to her. The gene could be weakening through the generations. So many possibilities…" she trailed off in a disjointed murmur.

I chugged the last few gulps of milk to wash down the crumbly remains of the cookies in my mouth. "Gran, I'm not sure you're firing on all cylinders here. I know what I saw, what I felt. I didn't just dream what happened to Sarah. I lived it. She died in the rapids." I said the words harshly, as though to drive them into her skull.

Gran refused to listen. "She's alive, Kate."

I decided to change the subject. "So how do we do it? Obviously it's part of our genetics? A slip in our DNA make-up?" I wanted facts, not shady theories. "Why can we travel and others can't?"

"Part of it is our DNA, yes, but since I don't have much of our family's history recorded I can't know for sure where it all started and why. The environmental factors have to be there, too. It took me a long time to figure out the sequence, but it has to do with the appearance of the aurora borealis, or northern lights as they are more commonly known, with the following of an electrical storm. Lots of lightning and magnetic activity. That's when the portals open up."

"Portals?" I echoed.

"The portals are where you can come and go between the worlds. My portal was in the river on my family's property. Then there's the Rapid River portal, and you discovered the one in the barn."

"Yeah, lucky me," I mumbled.

Gran narrowed her eyes. "This is real, Kate," she said, as if I needed a reminder. "This could change lives." As if I didn't know.

"Sorry, Gran," I said ruefully. "Keep going."

"It seems we can only travel within our family blood line. The only evidence I can tell that indicates the ability to travel is the birthmark. There aren't enough pictures to know, but it seems there is only one per generation, except the year of my mother and her identical twin sister, Vickie and Vivie." She tapped the picture again of the young women and the cluster of children. A light perspiration had developed on her upper lip and forehead as she became more animated in telling her findings. She sat back with a sigh and wiped her brow with the edge of a cloth napkin. She pushed the shoebox toward me, urging me to peruse the contents.

She drummed the tabletop with her fingers. "Maybe it's *where* you go through a portal that determines how you travel. The discovery of the portal in the barn changes everything!"

I grabbed another cookie. At this rate, I would be fifty pounds heavier before the end of the summer.

"Why don't you look through that tonight. Give yourself some time to think about it."

"Think about what?" I asked dumbly, forgetting the whole point of the conversation.

"Rescuing Sarah," Gran said simply. "I would go, but I think the ability to travel weakens with age. I wasn't able to leave the rest of the family before, and once so many years passed, I began to lose faith in everything I believed. I started to believe Sarah had died. Not in the river, you see, but back in the world she had traveled to. You coming here this summer is beyond good fortune!"

My interest came to a screeching halt. "Wait a minute, Gran," I interrupted, hating the way the light died in her eyes. "I don't want to go back in time again. Ever. It was scary, and really, really hard. I felt like I walked the edge of sanity the entire time." I tried to ignore the quiver in her chin and continued. "I'm not used to living life like that! Could you imagine if I went further back in time? Besides, you said I was *lucky* to have come back at all." Shifting uncomfortably in my seat, I fingered the edge of a napkin nervously. *Why did I feel like the bad guy here?* "Besides, Sarah could be dead. Probably is dead. It would be a colossal waste of time…and dangerous," I added trying to make her see my point. "Plus, what if I don't go back in a suspended form and end up spending years there like Sarah. You said yourself, the elements all have to line up perfectly. What's to guarantee that?"

"I know what I told you before- , about being lucky. But think about it; you don't travel the same way we do. You don't trade places with anyone. In fact, with your apparent link to Sarah, your chances should be better. It'll be like a dream." Gran sounded so sure of herself. I rolled my eyes to the ceiling. Was there a classification higher than crazy? Off your rocker, maybe? Gran wanted me to travel through time searching for someone who might not even be in their own body? Or dead?

Impossible. Absolutely bizarre.

The conversation died as a truck rumbled into the drive. Gran picked up the pieces from her box slowly and slipped them back inside, as though it took every effort to willingly stifle the only fragments of hope she had left. I cleared my throat and tried to ignore the way she almost caressed the worn photos and clippings, laying them gently inside like a baby in a cradle. A truck door slammed and excited voices broke the uncomfortable silence.

The two of us turned to peer through the screened door just in time to see Corey clambering from the truck, his gangly body all angles and sharp edges. The grin on his face as he held up the stringer of fish he'd caught broke the tension in the room and we quickly left the table to join the lucky fisherman.

When we reached the front steps, Gran gripped my shoulder, her fingers digging into my skin.

"Forgive me, Kate. You were right. It was a selfish thing to think, much less ask. Forget the whole thing."

I didn't answer but trailed her to the garage, where Dad was filleting the first of six shiny scaled walleyes. I couldn't help but feel guilty. Gran may have said the words, but I knew she didn't mean them. And now I couldn't shake the knowledge that I was the cause of the dead look in her eyes and the slump to her shoulders. I might as well have sucked all the color and happiness from the world.

Great, I had single-handedly killed Gran's hopes...again.

Chapter 3
A Change of Heart

I tossed and turned all night. Once, in the middle of a dream, I felt like I was suffocating; invisible hands surrounded my neck. Every person I came across tried to help, but still I couldn't breathe and the dream gradually grew dim around the edges as I fought for air.

I woke in a tangled mass of sheets wrapped so tightly around my neck it took several minutes to unwind them and get free. Gasping for air, I lay there in the dark, searching the night sky for the comforting light of the moon. Sweat had soaked the pillows and left oval stains of dampness in the pockets of the sheets. Frustrated, I tried flipping the pillows over and laying on top of the thin quilt, to no avail.

I knew why my dreams were a tormented mess. The guilt of the day still hung heavy on my shoulders. Was I doing the right thing? What if Gran was right? What if I could bring Sarah back?

I tried to think how awful it would be for Sarah stuck four decades in the past, away from her family and everything that was familiar. Arriving at the most vulnerable and insecure time of her life. Would she have gradually accepted her fate? Gotten married? Had kids? How she pulled it off was an even bigger mystery. Wouldn't someone wonder who she was? Where she came from? Why she was different? Unless she had become someone else. The idea of trading bodies with another stranger made me tremble. Yuck. I just barely tolerated my own turbulent, emotional body.

A whisper of cool air lifted the sheets on my bed, sending a temporary sense of relief through the humid room. No AC. Disgusting. Every morning I woke with the sense I had bathed in my own sweat, my normally curly hair a mass of frizzy tangles.

The blood red numbers on my digital travel clock read 3:40 am. Gran's box taunted me from the top of the dresser. Against my better judgment, I had carried it upstairs after dinner; a peace offering to Gran, sending her the message I would at least *look* at her findings. Big mistake. Because now I actually wanted to read what she had recorded. I felt like I owed it to my heritage…the ancestors with the weird traveling gene.

Crawling from the bed, I closed the door to my room and threw the quilt into the crack at the bottom, stifling any chance of light getting out into the hallway. The last thing I needed was for Dad to wake up and find me flipping through random newspaper clippings and freakish journals in the middle of the night.

The more I read, the more I became intrigued. Gran had done a substantial amount of research, especially on the occurrence of northern lights, their cause and patterns, and the level of magnetic and electric activity in the atmosphere. It seemed plausible that they could cause a portal to open, whatever that looked like.

I thumbed through several family photographs, some in color, some in black and white. The oldest photos were too faded to make out much for detail; the birthmark indistinguishable on anyone's face. But it was true, the birthmark seemed to carry through, one family member per generation, except the twins, my Great-Grandmother and her sister. Each one of them had a daughter with the same mark, but one had died in a tragic fire in 1910, and the other, of course, was Gran, not born until 1920.

Rummaging through the box, I pulled out an article on the fire of 1910, a fire so devastating it leveled the villages of Pitt, Williams, Graceton, and Cedar Spur, the townships of Baudette and Spooner, as well as burning over 300,000 acres. The fire had even jumped the wide river border into Canada. The article blamed the thriving logging industry as the cause. The dry harvested land plus a year of drought and possible sparks from passing trains all combined to make a trifecta of fire making power.

I dived back into my pillows, holding the article above my head with the pictures of Main Street, Baudette just before the fire, and the awful, devastating picture of the town afterwards. Rows and rows of buildings, homes and businesses had been reduced to ash. So many people had been left homeless on the cusp of winter weather months. The harrowing stories of survival both impressed and frightened me. It would have taken more than courage to get me through something that devastating.

A small paragraph at the end of the article caught my attention, the word *epidemic* jumping from the page like it glowed in neon letters. I read a little further and a chill raced down my spine. Typhoid? The town was going through a typhoid epidemic as well? I didn't know what typhoid was, but it sounded foreign and alien, where doctors wore suits with helmets in rooms marked 'biohazard'.

Gran's plea echoed in my mind. What if Sarah was forced to endure all of these horrible things, against her will, helpless and alone? I knew exactly what she would feel like. Well, maybe not quite to the degree of torture she would feel, but still. I had made a drastic jump from civilized city girl with technology at my fingertips, to rustic farm girl, carrier of water. It had been quite the shock to my system. Where had Sarah gone?

The picture of Great Grandma Vivie and her sister, Vickie, stood apart from the rest of the pile. I couldn't tear my eyes from the young women in the picture, their somber faces, the barren background. What if that was me? What if I had traveled to that time period instead of 1960? The grim aspect of the situation made my stomach tighten.

If Sarah had gone back, the chances of her being alive were slim. But what if she were alive? All that time I spent in 1960, I thought it was to prevent her from dying, but maybe it was to see she had gone through the portal. What if she was waiting for someone to try and bring her back, instead of figuring out how to get back herself?

My brain hurt from dreaming up all the possibilities. Everything was so bizarre and beyond rational thinking, that I couldn't make a simple coherent thought. The only true statement I could make was that I knew nothing for certain. Everything Gran had compiled was based on a theory with no way of trial and error.

Knowing that Gran spent the last forty years coping with the idea she might have a daughter somewhere, tugged at my heart. It was as though she were a prisoner of war, except Sarah would be a prisoner of time. What kind of person was I not to even try to help?

But giving in meant risking my own life. It meant giving up Dad and Corey. It meant, quite possibly, not being able to return. Could I deal with the consequences? What if I traveled somewhere in the 1800's or worse? How far back did the gene go?

This time would be different, I argued with myself. I would be ready, would know what's coming. If I succeeded, what a trip....I would be a heroine.

I had the sought after power that was only in myths and legends; the power to bring someone back from the dead. I held even more power than Gran. I traveled without losing time.

The thought was electrifying, intensifying by the moment. My body hummed with energy, my feet tapped incessantly on the footboard. The whole idea was preposterous. Inconceivable. Irresponsible. Dangerous.

But the idea was slowly becoming alluring. Fascinating. Tempting.

The confidence built slowly in my chest until it had become a solid knot, pulling my will together with finely taut strings. I could do it.

I could save Sarah.

Chapter 4
Crossing the Line

The smell of bacon floated up the steps and greeted my weary body, head hung over the side of the bed, arms flung wide as though I embraced the mattress like an old friend. Somewhere around five thirty in the morning I had fallen asleep, the black and white photo of Vivie and Vickie clutched in my hand. Now I sat in that fuzzy period between deep sleep and consciousness, processing minimal sounds and thoughts, trying to figure out why I slept on a bed without sheets.

Clattering pots and pans jarred me fully awake; the kitchen was already alive with activity. I squinted at the photo of Vickie and Vivie trying to make the image clear. Fear clutched at my belly. Was I really going to go through with this? Sarah's body could easily be at the bottom of the river. It was a more practical theory than she had traveled back in time. But Gran had been adamant.

Rolling from the bed, I threw on some clothes. I needed to tell Gran my decision before I changed my mind again. If anyone asked, I was blaming my irrational mood swings on my teenage hormone imbalance. There had to be something wrong with the chemistry in my body for even considering attempting the outrageous task of finding Sarah. I was only giving it one shot. That's all the time we had; there were only a few weeks of vacation left before my family headed back to Florida. I wondered what whopper of a tale Gran would dream up to explain to Dad my sudden disappearance? There was no way we could tell him the truth ahead of time; he would never allow it.

I found Gran frying eggs and bacon, her back to me as I entered the kitchen. Glancing around to make sure no one else was there, I crept up to her side and put my arm around her shoulders.

"Smells good." My heart began to accelerate, the closer I came to saying the words.

"Do you want fried or scrambled?" Gran asked, her voice back to its cheery self. She hummed as she flipped the bacon over, wiping the excess grease on her apron.

I looked out the window and into the farm yard where Corey was sprinkling seed for the chickens. Taking a huge breath, I whispered, "I'll do it, Gran."

"What was that?" Gran said as she turned the dials of the stove to turn off the heat.

Mustering the courage, I tried to keep my voice from wavering. "I'll do it. I'll try to find Sarah."

Gran's eyes lit up like fireworks, and then clouded over immediately. "No, Kate. I can't let you do it. It's too dangerous. I can't do to your father what was done to me." Shaking her head, she stepped away from me and carried the skillets to the table. "I should never have asked."

"What?" I hissed at her, irritated and crabby from my lack of sleep. "I said I wanted to do it. It means everything to you. Admit it. You've never been the same since Sarah disappeared. Let me do it, Gran."

She pretended not to hear me and instead poured coffee into three cups on the table.

Like cows stampeding toward feed, Dad, Corey, and Grandpa came through the screened porch, tromping their boots loudly, their carefree banter silencing any further argument from me. Annoyed at the lack of enthusiasm I expected from Gran, I slouched at the corner of the table and picked at my food. I had gone through agonizing hours of back and forth battles in my head before finally deciding, and now she was taking it back, wanting me to forget the whole thing?

Breakfast was a silent affair, save for the scraping of plates and clatter of coffee cups. Gran hardly ate a thing, but stared out the window at the cloudy morning sky. Sulking, I barely answered Corey's farm trivia, his usual incessant questions sparking the ire in my heart. I had stayed up all night battling the guilt demons in my soul, and Gran had made the decision without consulting me. It was my body...my mind.

Gran coughed and fiddled with the edge of her butter knife. "Say, Dean," she began, her eyes fluttering nervously to mine. I couldn't tell what she was thinking; she kept her face a mask of secrecy.

"I've been talking to Kate about going to this annual craft and quilt fair down in St. Cloud for the weekend. I go every year, and it's a wonderful time for the girls."

Dad's ears perked up and he shot me a covert glance, checking out my interest level. I shot up straight in my chair and threw him a smile and a nod.

"I know you don't have much time here left for your vacation, but I probably won't see Kate again for a long time what with college coming in a few years." Gran sent in another point for her advantage. Dad was a sucker for family time, and he always got misty eyed when the subject of college came up.

"I don't know, Mom. Kate, what do you think?" Dad turned on me, brow raised in inquiry.

"I thought it sounded neat. Who knows the next time I'll get to see Gran." I winced inside. When was the last time I'd used the word *neat*?

Dad looked unconvinced, like maybe I was just trying to appease Gran and say I wanted to go, when normally, it would be the last place you would ever find me. A quilt show? What was Gran thinking?

I stayed quiet. Just nodded my head and smiled dumbly.

Dad chewed an extra long minute on his last piece of bacon. "I guess it sounds like a good time. But you'll be back by Monday?"

Gran nodded and began to clear the table. "She'll be back before you know it."

I choked on my milk and spewed a rainbow of droplets across the table, coating everyone's plate in a milky shower.

Grandpa grunted in disgust and pushed his plate away. "Guess that means I'm done." He reached for a toothpick and a handful of red hot candies and left his tainted plate for Gran to clear away. He headed back out to the fields without another word.

"We leave tomorrow, Gran? Is that right?" I checked the calendar hanging on the fridge. A long weekend? That's all the time I had to master time traveling, find Sarah, and get her and myself back? But Gran had said yesterday, the northern lights were active in *three* days. That meant I only had two days to travel. I guessed the timing wouldn't matter if I never lost time to begin with. I would leave one day and return as if nothing happened. If the portals were open.

Dad and Corey started planning their all-boy weekend which I figured included a lot of greasy food, burping, and fishing.

Gran waited until I stood by the sink before brushing against my shoulder and whispering, "We will give it one shot. One. Bring me your suitcase, but leave it empty."

The plan had been hatched from its long incubation. In my mind there was no turning back.

***

Gran and I waved out the windows of her old Ford truck all the way down the driveway. The truck rumbled and jerked, the gears grinding in protest whenever she stomped on the clutch and shifted gears.

We hadn't driven two miles before she turned off the main highway onto a county dirt road, the gravel kicking up a hazy, rust colored wake in our trail.

"Are you going to tell me what changed your mind?" I asked, hanging on to the door handle for balance as we bounced over the low maintenance road.

"Are you going to tell me what changed yours?" She shot back.

We turned and eyed each other for a minute, and then burst into a fit of nervous giggles.

"It's a marvelous, dangerous power, isn't it," Gran said, her voice wavering. "I was tempted to try so many times…" she trailed off.

"So is the suspended time travel the same as the sustained? Will I have to do something to make sure I don't lose time?"

Gran turned sharply down an overgrown drive, low limbs and wild vines almost obscuring the entrance. Branches knocked against the doors as we plowed into the forest and down the darkened lane. She didn't risk a glance at me as she maneuvered the rough terrain. "I'm starting to think the difference is in the portals. The portal you found in the barn is a suspended time portal and the rapids portal is a sustained traveling entrance. That way we won't have to worry about you getting "stuck"."

Two deer jumped in front of the car and Gran slammed on the brakes, rocketing me into the dashboard; my hand braced against the windshield to protect my head.

"Nice reflexes," I commented, "for an old lady."

Gran snorted. "Nice reflexes," she threw back, "for a city girl."

"You were saying," I prompted, hoping she would finish the conversation. Everything she said sounded legit but I couldn't help but feel anxious. Who wouldn't?

"Oh, yes, yes," she muttered as her eyes scanned the trail. "I hope I didn't miss it."

"Aha!" she shouted triumphantly, turning the truck down another thick and unkempt trail. "Now," she continued, "there's one more thing about sustained traveling that I didn't tell you. I did tell you that I thought I had changed places with the person when I traveled. She became me, and I became her. And I believe you can only trade places with another traveler. But only if they are in or near a portal at the same time as you. The likelihood of this happening is extremely rare and probably explains why Sarah is unable to come back. I am hoping you can travel in the suspended form, find Sarah, tell her where the portals are and when they are active, and come back yourself. I am betting she has never put the environmental facts together with the place and time."

I swallowed hard. My mind turned, threatening to chicken out. "But what if I can't get back? How do I find Sarah? And who is she going to switch with?"

Gran pulled the lumbering truck to a stop just outside a small log cabin, or…the remains of what used to be a cabin.

"What's this, Gran?"

"It's your Grandpa's old moonshine shack. Oh, did he ever make some strong drink back in the day. Make your chest grow hair!" She laughed heartily. "We'll stay here for the night. Tomorrow is when the northern lights have been predicted to have a most powerful display, followed by a patch of thunderstorms in the early morning. That is when we will head to the portals."

"But how do I find Sarah?"

"What were you doing the night you were out in the barn with Corey? Were you thinking about Sarah? Did you pick something up? Say something?" Gran grilled me like I was some sort of criminal.

"Yeah, I guess I was bummed about being told I looked like Sarah. And I was mad at Dad for coming on her birthday..." *Actually I was mad for being made to come here at all, but who needed the details drawn out?*

"We won't know for sure, but maybe if you think of Sarah and channel your thoughts, you will be more direct in your traveling. Also, I brought this," she rummaged inside the duffel bag wedged between us on the truck's bench. She pulled out a long white dress that had yellowed with age. Lace lined the hem and neckline, and a pair of ivory buttons were sewn on the front. It looked like a doll's play dress except for the intricate lace.

"This was Sarah's baptismal dress. I made one for every child. All eleven," Gran said proudly. "If you hold this in your hands, it will link you to Sarah even more, possibly drawing you right to her." Gran could barely hide the tremor of excitement in her voice. "I'm sure the two of you hold some special ties to each other. I'm just certain."

It was as good a theory as any. Hesitant to touch the delicate dress, I remained seated, hands at my side. I wasn't ready to become one with Sarah...not yet. This whole secretive operation left me feeling shaky and uncertain. I wanted to help, I really did, but there were so many unknowns.

And the creepy, vine covered, ramshackle cabin with the boarded up windows wasn't helping matters.

It looked like something right out of a horror movie. I fully expected someone with an axe to come barreling through the door at any minute.

"Why here, Gran?" I asked, not even bothering to cover up my dislike of her choice in accommodations.

"No one has been here for years. Don't worry; I brought plenty of bug spray."

Withholding a groan, I stepped from the truck and into a crackling of brown, dead leaves. Sunlight, barely making it through the canopy of trees above, made its way down in tiny individual streams of light, as though actually piercing the shadowy forest.

Following Gran through the darkened doorway, I waved a stick in front of my face to loosen any blankets of cobwebs and frighten away any bugs. Gran had come prepared. She removed a lantern, two sleeping bags, and a Tupperware of food from her duffel bag. My suitcase carried bug spray, cards, a cribbage board, and a gallon of water.

"Are you really going to stay here all weekend until I come back?" I looked around at the broken, sloping ceiling. "This place might cave in on us while we're sleeping," I said, completely serious.

"No one can know what is going on. This was the easiest solution."

Somehow I doubted that. Getting a room in town at the local motel under a fake name and a little bit of costuming sounded much better.

Taking a hesitant seat on one of the rickety chairs in the room, I held my breath as it squeaked and groaned, then settled in to accepting its visitor. "Gran, you never answered all of my questions. Who do you think Sarah switched places with? Wouldn't that person have been stuck in 1960, wandering around Clementson? They would have stood out like a whore in church." I clapped my hand over my mouth. "Sorry." Gran winced at my vulgar expression.

"I don't have all the answers. Maybe they didn't make it through the journey. Maybe they wandered over to Canada." Gran avoided my eyes. "Let's focus on finding Sarah." She stared at me for a moment, taking in my tapping feet and twisted hands. "Don't be nervous. Remember, it will be like you never left at all. So no matter how long it feels like you are in the past, you will return to me good as new."

"Now what?" I said, a little impatiently. The more I thought about the insanity of what I was about to do, the more I was liable to give up. Waiting until tomorrow night was going to be torture. I smacked a mosquito buzzing across my face and blanched when blood spurted across my hand.

"Now we play some cribbage," Gran replied cheerfully, dropping a deck of cards onto a table with three legs and a broken hockey stick propping up the fourth corner.

Inhaling slowly and counting to ten, I clenched my hands in my lap. Thirty-six hours and counting…

Chapter 5
Tracing the Link

An eerie howl echoed through the trees, sending even the sturdiest of trunks into a humble bow. Throughout the day we had only emerged from the cabin to take walks, check on the cloud cover for the northern lights, and to use the outhouse- a horrible reminder of what my life might soon be like, even if only temporary.

The night did not disappoint. After a brilliant show of lights in hues of unbelievable greens and blues, the storm had arrived in full force, Gran's accurate predictions coming full circle. It was approximately two in the morning, but the adrenaline that pumped through my veins had me wide-eyed and hopping, like I'd had one too many espressos. Jumping at every sound, I sat in the chair and waited for the signal to go, my leg popping up and down like a jackhammer.

"Are you sure you want to do this?" Gran whispered, gripping my hand in hers.

I couldn't answer. The truth was, I didn't know what I wanted. After staying in the miserable cabin overnight, I was impatient, irritable, and apprehensive. Not a great trio of emotions. I managed to nod my head, Gran seeming to understand my difficulty in speaking.

"This will be hard, Kate. It will be demanding and you may fail. But I can't express the gratitude I have that you're willing to try. Whatever the results, I just want you to come back safely. Promise me you'll focus on getting yourself back as soon as the next portal opens. The northern lights will be very active this weekend, so it's your best shot. I don't want to risk any complications."

I nodded again, stilling my shaking knee with my hand. *It won't be real. It won't be real.*

"Wherever you end up, find out the year right away. Search for any clue as to where our family lives. Hopefully, if I am right, you will be drawn to Sarah- wherever she is. If anything, maybe you will be able to find out what happened to her."

If she's even alive. I flinched as I thought the words and coughed behind my hand. I looked off to the corner of the room and scolded my negative thoughts. This was no time to doubt Gran. "What if I become Sarah again? At a different age or time?" The walls creaked and groaned, seeming to pull at the foundation, straining against the rusted nails. Pine cones dropped randomly on the roof outside, sounding hollow, dull notes to match the thuds inside my chest.

"Leave her a note, a letter, anything to try and communicate to her. Leave it with a friend or family member to give to her. It's worth a try. " *But I can't change the future*, I wanted to argue. *Not the way I travel.*

Instead I nodded. Swallowing had become impossible. My mouth was dry as the dead leaves outside.

"Let's go then," Gran said. "The portals should be open by now."

"Wait!" I had thought of another question. *Just keep adding to the pile*, I thought miserably. "What if other portals exist? What if I keep traveling and end up everywhere but back here?" What if I spent decades traveling?

"It won't be real, Kate. Remember that. You're different. You have a special link."

Or a special defect.

"Just once, Kate. Travel once and then come home."

***

We had to drive with the lights off to the farm's back entrance. It was weird, sneaking around the place as though we were trespassing. I expected Rex to bark and give us away, but the rain kept him holed up inside his doghouse.

We made our way across the fields and snuck into the barn, our clothes soaked from the sudden onslaught of rain. Up the ladder we crawled, fumbling our way through the darkness that was only occasionally lit by a flash of lightning. My skin tingled and sang with electricity, the hair on my arms standing straight up. When we reached the loft, my head immediately began to throb, the familiar ache of before pushing against the confines of my skull. Nausea twisted the contents of my stomach and I was glad I had only eaten a sandwich for dinner instead of something heavy and greasy.

Gran grabbed the hatch handle and tugged the heavy door open.

"Stay back!" I warned, foolishly believing the hatch might actually suck her in, like a black hole lying in wait.

Inching forward, I took my time getting to the edge of the hatch. Though it was hard to see, I could tell that the hole had a filmy haze to it, sort of surreal and dream-like. I hadn't noticed it the last time I had jumped through the hatch, but I had also been afraid of nonexistent barn monsters attacking me in the night.

"Hurry, Kate. I don't know how long the portals will stay open," Gran urged, her gray hair glowing with another flash of lightning.

I didn't want to turn back, if I gave my doubts one inch of room they would run rampant and make me give up before trying. My body screamed with energy and the headache pounded to the beat of my pulse. Even the blood running through my veins seemed to speed up, burning a hot streak through the intricate maze of my body. I knew there was plenty of hay below so I wasn't worried about getting physically hurt if I jumped through and didn't enter the portal. Like looking over a ravine before rappelling down, I couldn't force my body to agree with my mind and take the plunge.

"Wait!" Gran screamed. She pulled Sarah's baptismal dress from her apron pocket.

Shuddering, I took hold of the dress and managed to choke out a shaky, strangled laugh that bordered on hysterical. I couldn't believe we had almost forgotten the dress!

"I love you, Gran. If something happens, tell Dad the truth. I know he would understand."

Before Gran could answer, thunder ripped through the sky. The barn walls shook and I took a deep breath. This was it. People didn't make history standing around waiting for something to happen to them…they took charge of their own destiny.

The flash of lightning came seconds later. As it lit up the barn, I closed my eyes and thought of Sarah, picturing her as I knew her best, the fifteen year old Sarah I had once been.

I heard Gran scream as I stepped into the hatch, gripping the dress like I would a hand, wishing it could pull me to safety. I fell like a feather, twirling and flipping through the air, feeling weightless and lofty, like I could be blown off course with a simple breath. My eyes stayed shut, squeezed tightly against the unknown; afraid to open and see what lay beyond the darkness. Biting the inside of my cheek, I kept down the rising bile and tried to keep my focus on Sarah.

Sarah Jane Christenson, I repeated in my mind until I felt the expected collision of my head and something unseen.

A darkness more oppressive than night swallowed me whole, crushing my senses and sending my mind to a perfect gridlock. My skin tightened and seemed to squeeze my insides like a tube of toothpaste. Pain exploded through all of my major joints creating a fiery hot pain that burst forth in sets like synchronized fireworks.

Then, just like before, I felt nothing…nothing at all.

***

I awoke in darkness, crippled with pain. Every movement, every breath sent waves of dizziness and tremors through my body. I ached to cradle my head between my hands; the throbbing surged in waves that crashed against my skull. A whimper escaped my lips. My bones felt as though they had been stretched unnaturally, my skin so dry and tight, like it had been sapped of all moisture for days. Even the blood coursing through my veins felt foreign and infected as it struggled to make its way through my body with the aid of my stuttering heart. Nothing seemed to be working right and I couldn't see a thing. What if I had come through the portal disfigured? What if my body couldn't handle traveling more than once?

With great difficulty, I focused on each part of my body trying to decide if I had any open wounds. A trickle of something warm ran the length of my neck, but my hands couldn't seem to find their way there. It was as though the limbs of my body were no longer connected to the mainframe of my brain.

One thing was obvious- I was no longer in the barn. But where was I? Who was I? Was I already dead? I could smell earth and stale air. Was I trapped in some sort of grave? I made a move to scream, but then closed my mouth in anguish. Even my tongue hurt.

A rhythmic thumping filled the quiet as my heart began to catch up to its normal beat. I breathed slow, even breaths, willing myself not to panic. There was still air to breathe and I wasn't dead….yet.

Something rattled overhead and grit fell from above and into my face and hair.

"Mama?" I heard a small voice call out.

"Mother!" A second voice echoed.

Muffled words and exclamations seemed to come from just beyond where I was laying, but they were above me, as though coming down from heaven.

I heard the heavy sound of wood sliding and scraping and then a thump. Another cloud of grit and dust floated down upon my head.

Great wide doors opened above, creaking and groaning, exposing a gray and cloudy sky. Raindrops, fat and heavy fell down through the open doors and broke upon the crooked steps in random splashes. Squinting, I could barely make out two silhouettes peering down into the dark hole, their halos of blond hair standing out against the dreary background.

I lay sprawled just beyond a stone staircase leading to the mysterious figures. Dirt walls and a dirt floor surrounded me; in the far end of the hole I saw a faint outline of shelves lined with glass jars and dried plants of some sort.

I tried calling out, but I had lost control of my voice as well. Had I traveled this far only to be completely helpless, a stranger and an invalid with no hope of being understood?

One of the shadows above came hurtling down the steps, a girl I could make out, her dress plastered to her shins.

Bold, blue eyes round as saucers, peered down into my anxious face. A shock of fear crossed her plain face and the girl stood and shouted to the figure left behind at the top of the stairs.

"Go get Dad, Ruth. Mama's hurt!" The fear in the girl's voice iced my heart on the spot, but the real chill came when I saw the girl's face dead on, the unmistakable mark standing out against her creamy white skin.

An hourglass.

The girl collapsed on my chest and pulled at my shoulders. "Mama! Get up!"

When I didn't move, she began to cry, throwing herself on the ground by my side and tugging uselessly on my lifeless hands. Rain came down harder, pelting my bare skin and soaking the girl's pale dress until it was translucent.

"Mama…..Mama," she sobbed. "Why won't you get up?"

I closed my eyes against the awful scene, then popped them back open in surprise. The girl had called me mother. Why would she do that? I looked nothing like-

A scream burst from my lips, my vocal cords finally freed from their gripping prison. I wasn't me. I wasn't even close to being me. Like some sort of alien, my body had morphed into something longer, curvier, and heavier than what I remembered seeing in the mirror. My legs shot down past the hem of my jeans, and my arms were a good two inches longer than the sleeves of my sweatshirt. My hips were wide, my feet like boats, and…shut the front door! I had breasts! My flat, barely A-cup, nothing of a chest had been replaced by rounded mounds of flesh that pushed at the front of my shirt like twin peaks on a mountain.

My eyes strained to see every part of me, the puzzle of who I had become getting more and more strange and frightening by the minute. I don't know what I had expected but I certainly hadn't expected this. I wasn't supposed to change bodies. I had gone through the barn portal. I wasn't supposed to change at all!

The girl continued to sob as my body tingled and burned; each breath a painful movement of my newly inhabited body.

A shadow moved across the doorway, darkening the gloomy room.

"Vickie?" a gruff voice called down the stairwell, sounding none too pleased to be my knight in shining armor. I heard the man grunt in surprise. "What the hell are you doing wearing pants?"

Large boots clomped down the stairs, the heavy tread matching the ominous booming of my heart. I rolled my eyes to the earthy ceiling. What had I gotten myself into?

Chapter 6
Sarah

The pain seemed to come from every angle, a massive attack that made her feel as though she had been hit by a team of horses and drug along the gravel road for a few miles.

But it had worked. After fifteen years, she knew exactly what had happened, remembered exactly what it had felt like. Finally, it had happened again. And no matter where she was, she was free from her life before. It had been a desperate fifteen years of waiting. Waiting for the perfect sequence of events. Waiting for another victim.

Nearby, the sounds of a storm raged. Thunder rumbled and rain plinked off the metal roof above. She felt around in the darkness, collecting her mind and calming her soul. She had waited for years, never believing it would happen again and now- even in excruciating pain, she could smile. Every time she had traveled had been different, but the last place she'd been stuck the longest and she had feared her days were numbered. She wondered if the portals had quit working, or if her body had given out. But now she knew for certain. It was all a matter of timing. And luck.

She recalled her last moments, traipsing to the root cellar for potatoes to fix yet another meal for her insatiable family. Shuffling through the canned goods and bins, she had watched as the walls had become fuzzy and unclear. She'd barely taken a step toward the swirling mass before falling into a vast, dark space, unable to move.

But the details weren't important. What mattered is that she'd been successful in her escape. Again.

She clutched her aching head. Where was she now?

The familiar brush of hay against her bare feet tickled her toes and stuck through the thin cotton of her night dress. A light swayed in the distance, like a large firefly spinning dizzily in the dark. It descended from up above, and Sarah could make out a body behind the bright sphere of light.

Suddenly, the figure was upon her, pulling her into a tight embrace. "It's ok, Kate. You tried. You tried."

The voice struck a chord in her heart, bringing back memories she'd buried and tried to forget.

The face hovered above her, worry creasing the ancient brow. Good grief, the aged face was as wrinkled as a raisin! But it was her. It was definitely her.

"Mom?" she croaked, reaching a hand up to caress the wrinkled cheek.

The face changed…became shocked, uncertain… afraid.

"Mom, it's me. It's Sarah." She rolled to a sitting position, clutching the arms of the stunned woman. "I've come back." She didn't expect her mother to understand what she was saying, but she didn't care. She had found a way home! A giddy feeling over took her, a joy so deep her heart fluttered and her stomach jumped. After forty years, her mother was right in front of her.

She scarcely could believe what time had done to her mother. The last time she had seen her, or any member of her family for that matter, they had been young, fit, in the prime of their life.

Her mother was shaking her head, her mouth open in silent protest. "Sarah? But you haven't aged? You look like Kate." She ran shaky hands over Sarah's shoulders and back, as though trying to make sense of the body before her. "But then, that would mean....no...no...this isn't what should happen. Oh my goodness, what have I done?" Wringing her hands, the woman stood and paced the floor. Then she seemed to remember Sarah crouched and confused on the floor, and she knelt, cupping Sarah's face in her hands. "Oh, my sweet Sarah, is it really you? I knew you were alive. I knew it!" Her watery eyes took in the sight of her, drinking her in like a prized possession. "How could this have happened so soon? Where is Kate?" Her mother pulled her into a warm embrace, and Sarah breathed in, her senses immediately picking up the smells of lilac and powder, smells she had associated with her mother for years.

Not understanding the constant rambling, Sarah ignored the train of questions and focused back on the immediate situation. Sarah looked herself over, carefully feeling up and down her body for the source of the pain that wouldn't go away.

"Eeep!" Sarah squeaked in disbelief. She hadn't had time to notice, but she had not come back as the beaten down, overworked mother of six. Her arms weren't marked with sun spots, and her legs weren't bruised and scarred. Her hair hung in beautiful, smooth curls around her shoulders, not in dry, graying strands the texture of hay. Lifting the hem of her dress, Sarah noted the smooth, thin calves that carried on up through her shapely, taut thighs. Not only had she traveled in time, she had gotten younger! She had miraculously regained the youth she had lost so long ago. She looked and felt....fifteen again!

Sarah's spirits soared. She'd reversed the powers of the portal somehow. She'd not only kept herself alive, but now she had found a way to make herself younger as well!

She had been reunited with her family. She would get to see her brothers and sisters; maybe she would find Travis…

Her wild dreams came to a crashing halt as she realized the absurdity of what she was thinking. Just like her mother sitting before her, everyone else would have aged as well. She would be the freak sister returned from the dead like some sort of horrific ghost story. Travis would be old and most likely married. A jabbing pain stuck her in the stomach like a knife, sending a wave of revulsion crashing over her flawless features. Dave Slater would be here. The same Dave who had tried to kill her. Who had taken her life from her in a way worse than death.

What would he say if he saw her? Could she forgive him after all this time? It was because of him that she learned the secrets of traveling. But, no, she couldn't ever forgive him. He had tried to kill her. In fact, if given the chance, she had an idea of what she would do to him. And it wouldn't be pretty.

Sarah wondered how she would tell her brothers and sisters what had happened. Would her family understand? How could her mother stand before her and not fall to the ground in fear or shock? All this time she had dreamt of returning to her family, and yet, they had to believe she was dead. They had gone on without her. They had lived their lives just as she had. She was no longer a part of them.

Ice cold hands gripped her face, turning her to look into the frantic eyes of her mother, breaking her train of thought.

"Sarah! Where's Kate? What happened?"

Sarah shook her head, confused at her mother's babbling and easy acceptance of her presence. Did her mother know about the traveling? Or was she dreaming? Sarah pinched her arm and pulled on the curls in her hair. Everything felt real.

"Mom, it's me, Sarah. I've been lost. Stuck in the past. I can-"

"Noooooo!" Trembling, her mother fell into her lap, letting loose with a piercing wail that echoed through the dimly lit barn. "I've lost Kate," she moaned. "I've lost Kate."

Sarah leaned into her mother's embrace and let the warmth of her arms wash away her fears and anxiety. This is what she had longed for, what she had missed all those years she'd had to be someone else, her childhood stripped from her like bark from a poplar. But who was Kate? Why was her mother concerned with a random girl when Sarah was sitting right in front of her, flesh and blood?

"Sshhh," Sarah whispered, rubbing her hands across her mother's arms. "Everything is fine. I'm home, now, Mom. I can explain everything." *Why am I the one comforting her*, Sarah wondered bitterly.

Her mother sat up, her cheeks wet with tears. "Sarah, you don't understand."

Feeling snubbed and frustrated Sarah snapped, "Well then help me understand! It's like you don't even care that your missing daughter is right in front of you!"

Outside, the storm had passed and the sun sat just below the clouded tree line, sending the first visible rays of sunlight out to warm the chilled, rain soaked grass. Sarah studied her surroundings, barely recognizing the farm of her childhood. Where were the horses? Where were the plows? The outhouse was gone, and so was the old water pump. The silo was missing, burnt to the ground judging by the ring of black on the ground where it used to be. The barn was faded and hanging on by sheer will, its walls leaning and broken from decades spent in the harsh Minnesota elements. From a distance, Sarah could see the house had changed. Additions on the front and back, to accommodate the large family that had since moved out and on with their own lives.

A screened door on the front porch opened and slammed as a man emerged from the house. He was too young to be her father. Sarah strained to see the stranger in the front yard.

Her mother sat up and gasped, wiping her face and nose on the hem of her dress. She no longer looked upset, but had moved to controlled terror. In jerky movements, she stood and pulled on Sarah's arm. "Sarah! We have to get out of here! Dean is coming. He can't find out. We have to hurry."

Sarah struggled to her feet and shuffled to the back of the barn, toward the door that led to the paths of the woods beyond. Tripping over the hem of her dress, Sarah slid on the loose hay beneath her feet. "That's Dean?" she asked, a tremor of excitement flowing through her. Her brother! All grown up and a man! And he was headed straight for the barn!

Sarah lurched away from her mother's steely grip. "No, Mom. I'm not leaving. I want to see Dean. I've been waiting for this moment my whole life. I can't just hide!"

"But you don't understand!" her mother pleaded. "He won't understand!"

Irritated, Sarah stomped her foot. "I am a grown woman." She looked down at her slight build and lack of a chest. "Well, in my head I'm a 'grown woman, and I can do what I want! I can't believe this. You're acting like you don't even want me here, like

I've done something wrong. I'm your daughter back from the dead! It's true, Mama! It's not something to be ashamed of. We should be celebrating! "

Her mother froze, looking at the open barn door to the shadowed corner in the back.

"We aren't supposed to be here!" she hissed. "Something went wrong."

Placing her hands on her hips, Sarah stuck her chin in the air. "I'm not leaving."

"Whatever you do, I'm begging you, Sarah. Don't tell Dean the truth. As far as he knows, you're Kate, his fifteen year old daughter. We were supposed to be at a quilt and craft show this weekend." Her mother said in a rush. "Just pretend everything is normal; I'll explain everything later. But *don't* tell him Kate is gone."

Convinced her mother had gone off the deep end, Sarah jerked her arm away. She was desperate to find out just exactly what had gone on in the time she'd been gone. "Fine, fine," Sarah said distracted by the grown man getting closer to the barn by the minute. How would Dean believe she was a girl named Kate when she so obviously was the fifteen year old sister he lost long ago?

Her mother eyed her warily, her voice calm and rational, no longer hysterical. "You have to pretend to be Kate. Dean's *daughter*. Do not say anything. I know you think I don't know what is going on, but I do. I know about the traveling. And there's been a big mistake. Please, just go along with what I am saying! We will have to fix everything later."

"I'm some girl named Kate, don't say anything. I got it," Sarah muttered, shrugging off the hand on her shoulder and turning to run from the barn "Nice welcome," she muttered, her ego bruised by her mother's slight. After forty years, she thought she would be revered and worshipped…fought over to be seen by everyone she'd ever known. Instead, she was being smothered and covered up, a dirty little secret her mother was afraid of getting out. Admittedly, the whole situation was bizarre and a stretch of the imagination, but it's not like they were living in a time of burning witches and prophets. People wouldn't lock her away in some ward. She had proof of who she was. She remembered her life on the farm like it was yesterday. But what was it her mother had said? She knew about the traveling? Maybe there was more to this than she had thought.

Sarah reached the door just as her brother Dean bent over to crawl between the poles blocking the entrance.

Startled, Dean jumped back and grasped a pole with one hand and his heart with another. "Katydid?" he called out, a huge smile breaking across his face. "I thought you were out of town with Gran?" Confusion knit his brows together, but he was obviously happy to see her.

Pushing around Sarah, her mother jumped between the two before Sarah could respond.

"I'm sorry, Dean. It was supposed to be a surprise," she interrupted. "Kate and I got back early from the quilt show and we were hiding something in the barn before you could see it."

Sarah raised her eyebrows. What was going on here? Couldn't Dean tell who she was? And her mother's lame attempt at a cover up was painstakingly obvious. Why would anyone be in the barn at this hour? Sarah waited, certain Dean would call his mother's bluff. He had to remember who she was, what she looked like the summer she had gone through the portal.

Dean looked far from convinced, but instead of questioning the two of them further, he scratched his head and turned toward the pig pen. "Dad was worried about the sow having her piglets early and eating them. He sent me out to check on her and then I heard you two and wanted to make sure it wasn't some teenage hooligans making mischief." He winked at Sarah. "Well, good, honey. I'm glad you're back. I just got a call from work last night, and we're going to have to cut vacation short. I need to get back home to prepare for a spur of the moment conference."

Sarah studied her mother, watching her face turn from flustered to horrified.

"Dean, surely you can't stay another week?"

Sarah's heart soared. Whether Dean knew who she was or not, she was getting out of there! And there was nothing her mother could do about it. Keeping her emotions in check, Sarah linked her arm into her brother's and placed her head on his shoulder.

"That's too bad," Sarah tried to sound disappointed. "Grandma and I were having such a tremendous time together," she drawled sarcastically. She turned to give her mother a look of satisfaction, who could only trail behind the two of them, clenching her hands with worry.

"Well, we leave in two days, Kate." Dean stopped to wait for her mother so the three of them could link arms together. "I can't tell you how happy I am you came around and actually want to stay."

When they reached the barn where the pigs were penned, he walked away in search of the pregnant sow, leaving the two of them alone.

Her mother's face was a mottled red, her eyes bulged in protest. Before she could say anything, Sarah held up her hand, silencing her mother's chastising. "Don't even try to stop me, Mama. I have dreamt of this day for forty long years. I'm finally going to get what's coming to me whether you approve or not." Sarah turned and headed to the farmhouse, leaving her mother frozen in shock.

Sarah took a deep breath. She didn't know quite the details of what was going on, or why she had to play someone named Kate, but she didn't care. This worked out even better than her being the freak circus sideshow that had returned from the dead. She could play the role of Kate, Dean's daughter, and she would cherish every breath she took. She had been given a second chance at her youth and wasn't going to let it pass by. Sarah couldn't believe her luck!

Quick as a wink, a trace of guilt flashed through her mind. Dean's daughter was obviously missing, and if she took the time to think about it, she knew exactly where the girl had gone. The two of them had switched places. It was the only answer, and the only way for a successful travel. Somehow, Dean's daughter had inherited the traveling link as well. Sarah was grateful the link had survived. It had taken so long for her to get out of the hell she'd been in before; she'd needed another traveler in the portals.

Sarah squashed the guilty feelings down deep and focused on the world around her. The opportunity she'd been granted was unbelievable. This was her time. And no matter how hard it was for her mother to let go of her precious Kate- she wasn't going back. She'd waited too long for this to happen. Kate was on her own, just like she'd been forty years ago.

Chapter 7
Misery Tenfold

I opened my eyes to a low, flat wooden ceiling, cracked and patched with traces of tar paper showing through. Sunlight filtered through one solitary window, casting a muted glow around the gloomy room. Curls of yellow, sticky fly paper adorned the ceiling in various corners, their corkscrew bodies covered with grotesque remnants of flies and other nasty bugs. Mosquitoes hovered near my ear, their incessant buzzing like an alarm clock, too annoying to ignore but impossible to silence.

As far as I could tell, the one room was the extent of the establishment, housing a few cots with limp quilts atop them, a glowing wood stove, and a sturdy log table with stumps for chairs. There were a few makeshift shelves and a crooked cabinet in the corner, but overall, the place was beyond rustic, bordering on caveman-ish.

The house reeked of earth and sweat, its airless confines practically smothering me in my sleep. Wiggling my fingers and toes, I gave a sigh of relief when I could swing my legs to the side of the bed. It seemed I had my body back. Or at least, I had *somebody's* body back.

A filthy mirror hung just above the makeshift bed where I had slept. Straining to see in the dreary space, I could barely contain my alarm upon seeing the grown woman that stared back at me. I had coarse, straight hair that grayed at the temples. Lines popped up across my face like a map when I grimaced at my appearance. Yellowed, crooked teeth peeked out from inside my mouth. No evidence of braces or whitening treatments.

At least the birthmark was still there, strong and dark in color against my pale skin and the only recognizable feature left from my old self. I ran my hands over my face and down my body. Someone had dressed me in a simple cotton dress that hung down to my ankles. Its plain gray color did nothing to boost my spirits.

I jumped as if I'd been stung. *Someone had undressed me*! I felt for my bra and underpants, but only felt the itchy lining of something like a bodysuit beneath the thin fabric. Someone had undressed me *and* seen me naked. A swift kick of mortification weakened my knees. I supposed that being seen naked wasn't the worst thing that could happen to me in this place. Even if it wasn't my true body, I felt violated. I had no idea what had happened to me in the last....who knew how many hours?

The thrumming pain in my head had quieted to a hum, and the aches that had consumed me upon passing through the portal had dulled considerably. Having the body of a grown woman was taxing and overwhelming. I would probably freak when I actually took my clothes off.

Muffled voices just beyond the front door startled me into action. Where to hide? I looked around the barren room, its bleak emptiness giving me no consolation as to my predicament. What was I thinking, trying to find Sarah, I thought miserably. This situation was infinitely worse than 1960. This was like arriving on the doorstep of a pioneer woman, sans the covered wagon.

The door slammed open and a woman bustled in, her skirts swishing in a frenzied manner.

"And I told you she's fine," the woman said to the dark shadow of a man blocking the doorway with his broad shouldered frame.

I blinked back surprise. As soon as our eyes met, I knew exactly where I was. I knew *who I was.* The women from Gran's photo. The twins- what were their names? Vickie and Valorie? No, Vivie. Vickie and Vivie. The unmistakable reality of facing your own identical twin left no doubt in my mind.

Terror ricocheted from my heart to stomach and back. But which twin was I? It made all the difference in the world. One of the twins died in the 1910 fire. And the other, was Gran's mother.

"Vickie, we need to go now! Martha is about to birth her child any minute and she needs help. Dr. Clark is away in Williams and won't be back in time."

The man who had rescued me from the root cellar stomped into the crowded room, taking up what little space there was for breathing. "And I said she ain't going nowhere." He pointed straight at me and scowled. "She couldn't even move yesterday. What are you doing out of bed?" He directed the last statement at me, taking two strides to close the gap between us. "She might have the typhoid."

"She does not have typhoid. She just had a bad fall is all." Vivie clucked her tongue and pushed him aside. "Evan, you have two capable boys to run this household. Take your load of timber to the river and quit worrying. You can't feed this family with sticks and stones." She shoo-ed Evan to the door. "I promise I'll have her back to fix your dinner."

Evan rolled his eyes in my direction, eyeing me with a tired wariness like he'd had this fight one too many times. He grabbed a floppy brimmed hat from a hook by the door and left without another word.

My stomach pitched and churned, the realization that I had traded places with Vickie, my great grandmother's twin, turned uneasily in my stomach like I'd eaten a load of greasy eggs and topped it off with a glass of lard. *Of course I couldn't have traded places with Vivie…the one who lives*, I thought derisively. Bothered by Evan's stormy retreat, my stomach gave another lurch. Vickie had a husband! Oh, heaven help me, I was married…and remembering the black and white photo from Gran's box, I had children, too.

Vivie tugged on my arm, startling me from my train of thought. "We have to hurry. Johan says the pains are only minutes apart."

Digging my feet into the ground, I held fast, trying to process what Vive was saying. The walls seemed to lean and weave, the room spinning in a tilt-a-whirl fashion. I grabbed on to Vivie's arm to steady my shaking legs and clear my vision.

"You want me to help deliver a baby?" I asked incredulous.

"Well, you've done it six times. I think you've got a handle on it."

"Six? Six times!" I repeated, wondering where the mysterious brood could be. Two of them would be the girls from the root cellar, but six children? In my care?

"What about you? Don't you know what to do?" I babbled, stalling for time. I was just getting used to my body; I wasn't ready to take on any responsibilities. "I'm still not feeling very well." That statement made me want to laugh and cry all at once. Not feeling well? Having the flu was not feeling well. There wasn't a word to describe my condition.

Vivie shot me a look, eyeing me up and down as though trying to see through me. "Every time I deliver another baby to someone else, their happiness equals my despair. I needed you to come with me….not for help with the baby. I want you there for me."

Puzzled, I followed her from the house, afraid to stay in the gloomy, rickety home alone. What would I do if Evan came back? And what was I supposed to do with six children? There was barely enough room in the shack for three grown adults! A brief flash of Sarah's face came into mind on the tail end of my barrage of questions. And how was I supposed to find Sarah? Would she even be here?

"I'm sorry," I heard myself say over the roaring battle of confusion in my head. I had no idea what she was talking about but she was my first and maybe only link to figuring out where I was and how I could find Sarah. I sure wasn't going to ask Evan.

"It's just not fair. You're fertile as the Garden of Eden and all I'm asking is for one child. One."

I had no idea what to say. I kept my head down as we continued down a pitted, dusty trail that could only be fit for horses, passing several homes dotted haphazardly along the river's route. I recognized the river, as well as the familiar line of buildings across the wooden wagon bridge. It was as though the photos from Gran's box had come to life.

I had traveled to Spooner, Baudette's twin town of the early 1900's. Across the bridge would be Baudette, its main street lined with severe whitewashed storefronts and the occasional horse and cart. The towns reminded me of a rough and haggard western movie setting, minus the cactus and tumbleweed.

The snake-like Baudette Bay ran between the two towns and turned into the Rainy River to divide the state of Minnesota from Canada. In the distance, black puffs of smoke rose from the trains traveling between the two countries, darkening the brilliant blue sky.

The domed roof of Spooner's large saw mill stood on the edge of the river with logs of varying size taking up most of the wide river's path. The smell of burning peat and charred ash filled the air. Not too far from our shack lined street, majestic, two-story homes lined the streets of downtown Spooner, their creamy painted walls and shuttered windows a drastic slap in the face to the meager homes behind us. I surreptitiously kept pinching myself as we walked. To look at it now and know that a hundred years from now, Spooner wouldn't exist made me shivery and weak. The people, the buildings, the massive saw mill, it would all be gone.

Screams tore me from my observations of the rustic towns. We had reached the house of Johan and Martha Olsen, and it was apparent we were just in time. I assumed the stout, red haired man pacing outside the doorway was Johan, his hands running through the length of his hair in manic strokes; sweat stained the pits of his shirt and formed an oval ring down his back.

When he spied the two of us approaching, relief like I've never seen crossed his face. "Please, come…come," he said in broken English.

Entering the house took every ounce of will power. The grimy, filthy home was worse than imagined; its porous walls and crooked roof the least of the structural problems. A gamey, animal stench filled the restricted space, causing my eyes to tear and my throat to convulse in dry heaves. Vivie pushed me from behind, blocking the door to keep me from running.

A girl not much older than my real self, perhaps, sixteen or seventeen, writhed on the bed in obvious agony, her face contorted in a grotesque mask of pain. The linens on the bed were filthy, stained with blood and a foul smelling, colored liquid. The stuffing of the mattress, hay and feathers, had come loose from the girls' thrashing and had reduced the mattress to a thin barrier between the wooden frame and her heavy, pregnant body. It looked as though a chicken had exploded beneath the girl's feet and I felt a laugh bubble to the surface. Suppressing it with my fist, I stumbled to the side and watched Vivie take over. The scene instantly changed as I witnessed the next blood curdling cry.

Frozen in sheer horror, I stood away from the screaming girl and watched as Vivie consoled Martha, lifting her skirt and checking the baby's progress all while stroking the girl's perspiring head. Unwillingly, I flinched, looking to the ceiling to keep from invading the girl's privacy. Not that she looked like she cared. Martha had her eyes squeezed shut and her teeth bared like a lion's. I wasn't sure she even knew we were there.

Vivie eyed me expectantly. "What are you waiting for? She's almost fully gone. Run and fetch the water from the stove and some clean rags. And get me some more light." She squinted in the dim light at my still form. "Go on!"

"Clean rags?" I muttered dumbly, eyeing the place. There wasn't a clean thing in the house, and I wasn't about to look under anything or *touch* anything to make sure. I felt contaminated just breathing the air.

Martha screamed again, a deep guttural scream that shook my bones and sent my skin tingling. If ever there was an ad for birth control, this would be the ticket. If my high school back home showed every girl a glimpse of the scene I was witnessing, teen pregnancy would be eradicated.

Biting my lip, I searched the one and only cupboard hanging above the woodstove. The fire inside the woodstove had gone out giving us a reprieve from the added heat in the stuffy room, but this meant the water on the stove had cooled and a fly floated lifeless on the surface. Remembering my first trials with a woodstove on Gran's farm, I opened the door and fluffed the gray ashes a bit. Tiny red embers lay beneath the ashy surface, and I blew into the open door while adding some sticks and kindling from a basket nearby. Puffs of acrid smoke blew back into my face as I urged the fire to light. Behind me, Vivie tried to help Martha sit up to remove the soiled sheets beneath her while wincing in pain as the girl pulled and clutched at her arms.

"Vickie, go get some clean linens from the neighbors. And some cool water from the well for Martha." Vivie was all business as she situated Martha back down on the bed.

"But the fire-" I started, arguing that the sterilized water was more important than a clean blanket. Martha was just going to soil the next batch anyway.

"I'll tend the fire. This girl needs something to bring down the heat in her body. She feels feverish to me," Vivie said, her voice carrying a hint of worry.

Hurrying from the house, I brushed past Johan who still paced by the door.

"Baby come, ja?" he asked, hope lighting his face.

"No, baby not come," I said irritably. "Thanks for being such a big help," I muttered as I continued down to the river, grabbing an empty pail on the way. How was it that Johan was allowed to just stand around worrying instead of...oh, I don't know...help haul water or hold down his flailing wife? Bitter and overwhelmed, I pushed through marshy grass and prickly pines to the edge of the Baudette Bay where the shallow, brackish well sat firm in the breeze. I splashed a round of cool water on my face to ease the surge of heat. Everything was happening so quickly. I didn't want to do this. I wasn't supposed to be here.

Heaving a full bucket from the well took only a moment, but I paused to stretch and reassess my surroundings. Maybe I was mistaken. Hopefully I was dreaming. My eyes moved over the banks, looking for more proof that what I was seeing was real.

It was then I noticed the outhouses dotting the shoreline of the bay.

"Oh, no. Oh, no. No.. no.. no," I repeated as I picked up the muddied hem of my dress and hauled myself back to the cabin as fast as I could. The outhouses were lined up to drain right where the women got their drinking water and did their wash. It was a recipe for disaster…and disease. The newspaper clipping from Gran's box noting the typhoid epidemic haunted me as I rushed back to the cabin.

The screams met my ears before I had made it through the trees. Bursting through the door, I saw Vivie holding something limp and bloody, looking very similar to an alien life form, and Martha wailing behind her, clutching her stomach in pain. *How long had I been gone?*

"Do you have any idea how disgusting that water is? And dangerous?" I yelled. "Everything will have to be boiled and sanitized-"

"What took you so long? Where's the water?" Vivie interrupted, her eyes wide with terror. "The baby's just come and it's not breathing."

Dropping the bucket, I approached cautiously as though the still form were a venomous snake. Sure enough, the skin had a mottled blue color tingeing the bloodied skin. Vivie had tried to clear away the face with her dress, wiping the mucous and cleaning out the mouth and nose, but the baby's chest did not move.

"What happened?" I said, fear clutching at my throat. Would Martha and her husband blame us for the baby's death?

"The cord was around the neck when I pulled the baby out," Vivie answered, clearly distraught. Martha's moaning and wailing did nothing to calm my nerves. What did I know of childbirth?

The only answer came to me from tenth grade health class. CPR was about the only thing I could do, and I couldn't do it well. I failed out on the test dummy three times before finally passing.

"Give her-" I glanced down between the baby's legs, "I mean *him* to me." Without another thought other than the need to do whatever I could to get the hell out of there, I flipped the baby over onto my arm and angled his head to the ground. I beat on his tiny back three times and flipped him back over holding him in the crook of my arm. Everything around me became dim and far away; sounds became distorted and I felt robotic in my motions, repeating what I had seen and practiced before with no emotion.

I placed my mouth over his tiny nose and mouth, letting his head fall back slightly to give me a better angle. I couldn't remember the number of breaths to compressions. At this point I didn't think it mattered.

Numb, Vivie watched me work methodically, pushing on the slippery chest for several seconds. Once, she tried to protest, but I held her back with my elbow, refusing to let her take the baby from me until I had given it a full five minutes.

"What are you doing?" Vivie shouted in the background, her eyes bulging with hysteria. "Stop it! Vickie! Are you crazy?" She pulled at my arms and fluttered nervously at my side.

Martha had fallen back weakly in her bed and turned to the wall to avoid looking at the still baby. I turned my back on the both of them and tried to give myself some breathing room in the confined space.

Vital seconds passed. Whispering a prayer, I decided to give one last try. I breathed deeply into the infant's mouth and nose, its chest rising ever so slightly. I closed my eyes and listened. A gurgling cough, followed by a cry that sounded like a baby lamb came forth from the baby's lips. His arms jerked and his fingers curled in protest.

Immediately, Martha stopped sobbing, intent on the sound of her newborn child. She rolled to face me, eyes wide with a mixture of fear and wonder. Shaking, I handed the baby to Vivie, his bloodied skin already taking on a pinkish hue. Martha made the sign of a cross on her chest and eyed me suspiciously, as though I had somehow transformed into a witch or magician-something from the devil itself.

Vivie didn't waste time on praise. She washed the baby with the water from the woodstove, now orange and fiery red inside. When she placed the infant in Martha's outstretched arms, the room lost its tainted, contaminated feel and became a haven of security and love. But only for a few minutes. It didn't take me long to remember where I was and what I had just done.

Johan finally made his appearance, his cap clasped nervously in his hands having not an inkling of the brush with death that had occurred only a few feet from his presence. Vivie and I left the two of them huddled together over the baby, Martha forgetting my impossible feat- distracted by the mews and cries of her newborn son.

After cleaning the soiled bed and washing Martha the best we could, Vivie promised we would return the next day to help clean up the place and teach

Martha some simple caregiver tips. She escorted me through the doorway in a daze.

My hands trembled and my knees shook. I kept going back and forth between the outcome and what could have happened. Dry heaves caught at my throat as I held back the anxious retching I had been desperately trying to hold in.

How on earth had I saved that baby?

Vivie practically interrogated me about my display of unorthodox methods. How did I know how to do that? Did I whisper a spell before I breathed into the baby? Did I care that by tomorrow, Martha will have everyone thinking I was a witch or crazy healer woman?

I walked alongside her, mute with exhaustion and awe. I kept looking at my hands...hands that weren't really mine, and I wondered if the outcome would have been different if I hadn't been there. Had I changed the future?

Suddenly, I was suffocating, the air impossible to draw into my lungs. I clawed at my throat and pulled at the tight neckline of my dress. The shacks along the road teetered and moved in my peripheral vision; the trees turned soft and hazy, waving and bending as though turned to rubber. I gasped and gasped for air, clutching my stomach and bent at the waist while Vivie barely noticed my distress in her harried replay of the recent events. Everything came crashing down on me- the vision of the blue tinged baby, Martha screaming, the filthy house....the fact I had no idea how to find Sarah.

I rushed past Vivie, stumbling toward the bay's edge, disregarding the possibility of contamination. My body was soiled anyway; streaks of blood and who knew what else ran the length of my dress and onto my skin. Crashing into the river, I tore away the restrictive clothing and dove beneath the frigid water. I swam out to the bay's current, where the water rolled swiftly along. I pulled through the murky depth in strong, sure strokes, trying to ease the tension rooted in my bones. This was a lot to handle. Much more so than the average fifteen year old would have to experience. This was insane.

And it wasn't even close to being over.

Six children and a husband that resembled a heavyweight boxing champion were waiting for me to take care of them. There was no way. No freakin' way.

Kicking free of my dress, I finally surfaced and was able to pull in gratifying gulps of fresh air. I flipped onto my back and kicked lazily, spent from my mad dash and swim. I could hear Vivie shouting hysterically from shore. What was I going to do?

I couldn't leave. I wasn't even sure I could leave if I wanted to. Gran said to watch for the northern lights and a lightning storm. We had made sure about the portal being open in the future....but we never thought about the portal in the past. When would those two things occur back to back? Tomorrow? In a few days? A few months?

I sank beneath the surface, gritting my teeth against despair. We had not thought this out at all. We knew nothing about time traveling. Nothing was constant or certain. There were no rules or boundaries. Gran's research and theories meant squat.

And possibly the worst part, the part that threatened to break my sanity, was that I hadn't traveled in the suspended form like we'd thought.

This wasn't pretend.

And my real life, the one I'd left behind, was going on without me.

I moaned into the water, the eerie haunting vibration running through the ripples. For the tiniest second, I considered not coming back up.

Chapter 8
Living the Good Life

Sarah breathed out an exaggerated contented sigh. She had taken a well-deserved nap- her first in forty years, and she felt just short of princess stature in the cushy mattress. Overwhelmed by all of the modern conveniences she had never seen, and relieved to see some of them she'd had as a child, Sarah couldn't believe how easy life had become.

She sat up and reached for the string above her bed. With the slightest pull she had an immediate flooding of light! How luxurious to have electricity again. Sarah slid from the bed, eyeing the door. She wondered if her mother was waiting for her in the hall; she had looked none too pleased when Sarah had left her behind and slunk off to bed with the excuse of a headache. There was no way she was going to give her mother the pleasure of a lecture in the first few moments of her return.

Rooting through a suitcase laden with piles of unkempt laundry, Sarah marveled at the shocking change in clothes and shoes, bags of make-up and underwear in colors that would have had the women of 1910 swooning. Sarah held up one thin, stringy article of clothing, unsure of what it was. It resembled underwear, but hardly had enough fabric to operate as such. Maybe it was a fancy sort of hair ribbon. Finding Kate's purse, she flipped out the contents, amazed at the amount of money in the wallet. The girl was just plain spoiled, Sarah figured. Kate had more with her on vacation than Sarah had owned in her entire life.

Sarah chose a soft, stretchy short sleeved shirt and denim jean shorts that had been hacked off high on the thighs, the white of the pockets peeking out right at the hem line. Admiring her slim figure in the mirror, Sarah twisted and turned, eyeing herself from every angle. The feeling of freedom practically oozed from her pores; she didn't have to wear a stuffy, tight corset, or have her hair tied up in a bun. She didn't have chores to do, wood to chop, children to feed, meals to cook…she just had time. Plenty of time.

"Hey, sleepyhead." Dean poked his head into her bedroom and smiled. "Your weekend with Gran must have worn you out. Why did you guys drive back so quickly? Was there a problem?"

Not for me, Sarah thought. Ignoring his questions, Sarah laughed and sprinted to give Dean a huge hug. Like the climax to a firework, the elation she felt practically exploded from her chest. She held onto Dean and closed her eyes thinking of the new life she was about to start. And who better to start it with than her own brother?

"I can't believe it's you," she sighed. "Sorry I slept so long. What are we going to do today?" Sarah asked, snuggling her face into Dean's chest.

"Well, unlike some people," Dean laughed and raised his eyebrows at her, "some of us have already been out and working today. You slept past lunch, Kate." He untangled himself from her embrace and seemed to look her over. "Are you sure there isn't anything wrong? Gran seems upset, or worried about something. And you don't usually hug me like this unless you need money. Or are in trouble." He waited for her to explain.

Sarah blinked. She had almost forgotten she had a role to play. "Nothing happened. I swear! I felt a little sick and we had to come home early. We drove late in the night, got here this morning, and hid something in the barn from Grandpa. A quilt." Sarah thought quickly. "For his birthday. I had to sleep off a headache. That's it." She peered up at him with wide, innocent eyes.

Dean sighed and turned to go back downstairs. Jumping ahead of him, Sarah held Dean's hand and practically pulled him down the stairs to the kitchen. A plate of leftovers and a glass of lemonade waited on the table for her. Everyone else was outside finishing chores.

"Maybe you could spend some time with Corey. Take him fishing at the rapids," Dean suggested as he slid tall, rubber work boots on. "We're leaving soon and he keeps complaining that you haven't played with him much."

Sarah nodded, taking everything in. Play with Corey? That was her job for the day? Sarah stretched her arms and twirled around the kitchen, drunk with giddiness. Kate had to be about two minutes from killing herself right about now, Sarah figured. If this was the life Kate had left behind, she was in for a huge shock. She was probably knee deep in dirty diapers and swampy marsh shores, or busy trying to figure out how an outhouse worked. Sarah giggled to herself. Oh, how the tables had turned.

Dean left the kitchen with a wave and look of bewilderment on his face, like Sarah had grown another head. The way he watched her…it was as though she were an intricate puzzle with the pieces jumbled on the floor. Sarah did a mental check, erasing the wide smile from her face. She would have to try hard not to do anything to throw things out of whack. She had a life to figure out and she had to figure it out quickly.

Sarah scarcely recognized the kitchen, or the rest of the house for that matter. Since she had vanished, a bathroom had been built inside, a modern washer and dryer stood in an addition behind the kitchen, and the sink had working plumbing-with hot and cold water at the turn of a knob. The room had a radio tuned to a lively country station, an electric mixer on the counter....and a stove that didn't require someone shoving wood into it every half an hour!

Unwrapping the paper towel from around the sandwich left on the table, she took a huge bite, relishing the soft, white bread and the thinly sliced ham and cheese. Her mother had left her a cup of pistachio pudding as well, her favorite. Digging into the pudding with the tips of her fingers, she licked the bright green glob and groaned in ecstasy. She hadn't had pudding in so long.

Sarah cleaned the cup and swirled her finger around the edges for good measure, getting any last traces of pudding. Outside the window, a small, gangly boy crossed the yard carrying a slingshot and a fishing pole in his grubby hands. His confident swagger and thick thatch of hair reminded Sarah of a young Dean, around eight years old. The age he was when she had disappeared. It was fate, Sarah decided. Everything had come full circle. She was getting her life back almost the same as she'd left it. And it would be perfect.

Maybe her time traveling days could finally be over, at least for a decade or two.

Dropping her empty glass into the sink, Sarah slipped on a pair of bright pink flip flops, approving the bright hue as compared to the browns and blues she was so used to. She headed onto the porch and called out to Corey, stopping him in his trek. Hurrying down the steps, Sarah raced to catch up with the little boy who would now be her brother, ignoring the pointed looks from her mother who was busy hanging sheets on the clothesline. She knew that her mother wanted to talk with her, try to change her mind. But it wasn't going to happen, and it hurt that she would even try.

Didn't her mother want what was best for her? What she deserved?

In the end, it didn't matter what anyone else wanted anyway. She only had two days to steer clear of any guilt heavy discussions, and then she was free and on her way to Florida. A whole new state! Near the ocean! She had never dreamed something so outlandish.

Shaking her head clear of any negative thoughts, Sarah focused back again on Corey. Spending time with him wouldn't be the chore Dean was making it out to be. In fact, Sarah figured, Corey was the best place to start on learning who Kate was and what she had to do to be like her. Sarah needed facts on friends, hobbies, her missing mother? Boyfriends (hopefully), and clues to high school survival-: hang outs, fads, and clothing. It had been ages since she'd been inside a school. When was the last time she had gossiped with friends, or shopped in a decent store. The possibilities were overwhelming. She couldn't be more surprised or thrilled if she'd woken up on the moon.

In the beginning, she would have to stay on the path Kate had carved out for herself; it was necessary, if only to establish some ties to her new family. She hoped Dean would understand her eventual transition or blame it on raging hormones. Sarah would give herself a month or two in Kate's shoes, but after that she was on her own, creating the life for herself that she had never had.

And what a life it would be.

Chapter 9
A Friend in Need

"Are you trying to cause a scandal?" Vivie chastised as I emerged from the icy water, my undergarments soaked and transparent, leaving nothing to the imagination.

Teeth chattering and covered in goose bumps, I let Vivie put her arm around me and hustle me down the dirt trail toward Vickie's home.

"Are you trying to catch the death of you?" she continued, eyeing me out of the corner of her eye with displeasure. "It's bad enough that every other house has typhoid, you want to add pneumonia on there, too?"

The house was empty when we returned, the four walls and roof looking as though it could blow away in a strong wind. Before I could protest, Vivie stripped me clear of what was left of my clothes, leaving me standing naked and shivering. Shoving me onto the bed, Vivie covered me with several quilts, pulling them straight up to my chin.

She moved around the room, stoking the woodstove, adding a few pieces of a wood, and then putting an old scratched tea kettle on the stove to warm.

"Looks like we're out of mint leaves. And honey," she said, pawing through the few tins stacked in a row on a makeshift shelf next to the stove.

I answered with a noncommittal groan and clacking teeth.

Vivie pulled a trunk from beneath the bed and pulled a dress from within the folds of fabric. It was brown and faded with cream colored flowers embroidered around the hem.

"Put this on. You'll have to wait for your underclothes to dry." She still sounded like she was lecturing me.

Finally, I tried speaking. "Th...thh... thanks. I don't know what came over me. After the baby-" I paused and took a deep breath, trying to ignore the image of the blue tinged baby in my head. "I just couldn't breathe. I had to get out of that house."

Vivie grabbed a couple of mugs from the cupboard; both had chips taken out of them and they didn't match. She filled them with steaming hot water and dumped a scoop of sugar in each. The spoon scraped the bottom of the tin as she scooped the last of the sugar granules into the water. She dropped a few withered leaves on top and carried the mugs to the table.

She waited on a tall wooden stump, her hands clasped around one of the mugs for warmth.

Embarrassed, I stayed beneath the sheets hiding my naked body. I hadn't even had time to really examine my new curves and already Vivie and Evan had seen me in all my glory. My cheeks flashed red at the thought of Evan. He was a full grown *man*, not some lanky, acne prone, high school boy with barely a mustache to show for himself. He would have needs and expectations. I gulped and swallowed hard. That was not something I had considered, even after my experiences with Dave and Travis.

Vivie cleared her throat and nodded at the dress. I pulled the coarse fabric under the quilt and tried to slide it over my head. Vivie snorted with laughter as I wiggled and squirmed beneath the heavy quilt. Finally, I gave up and rolled from the bed, wincing as the wooden side boards dug into my side. Pulling the dress over my head, I shook it down to the floor and slipped my arms through the long, tapered sleeves. Vivie rose and helped me button the back, all fifteen buttons. I was still shaking and not just from the cold. Fear had settled stony and hard within me, coaxing a deep, icy, unsettling panic in my soul.

We moved to the table in silence. I had to refrain from pushing the dress between my legs, the lack of underwear so foreign and uncomfortable; it was like an outdoor market down there, breezy and without boundaries. I sat closest to the woodstove, hoping the stoked fire would help ease the tightly coiled spring of emotions inside.

We sat across from each other holding our steaming mugs of…whatever Vivie had whipped up.

I choked down a mouthful of the bitter drink, wincing as the heat burned the roof of my mouth and tongue. It seared a blistering course down my throat and settled in my stomach trying to break the ice within. I coughed and sputtered and slammed the cup to the table.

"Ok," Vivie said, "I think we better start with you telling me who you really are."

I coughed again, gagging at her blunt, take-me-off guard brashness. "What do you mean?" I wheezed. My eyes welled up and leaked at the sides as my stomach heaved in an attempt to get sick.

"This is no time for games," she said simply, sending me a look of reproach.

"How did you know?" I gasped, relieved I wouldn't be alone in this mess. I didn't even bother trying to hide. Vivie was right; there wasn't enough time for the charade and games. I had to find Sarah and get out of there.

"The same thing happened about fifteen years ago. I'm a twin. I have senses. I have a connection with my sister that goes beyond emotions; it's practically tangible the ties that bind Vickie and I." She took a sip of her drink, contemplating her words. "At first, when Evan brought you out of the cellar, I thought Vickie had found her way back. That's how it happened the first time. But that's obviously not the case at all. I wasn't sure at first." She wagged a finger in front of my face. "I knew for certain when you brought that baby back to life. And you got upset about the water being dirty. Vickie and Sarah would never have done something like that. They've lived this way for years. " She stared at me, waiting for my confession. "Vickie couldn't swim. And Sarah only swam at the lake. So-"

My ears perked up and my mouth went dry. Fifteen years ago? Sarah? "Wait a minute. What happened fifteen years ago?"

"A girl named Sarah appeared one day in the root cellar, same as you, taking over Vickie's body like some sort of spirit. It took me awhile to figure out, but when I did, she broke down and told me who she was, where she had come from. She said she had some special time traveling gene?" She looked at me with eyebrows raised, even though she knew the answer.

I nodded.

"Apparently, she had been to other places, other times. You know, within our family lines. She made it sound fun, like a game. But when she got here she sort of became stuck. She didn't know how to get back to her family, or anywhere else for that matter. And she couldn't tell me what had happened to Vickie either. Eventually, I had to accept her as my sister and carry on the lie for all these years. Vickie has never come back." Her eyes became pools of azure and she blinked and turned her head. "Do you...do you think Vickie is still out there somewhere? In someone else's body?"

The words poured from Vivie's mouth on deaf ears. A cold stone of dread had replaced my heart. Sarah had been here? As Vickie? Which meant…

"Oh no!" I cried, dropping my head into my hands. Sarah wasn't here, but she had been. Did that mean she arrived at the farm in my body? Fear took over, crushing in on my sides until I could scarcely breathe. I had done the improbable. I had traveled like Gran and Sarah.

I could be stuck here forever.

"Honey, it's ok," Vivie murmured, rubbing my arm. "We'll figure something out." She sighed and stared out the window.

"You don't understand," I wailed, only the words came out muffled between the folds of my arms. Tears welled up and overflowed from my eyes, darkening my sleeve in round blotches.

"You're right," Vivie said, "I've never time traveled. I don't think I can. I don't know why Vickie could do it and not me." She sounded slightly jealous. "I swear it's like you all really are witches."

I cried harder, my shoulders shaking the table.

"Look, let's start this over. Who are you? Where do you come from? How did you get here?"

I lifted my head and stared through watery eyes. I had someone on my side, someone to share my secret and I felt a hundred times worse. Sniffing, I wiped my nose on the sleeve of my dress and blotted my eyes dry.

"My name is Kate Christenson. I'm your great-granddaughter. I'm fifteen and from the year…wait. What year is it now?"

"1910. Did you say great-granddaughter? That means I will have children!" Vivie clapped her hands together, forgetting the intensity of the moment. I could see her doing the calculations in her head, picturing the limbs of her stilted family tree. "You've actually met my own children before me, imagine that," she mumbled, scratching her head. "Sarah never did tell me the exact family lineage. I knew we were related but I didn't know how."

I sat back, resting my hands in my lap, dazed with shock. The fire of 1910 that had obliterated every town and forest for miles and taken Vickie's life had not yet happened, but it was in the near future. The redundancy of my time traveling into death's hands was unsettling. Was there a pattern? A purpose? Was I supposed to save Vickie's life, or was it all to be in vain? I thought I had been meant to save Sarah before, but that had been wrong. Was this another traveling incident headed for death? How tangled was this mess of a web I was in? The questions whirled around in my mind.

"What month?" I asked, visibly cringing as I waited for the answer.

"It's August 28th." Vivie stretched out her hand to grab mine. "I can't believe I am talking to my great granddaughter." She was disturbingly distracted from the focus of my plight, caught up in the magic of realizing her own dreams.

I racked my brain. There were much more important things to discuss. When was the fire? It had been at the end of the summer. October maybe? Where had Sarah gone? Would Vivie help me pull off a convincing role as Vickie? If Sarah and I had switched places, would she come back for me? Would Gran figure out what happened? The questions swirled and collided at a dizzying rate, causing a nauseous, seasick sort of effect. I knew the local general store didn't have Dramamine.

Squeezing my eyes shut against the epic battle in my head, I took a steadying breath. At least I had time. It's not like my death sentence was tomorrow, or even next week. I had time to figure out the portals and get back home. It could have been worse.

Vivie shook my arm, bringing me back to the present. "Kate, I can't imagine what you must be feeling, taken by surprise and ending up here."

"That's the thing, it wasn't a surprise. I was trying to find Sarah. I was going to bring her back, to the time I'm from. Back to where she should be. Except," I bit my lip to get control of my wavering voice, "everything went wrong!"

Vivie put her hand on my arm. "We have much to talk about. But it will have to wait. The kids will be home from the neighbors soon, and Evan will be back tonight. I need to fill you in on what you need to know, and then later, you're going to fill me in on the rest. I promise I will help you the best I can. Kate?" She bent her head to look into my downcast eyes. "Can you do this? Can you be Vickie?"

Before I could answer, the door burst open. Two boys raced into the room stopping just short of the table, their eyes eager and expectant. One was tall and lanky with dark hair, and the other was stout and broad shouldered, a patch of curly brown hair on his head. Their pants and shirts had been stitched and patched several times and they lacked shoes on their feet. When they saw the table empty, their smiles turned to disappointed groans.

"Ma, where's dinner? We're starving. Mr. Arneson made us haul two fields of brush today."

A thin girl with scraggly blond hair came through the doorway on the boys' heels. She carried another girl on her back and led two more children by the hand. Their serious faces were haggard and drawn after a long day's work. I stared hard at the cluster of children until I spotted the girl with the hourglass birthmark. Mary. Unintentionally, my hand reached out of its own accord, trying to make contact with the tiny symbol.

Vivie jumped from the table, stopping me with a slight squeeze of my arm.

"James, William," she nodded at the older boys. "Go down to the root cellar and bring me up some potatoes and lard." She turned to the others and addressed them as well. "Ruth, change Gracie's diaper. Mary, fetch some water from the well. John, go check the garden for any leftover onions we may have missed."

The names swirled inside my head but vanished as soon as the children left the tiny cabin. How did they all fit in here?

"We need to whip up something to eat. Can you cook?" Vivie asked as she pawed through the lone cupboard by the woodstove.

Panic rose again as the enormous weight of responsibility took up the tiny spaces left in the cabin. My hands shook as I rose from the table.

"Vivie, I can't do this. I'm fifteen! I come from a time where there are lights in the house, and microwaves, and fast food!" I paused for breath. Vivie wouldn't have the slightest idea what I was saying. "I can't raise children. I'm a child myself! And I can't be a wife." I shuddered thinking of Evan wrapping his solid arms around my waist.

Vivie spun around, her eyes wild and bright with intensity. "You're going to have to, Kate! These are people's lives we're talking about. And there are plenty of girls these days who are married and have children at fifteen. This is your fate. Deal with it. Sarah did."

She heard my intake of breath at her harshness and she paused as she adjusted a large cast iron skillet on the woodstove

"I'm sorry, Kate," she whispered. "You're not the only one this is hard on. I've lost my sister twice now. It's like starting all over again, losing someone you love. Sarah felt like a sister to me, not like a twin, but a sister. And now you're here, and I still don't have answers. Vickie's still missing."

Little John returned first, his hands grubby and full of tiny onions pulled from the family's garden plot behind the house. Vivie held her hand up to signal he was five years old. I made him wash his hands in a bowl of water leftover from the reservoir on the woodstove before touching anything in the house. I didn't know much, but I did know something about sanitization. The world I came from was nothing but spotless floors and travel size anti-bacterial lotions.

Ruth and Gracie arrived next; Gracie's soaking wet cloth diaper left outside the front door. Vivie signaled nine and two. They also were treated to a quick hand and face wash, their cheeks turning bright red from the scruffy swipes of the hem of my dress.

James and William came through the door, their arms loaded with potatoes and a glass jar full of lard. Vivie mouthed eleven and thirteen. The two older boys protested to washing, but Vivie silenced them with a look and sent them back outside to chop more firewood for the stove.

"You're going to have to be strict and lay down the law right away. They're going to take advantage of a soft mother. They have chores and work to do every day."

"I don't know the rules. Or the law," I hissed back, fumbling with the large bowl of potatoes the boys had left behind. "And I am the furthest thing from a mother!"

"It'll be easier when school starts."

"I better not be here when school starts," I murmured to no one in particular.

Mary was the last one to appear, her blond tresses standing out like golden strands of corn silk against the dreary dark walls. She carried in a full bucket of water and set it near the stove.

"I heard someone has a birthday next week," Vivie said, mischief in her voice.

Mary looked up, her blue eyes shining with innocence. "It's mine, Aunt Vivie. It's my birthday!"

"And you're going to be, what? Four?"

Mary giggled loudly. "Aunt Vivie! You know I'm gonna be eight!" Her cheeks flushed with pleasure at being noticed and remembered. Mary turned her saucer sized eyes on me. "Mama, are we gonna have a cake?"

My heart jumped into triple time. *Could I promise her a cake?* It's not like the house had an ample pantry; I didn't know how to make anything but a Betty Crocker mix in a box. But it wasn't like she was asking for the world- the poor girl only wanted a cake. For my last birthday, I had asked Dad for a trip to Universal Studios in Orlando. Slight difference.

Vivie soared into the silence to save the day. "Of course your Mama's going to make you a cake, honey. It's a special day for a special girl."

Mary's birthmark stood out like a neon light in a bar window. *If she only knew how special she really was.*

The rhythmic thud of chopping sounded outside the window. Thunk! And I couldn't help but flinch. I paced the narrow space of flooring chewing on my bottom lip. Children were everywhere! Like cockroaches hidden in the crooks and crannies of a palm, they scurried and fluttered around the house in a frenzy of motion. A headache began to form behind my eyes. It was true I had lived with my Dad's ten brothers and sisters for a time, but being in charge of brood was something else entirely.

Sensing my state of overwhelmed emotion Vivie sent the children outside to play, with what I didn't know. Apparently, all the children needed was a ball of twine or a rusty can for a rousing game of kick-the-can or stickball. Sometimes they played hide and seek for hours, Vivie assured me. They weren't allowed in the house except for eating and sleeping, and the occasional rain storm- which explained why the quarters could be so small. I wondered what they did in the winter. How did they keep from going stir crazy and killing each other?

Vivie put me to work peeling and slicing potatoes. She threw some lard into the cast iron skillet and fried the potatoes with bits of onion. She checked a woven basket that had been stashed on the shelf with the sugar tin. She pulled two eggs from the folds of a checkered cloth and cracked them into the potatoes and onions. A pinch of pepper and salt over the entire works and that was it. Dinner for the family was done.

"Look," she said, "I'll come over and help with meals for a few days, until you get your feet wet. I'll show you how to do laundry and where to shop for your food items like milk and eggs, flour and sugar. Some food we trade work hours for. As far as clothing, we wash the children's clothes together during the days while they're at school or working for the neighbors. School starts soon, so we'll fashion some flour sack dresses for the girls and pants for the boys. I'm assuming you don't know how to sew; I'll help you with that. Shoes will have to be charged at the store."

Vivie looked to the ceiling, trying to figure out what else I needed to know.

"When do the kids eat? When do they bathe? How do they bathe? What about Evan? Where does he work? When does he come home? What chores do I have?" My words were frantic, pouring from my mouth like liquid fire, hot and fast. I was afraid to voice the most important question. What about how I was going to get home?

The door slammed open and I jumped, slamming my head into the shelf above the wood stove. Stars blinked fuzzy patterns inches in front of my face. Evan swept into the room, his massive shoulders scraping the frame of the door.

"You're not going to believe what just happened, V." He sounded excited, and he held a roll of paper clasped tightly in his hand. "I ran into Helic Clementson just outside the Minnesota hotel downtown. He asked to meet with me, hearing as I've been foreman of the Mathieu sawmill for a few months now." Evan paused, his mouth working past a smile as wide as the room. "V, he offered me a position out at his mill on Clementson! A promotion, an increase in pay, and get this, he's giving us some of his property to build on! Can you believe it?" Evan grabbed me into his arms and swung me around, my feet nicking the nearby stumps around the table. "We'll finally have our own place. A place to farm! And a real house, like you've always dreamed."

His deep, velvety laughter echoed and reverberated through the tiny space, sending goose bumps up my arms. I remained stiff and on guard, not knowing what to say, afraid that if I smiled my face might crack in two.

Again, Vivie saved the day. "Evan! That's great. Just great. How happy you must be after all your hard work."

Evan seemed to notice Vivie for the first time. "Vivie, you need to run home and talk to Bertel. The property's big enough for the both of us to build. It's right in the prime area where all that white pine will be logged off. It's close to Rapid River and a general store. Even a post office!"

"Rapid River?" I echoed, thinking of the bridge and Dave Slater and portals. Bile burned the back of my throat and I grimaced. It just kept getting worse.

"What's the matter, Victoria?" Evan cradled my face between his large, calloused hands. "We can finally get the kids out of this hole. There's a good school for them to attend in Clementson. Everyone wins." He spread his hands out, waiting for my jubilant reaction that would never happen. "It's never gonna happen any other way." He unrolled the paper in his hands and spread it out on the table, taking care to smooth the creases. "Look at the plot he promised us, V. Look at it!"

Vivie moved away from the stove and called to the kids through the still open door. Hordes of mosquitoes and flies took it as an unwelcome opportunity to flood the warm room, buzzing and swarming, on the prowl for fresh blood. Vivie grabbed a towel to shoo away the pests while peeking over at the crude drawing on the table. Her eyes beckoned me closer, urging me to be more receptive to Evan's announcement.

Cornered in the kitchen, I stood helpless and mute. I had lost the feeling in my legs and needed to sit down. *Get a grip on yourself, Kate. Grow up,* I lectured myself. *You got yourself into this, you can get yourself out.*

Tentatively, I made my way over to look at the drawing. Amazing. I recognized the Rapid River, the crossroads where Slater's Farm store would someday be and the plot where Gran's house stood. We would be moving onto Gran's land.

I gave a curt nod of approval and forced a shaky smile.

"Vivie, why don't you head on home and tell Bertel. There's plenty of space for us both to build. I could get him a job at the mill." Evan's meaning was clear. He wanted privacy.

I spun around, desperate for an excuse to get her to stay. The moment was about to get beyond awkward. A sudden howl, high pitched and eerie filled the air stopping Vivie in her trek to the door.

James and William burst through the door, William clutching his hand in agony as a river of blood ran the length of his arm to splatter unheeded to the floor below.

"I didn't mean to!" James yelled, trying to outdo his brother's shrieks. "It was an accident! He knows better than to…"

"What happened?" Vickie squatted eye to eye with William, wrenching the bloodied hand away from his chest and into view. Her gasp was telling enough. "Oh, my sweet Lord."

William's face was ashen and his shrieks louder when the evidence of his injury became clear. Snot bubbled from his nose and dirt mixed with tears, as he writhed in front of Vickie's probing gaze.

"Evan, run next door and get the mercurochrome from Mrs. Klakeg."

He shot me a curious glare before racing out the door, and it was only then I realized how odd it must seem for William's *mother* to be standing in the background, mute and motionless with terror.

The rest of the thunderous herd soon followed in the wake of the emergency. They crowded around William, who was now sloped over the table, his legs giving out as the true sensations of pain and fear took over. The room filled with animated chatter, tattling and whining, peering and the throwing of elbows as the group jostled for attention and the ability to see in the tight space. John had prickers and burs all up and down his pants and a rip four inches long through the seat, Mary had a red, angry scratch on her cheek looking to be from a stick or branch, hopefully not a set of fingernails. I did the only thing I could think of- I put the hot cast iron skillet on the table and ordered the children to move away from William and eat their dinner.

"The show is over, children," I admonished. "Your brother doesn't need you crowding around him right now."

But the show was far from over. Through the grabbing and shoveling of food, Evan reappeared with the mercurochrome, handing it to Vivie while wiping the sweat from his brow. She peeled back the cloth she had wrapped swiftly around William's bleeding hand, and the entire room filled with shrieks and gasps of horror.

The tips of William's three middle fingers on his right hand were missing.

Without a second thought, Vivie doused the open wound with the mysterious brown liquid whereupon William promptly sat straight up, arched his back in agony, and fainted dead away on the floor- the whites of his eyes showing brightly in the cracks of his opened lids.

Stars blinked before my eyes. I needed to escape. But instead, it was Evan who got to escape. He stormed from the kitchen rattling the plates on the table as he slammed the door.

Vivie ripped a hand towel into shreds to bandage and staunch the bleeding of William's arm. She lifted him into the closest bed and took to washing the bloody evidence away. Arms clasped around my legs and pulled at my skirt. I patted Gracie's head absentmindedly, bothered by yet another mud smudged face and tousled hair. Was nothing ever to be clean? Did it even matter if it was clean when children's fingers were getting chopped off?

The skillet was empty in less than fifteen minutes. Vivie, Evan, and I hadn't eaten one bite. I ordered the children to wash again after their meal, taking special care to clean Mary's scratch. John handed me his torn pants and wiggled into his only spare pair hanging from his bedpost. I guessed he expected me to mend them. *Awesome.*

There were complaints I had forgotten to make bread and the children grumbled they were still hungry. Their lean frames stood out in their ill-fitting clothing, but they were sturdy children used to hard labor. They wouldn't bend or break from lack of one full meal. William hadn't moved on the bed, but the color was returning to his face. I glanced at each one of them trying to summon the courage to speak. To take charge.

"I... I'm sorry," I stuttered. "I didn't have time to bake bread. I had to deliver a baby today. There was trouble. I... I..." I couldn't finish. The weight of ten expectant eyes boring into my skull was enough to make me want to run screaming down the street. They didn't care about the blue baby that I'd had to save, or the filthy living conditions, or the tainted water supply. They had almost forgotten their brother, missing parts of his hand, for heaven's sake. They cared about their stomachs and having enough to keep them full through the night. Living in the now. Surviving the present. That was the motto.

Because in reality, for many people of this time, there might not be a tomorrow.

"There's a few pints of blueberries left in the cellar," Vivie said. "James, go get the berries and you all can share them outside." The children cheered as though they had been offered cotton candy and ice cream cones. They rushed from the room, their bare feet pounding the wooden floor in resonating slaps.

"Are you ok?"

Was I ok? I still had all my fingers, but I wasn't ok. Not in the slightest. I sighed and leaned up against the bed frame furthest from the table. "Vivie." I couldn't manage another word. Didn't want to taste a single word in my mouth. Suddenly I was so tired, so overwhelmed I could scarcely stand, let alone carry on a sensible conversation. What did I expect? To live like the show *Little House on the Prairie*? For everything to come and pass, all with a tidy ending where everyone lives happily ever after? For this trip to be easier than the last? I could barely pass as Sarah, a fifteen year old from the 60's. There was no way I could pull off a grown woman from the 1900's, married and with children. How could I have possibly known? But then again, why hadn't I thought out all the possibilities?

A small framed sampler hand stitched with red roses and green vines hung on the wall, the only hint of décor or attempt at claiming the shack as home. The background of the sampler was stained and far from its original white color, but the words were legible and completely appropriate. I read the words over and over again until I could breathe normally. *This too shall pass.*

It was all a matter of priorities, I decided. Struggle through the everyday chores enough to get by. Pay attention to the weather and watch for northern lights. Keep the family from starving to death. Breathe. Probably all of those things, in the reverse order.

It was the best I could do.

***

I lay stiff as a board in the cramped, uncomfortable makeshift bed that Evan and I were supposed to share. I might as well have been lying directly on the pine board bottom as much cushion as the lumpy mattress stuffed with straw offered. Evan still hadn't come home after his abrupt departure earlier today. I had busied myself straightening and cleaning the small space while he was gone.

As soon as the sun had gone down, the kids expected supper. Vivie and I fried up the last of the cellar's potatoes with onions, same as we'd had earlier. Again, there was grumbling at the lack of bread for which I had no answer. It's not like I could run to a store, or whip something up with a few random ingredients. I had no flour, sugar, eggs, not even some milk. I hoped I could fill the pantry soon; I sensed the children plotting mutiny.

Vivie had stayed as long as she could, before taking off to make dinner for Bertel. She had waited until William had woken, tended to his throbbing hand, promising a dose of pain medicine in the morning, if she could find it. She had offered him a mix of weak tea and whiskey, procured from the neighbors, to help him through the night, and thankfully he lay sleeping next to James and John on the thin bed, his bandaged hand elevated on a pile of quilts. All six children were sound asleep, three to a bed, some snoring softly while others breathed evenly, their mouths slightly open. Arms and legs criss-crossed over each other, while random feet hung over the sides. They looked like a ragtag bunch, worn-out from their hard day's work hauling brush into bonfire size piles, their hands still stained and somewhat sticky from the pine sap. Poor Gracie had burs and stickers all through her hair. I'd pulled most of them out despite her cries of protest. How was it a two year old was allowed to romp unsupervised in the woods with children barely old enough to cross a busy street?

Earlier, when the sun had gone behind the shelter of giant pines, darkening the already gloomy room, James had lit and turned down a kerosene lamp for me so I could wash the dishes. I had yet to extinguish the warm glow, leaving it on out of respect for Evan, but more so as a deterrence to my nighttime fears kicking into gear. Wolves howled and the house creaked when strong winds passed through the bay. Doors slammed and drunken shouts could be heard as loggers returned home from the Spooner bar. I tossed and turned, pulling the bedding free of the mattress and up tighter around my chin to form my own sort of shield. Minutes passed. I was itchy with anxiety. Would Evan stay out all night? Would he come home drunk and beat me? Or try to sleep with me? At this point, I wasn't sure which was worse. I wished I had a clock to know the time. It had been dark for so long, it had to be past midnight.

Rolling out of bed, I stepped over to the window to peer down the darkened street. I couldn't make out anything but dark lumps and shadows.

I went around checking on the children, holding my hands to their foreheads to make sure they were neither too hot nor too cold. With the woodstove stoked and loaded for the night, it kept the room toasty, despite the errant drafts.

Most of the children looked like me, dark curly hair, strong cheekbones, lanky frames. Mary and Gracie had blond, wispy hair and sturdier, solid bodies, maybe from their father's side. It struck me that all of these children weren't even Vickie's. Adding up the time when Sarah had arrived versus the eldest child James, who was thirteen, meant that all of these children were Sarah's. I thought about her and where she could possibly be. Was she devastated at losing her family, losing her identity? I wondered how it felt to travel to a time and be forced into a marriage to someone you didn't love. Someone you'd never met. Like some bizarre arranged marriage without the exchange of money or property or a written agreement. What had it felt like to be pregnant and have a man's family, the whole time knowing it was all a lie? That *she* was a lie.

I stopped to look at Mary, resting my hand next to the hourglass shape above her eye. Like one of those plasma balls with trapped electricity inside, I half expected a blue streak of light to run from her body through mine, a sort of special kinetic energy that could be felt and seen but only through us travelers. But nothing happened. She didn't even stir in her sleep. It was weird to think that if she and Vickie survived the fire, there might be another time traveler in my generation-a freak cousin just like me.

I could change the future. That's what Gran believed anyway. Since I had traveled in the sustained form instead of the suspended, Gran seemed to think I had full control over my decisions and outcomes. But it also meant time was passing in my world without me. I had already saved one life today, how would that affect the future? I looked at myself in the mirror and then at Mary. What if I saved two more?

The door opened softly behind me. A gust of cool night air rushed into the room like an unwelcome guest sending sparks flying helter-skelter inside the woodstove. I spun around to find Evan, slumped and weary, with barely the strength to hang his hat.

"Why are you still up?" he asked, taking a seat at the table. His strapping frame bulged against his sweat stained shirt as he bent over and placed his head on his arms. "How's William?"

"He's fine. I think." My whisper was hoarse and gruff. Unsure of my place, I waited a few steps away. It was plain to see he hadn't been drinking or at another woman's house. He reeked of sweat and oil, burnt wood and earth. His hands were caked with dirt and his hair stood up on end from the greasy hands that had run through the strands all day. He had been working. Probably to make ends meet.

My heart lurched out of compassion for the weary, exhausted man at the table. He had been so excited today, a brief smile and a surge of joy, all forgotten now because of aches and pains and a wife who didn't support his dream. But he had also stormed out on me in the middle of a crisis. Who was this man?

He hadn't said anything since sitting down, hadn't moved a muscle, and I wondered if he had fallen asleep right at the table.

"Evan?" I whispered not wanting to wake the motionless bear of a man.

He grunted. "What?"

Startled, I searched for something to say. "Would you like something hot to drink? Or would you like me to warm up some water so you can wash?"

"How about a shot of whiskey and a warm pack for my shoulder?"

Whiskey? Warm pack? And I got those... where? Vivie had used the last of the neighbor's whiskey in William's drink.

Against my instincts, I grabbed a hanging towel from a line above the stove, poured some water from the reservoir into a bowl and carried it to the table. I lifted Evan's meaty, calloused hand, dipped the rag in the water and began carefully, methodically washing and massaging the grime and grit from his skin. It wasn't awful touching him. And he seemed to appreciate the gesture. He never moved; just let me work around him like a nurse to her patient.

When I finished his hands and neck, Evan lifted his head and with great effort, pulled the shirt from his back. He threw the soiled shirt to the floor and scooted closer to the fire, giving me ample room and access to his bare torso. His head lulled forward, his chin almost touching his chest. He shut his eyes, giving me a moment to gather my courage. How far would this go? The way he looked, not very...but boys were boys and men were men. They could be awakened from hibernation easily with the promise of a girl's attentions.

Evan sighed, not from fatigue but pleasure. "We haven't been alone like this in a long time." When he felt the first brush of the warm towel against his chest, he growled like an animal. "Victoria, I love you."

Fire raced to my cheeks, igniting them like a match to kindling. I couldn't tear my eyes from his muscled chest, the way his waist narrowed at the hips, the rippled pink scars scattered here and there over his body like a warrior's marks of battle. A trail of dark hair started just above his belt line. I felt my eyes travel the forbidden path down past the belt and to the dark, shadowed regions of Evan's pants, unable to stop myself. Evan was all man.

"I'm sorry I ran out on you today. I just felt so... useless. You know how I feel about blood."

I offered a soft smile of understanding. Clearing my throat, I murmured, "Would you like something to eat or drink? You missed supper." I threw the rag into the bowl and moved away toward the kitchen, choosing the heat of the woodstove versus the heat that was building up by my close proximity to Evan. Suddenly, it was awful easy to imagine Sarah becoming Evan's wife-in every sense of the word. He was rugged, quiet, mysterious, and attractive. In a brooding lumberjack sort of way. I yearned to know the secrets of a woman, but was scared out of my mind to imagine them actually happening to me.

"Nah, Mr. Wheeler's wife fed me again. Only another week and this job will be over." He paused, seeming to deliberate over something. "I'm sorry about surprising you today, about the land and all. I know we should have talked about it first, but I didn't want Helic to ask someone else."

I waved at him like shooing a pesky fly. "No, I'm sorry. I should have been more supportive or excited. It's just that I'd had a rough morning. And rough afternoon. And-" I stopped. It sounded like a stream of weak excuses in comparison to the day Evan must have had.

"Come here, V," Evan beckoned, leaning forward and opening his arms. "You and I both had bad days."

My mind went blank. I couldn't think of a single reason why I wouldn't go to him. A normal wife would. I shuffled my feet toward him, my eyes flickering from his chest, to his drowsy, half-mast eyes, to his large, massive arms that could crush me in an overzealous embrace.

He pulled me onto his lap and rested his head upon my chest, his fingers working up my back to tangle inside my hair. He breathed in the scent of me, turning his nose into the cleavage of my chest, and his arms relaxed, becoming warm and boneless; his weight sagged into me like a heavy sack of grain. I struggled to stay upright.

"Go to bed, Evan," I whispered, nudging him with my elbow. As much as I didn't want to share a bed with a stranger, Evan didn't look like he could hold a candle, much less take advantage of a teenage girl impersonating his wife.

"Mmmphphh," was the muffled reply inside the folds of my dress.

I climbed from his lap and Evan staggered to the bed, climbing beneath the covers after shucking his boots and pants to the floor. Averting my eyes from his almost naked body, I turned down the kerosene lamp and felt my way by memory, trying to avoid knocking my toes or knees on the children's beds. I slipped in next to Evan, squeezing my eyes against the possible rush of groping hands.

But Evan was already snoring, his head dug deep into his pillow, the quilt pulled to his chin. I let out a huge sigh of relief. One night down. Who knew how many left?

But having Evan beside me, warm and safe, a guardian and protector- helped me to sleep almost immediately. His solid form put off plenty of heat, and as the night wore on, I snuggled up next to the small of his back, using him like I used my stuffed teddy bear on a stormy night- for comfort and strength.

Surprisingly, I didn't wake until the chilly morning air touched my cheeks, the woodstove having gone out sometime in the early morning.

Another day.

Chapter 10
A Strange New World

The whirring of tires on even highway lulled her to sleep before they passed the county line. She had waved goodbye with little remorse. Her mother's tearful departure was lost on Sarah. She was about to begin the greatest adventure of her life and after everything she had done, that was saying something.

Inside the car, Sarah had surrounded herself with all of Kate's treasures like a pack rat in the middle of its nest. She reveled in all of Kate's comforts and could hardly believe how things had changed since 1960, the last time she had felt part of the real world. A satin lined blanket, lotions and polishes, books and magazines, a hand held video game of some sort she barely understood, and a phone the size of her palm that didn't need a cord to operate! Sort of hard to believe, but from what Corey had told her, there were all sorts of automated things now. She could scarcely take it all in.

She had to remember that this was all supposed to be normal for her: the dishwashers, the television set, the microwave and flushing toilets. It was hard to keep from going around with her mouth hung open in wonder; everything was amazing and so much better than she could have hoped. Food tasted better, clothes fit better and were softer, traveling was easier…the list could go on and on.

Her mother's face appeared large and hazy in her dreams, stirring her from sleep. Their last private discussion had ended badly, with her mother in tears and Sarah disgusted beyond any possibility of forgiveness. She could hear her mother's pleading voice, her dream replaying the conversation as vividly as though it were happening now.

"Sarah, you can't do this. You can't go to Florida with Dean. You and I both know this is a disaster destined to get worse. You have to go back for Kate."

"How can you say that! You don't know anything about me! About what I went through! I'm your daughter! A daughter, who at fifteen years old vanished from this world and eventually ended up in the arms of a man I never met...never knew. And I was forced to sleep with him. To bear his children. To cook and clean and scrub until my hands were raw! Half the time we never had enough food to eat or clothes to wear." Sarah felt the tears burn crooked trails down her cheeks. "My innocence....my childhood....was stolen from me!"

"So you would subject Kate to the same fate?" Sarah could hear the disappointment and disgust in her mother's ancient, shaky voice.

"I'm never going back. It took me years to leave that prison. I lived in a shack, mother! A horrible, drafty, disease ridden home that was never clean, no matter how hard I tried! It was awful, despicable! Light years from the way we lived in 1960 when I left, and that was bad enough." Sarah trembled and shook. Why was she defending herself? The whole thing was insane. The sooner she left the better.

"I won't let you do this, Sarah. Let's figure out a way to save both of you; bring both of you here to stay."

"This is so typical," Sarah accused. "You weren't around to help me then, and you refuse to help me now. How easy it is to turn a blind eye to my troubles, but when YOU need something...." Sarah closed her eyes against the hard memories of her past.

Of Dave's abuse. Of everyone's acceptance and willingness to ignore what was really going on. And she had only been a child then. Sarah had endured much worse than that, not that her own mother cared.

"What are you talking about?"

Sarah stared at her mother, eyes narrowed and hard as steel. How dare she have the nerve to look offended and innocent? She shook her head. "Nice try. But I'm not going anywhere near those portals. Once I leave for Florida, you'll never see me again. It'll be like I died all over again. And it will be your fault."

Sarah turned to leave the room, her mother now hunched at the waist, sobbing. "Just because I left all those years ago doesn't mean you get to stop being my mother. If you even know what that means."

Sarah thought she'd had the last word, but as she disappeared around the corner, her mother called out in hitching sobs. "You are a mother, too! How easily you have forgotten and left your children in the past! Will you turn your back on them as well? You are a hypocrite, Sarah. You're not the girl I raised!"

Sarah barked out a harsh laugh, born out of years of pity, grief, and regret. "I raised myself," she sneered, slamming the screen door as she stormed from the house.

Sarah twisted and turned trying to erase the bitter conversation from her mind. Studying the passing signs, she exhaled in relief. They had traveled four hours and the Wisconsin border line wasn't too far away. She had never been anywhere but Minnesota. Once they crossed the state lines, Sarah knew the weight on her shoulders would disappear. One thing was certain; she hadn't expected her unlikely homecoming to have gone so badly. She had been prepared to deal with shock and disbelief. Maybe endless questions on how she could travel or what it felt like. But she had never expected the shunning. The secrecy. The incessant efforts to send her back where she had come from.

In Sarah's mind, things couldn't have gone more perfect. She had waited a long time to perfect her traveling- to reach the ideal moment in time. If it were up to her, she would spend her entire life traveling, inside and out of people's lives, making herself immortal. Except for the fact that she never wanted to go back in time ever again. Not once she'd seen how spectacular the new world was.

Duluth, Minnesota came into view. The steep hills gave way to the impressive span of the harbor below; the expanse of bridge connecting to Wisconsin in her sights. The little car wound through the city and Sarah could hardly keep from shrieking in delight. Buildings rose up from the ground to touch the clouds, lights and sounds came at her from every direction, people and cars flooded the streets! Sarah rolled down the window for a better view. She had found her calling! City life was amazing, and she had only caught a glimpse of it.

"Where do you kids want to eat?" Dean called to the back seat.

Sarah scanned the shops and local storefronts, looking for something to catch her eye. The choices were overwhelming.

"McDonald's!" Corey yelled, without taking his eyes from the screen of his video game.

Dean groaned. "Not again, Corey."

A bright striped awning caught Sarah's eye. "How about Tagee Friday's?" *Strange name, but looks classy,* she thought.

Dean rolled his eyes in the rearview mirror. "Seriously, Kate? Is that what you kids call it? T.G.I.

Friday's is better than McDonald's though," he said, turning into the first available lot along the road.

Corey offered up his own groan at being outnumbered. "I get next pick," he grumbled.

A buzzing sound followed by a vibration in her lap sent Sarah shrieking out of her seat, bouncing her head off the car ceiling and rocketing her limber legs into Corey's lap.

"Hey! You just made me die!" Corey complained, throwing his head into the headrest.

Dean swerved and jammed his foot on the brake. "What was that all about?"

Sarah noticed the phone she carried was lit up and pulsating, practically jumping from the seat like a flea on caffeine.

"I thought I saw a spider," Sarah murmured, giving off a slight laugh of embarrassment.

"Aren't you going to answer your phone?" Corey asked, prying his eyes from the screen of his game for a moment. "That buzzing noise is annoying."

Sarah stared hard at the compact, electric pink phone. How did she answer it? Who would it be? What would she say?

"You answer it, squirt," Sarah offered. "It'll be like a prank." She knew Corey couldn't resist a good prank and it was the only way she could think of finding out how to operate the thing.

"Really?" Corey's eyes lit up and he dropped his game to the seat before another word was said. He flipped open the phone, pressed it to his ear and said in a high, unflattering voice, "Hellooooooo?" He burst into giggles and handed the phone to Sarah. Some prankster. He couldn't carry a joke for longer than two seconds.

Dean laughed from the front seat. "Very convincing, Corey. You sound just like your sister."

He parked the car in a tight space between a large silver truck and a tan suburban. "Not too long, Kate. I'll go in and get us a table." Dean opened the door and performed a limber backbend to squeeze out from his seat in the tiny space.

Tweaking Corey's ear, Sarah settled into her seat and brought the phone to her ear hoping she could hear over the pounding of her heart. This was another test. Would she pass or fail miserably? So far, in the technology department she might as well be a caveman. Kate's friends would probably disown her in a week.

Which would be better in the long run, Sarah thought. *I'll make my own friends.* There was nothing to say she had to do everything the same as Kate. People changed all the time. In this case, quite literally.

Sarah smiled and leaned her head back to rest in the space between the seat and door. The game had entered the next phase. "Hello?" she said. "This is Kate."

***

The drive had been excruciating at the end. A billion times better than horse and cart, but thirty-some hours in any contraption was cruel punishment to the mind and body. Sarah had to blink and pinch herself twice when the car pulled up to a monstrosity of a house, its lush, landscaped yard with a fountain in the front and a fenced in pool around the back just visible from the driveway. The house seemed to go on forever; Sarah had never seen such a thing. And every house in the neighborhood was the same- two stories, manicured, room enough for ten families. Sarah felt a bubble of excitement, the elation of her situation almost too much to contain.

She carried her bags inside, waited for Dean to disappear around the corner, and then jumped up and down with joy. On her left, the entry opened to a great room full of plush leather furniture and a grand television the size of a baby's crib. Ahead, a huge kitchen gleamed and shone with stainless steel appliances and miles of countertop that looked like polished stone. To her right, behind closed French doors, was a library bordered with mahogany trim, its shelves lined with books of colored bindings, and a massive, solid desk in the very center with a computer on top. Corey had explained all about computers...and something called the Internet...and video games...and cell phones. The world was a blip away from everything. Information and access to anything at the tips of your fingers. Sarah didn't understand how it worked, but she couldn't wait to learn.

Sarah gave a low whistle of approval to her new living quarters. "My, how times have changed," she said with a happy sigh.

She made her way up a wooden staircase, past a bathroom and laundry room, to the end of the hallway. A door covered in posters of half-naked men and a license plate with the name 'Kate' revealed a bedroom behind it that surpassed any of Sarah's dreams.

A canopy bed stood front and center to the spacious room, its comforter and pillows looking like an ad for exotic animal slaying. Cheetah and leopard print pillows, zebra striped blankets, a giraffe shaped body pillow. It screamed animalistic and wild- what every teenager ached to be. Yards and yards of gauzy black tulle hung from four corners, enveloping the entire bed in a swarthy hug. *Sort of dreary and morbid if you asked me*, Sarah thought, critiquing the immature sense of style.

Sarah walked the length of the room to a huge bay window with a padded window seat. The room had to be as big as her entire home had been in 1910.

Outside, the window revealed a beautiful view to the pool and lush green yard below. Despite their long absence, every tree and bush and flower was trimmed to perfection. Like a picture in a story.

Kate's walls were painted in soft hues of pink and cream, evidence of her innocence and childhood, but were now layered with posters, pictures of friends, and floor to ceiling mirrors. Sarah ran her fingers over every shelf, fingering tubes of lipstick and hair brushes, dusty athletic trophies and tiny glass figurines of dolphins and sea turtles. Someone had written in nail polish on the giant, obscene-sized mirror and drawn with some sort of puffy paint across her dresser. *Go Falcons! Kate Christenson # 13 Rocks!* Then someone had kissed the mirror multiple times in different shades of lipstick and signed *LYLAS-Raven*. What kind of name was that? A montage of photos cluttered up a corkboard mounted next to the mirror. Kate with her friends. Kate playing softball. Kate making goofy faces. Kate and Corey at the beach. Sarah grimaced. The girl was an island of herself.

Sarah paused at a pair of photos framed in silver and decorated in the corners with ornate roses and buds. She recognized Dean in the photo immediately, along with a younger version of Corey and what must have been a pre-adolescent, but sulky version of Kate. The three of them stood with the backdrop of a giant canyon behind them; hiking packs decorated their backs and Dean boasted a tall walking stick in his hand. In the second picture, Kate and Corey posed by the ocean with a woman Sarah could only guess was their mother. Kate was younger in this photo, still smiling, her eyes twinkling and free of her teenage jaded stare. Corey was just a toddler.

Sarah wondered what had happened to Dean's wife. It wouldn't be long to drag the details from

Corey, but it was a delicate situation and needed to be handled as such.

Staring intently at the woman's face, Sarah's mouth opened in surprise. Her eyes narrowed and she pulled the picture closer, just to make sure she wasn't seeing things, a smudge or scratch in the picture. But it was there. Sarah couldn't believe it. *Interesting.* Sarah stepped away, biting the inside of her lower lip. *This changed things.* Shrugging, she moved on through the room. She had time to worry about all the details. Plenty of time.

Sarah found a radio with a stack of circular discs Corey called CD's. She pushed the power button and stepped back to listen to the immediate flood of music, pumping and pulsing from the speakers. It wasn't the kind of music she was used to, but it had a catchy beat and a feeling to it that closely resembled Kate's bedspread. Sarah posed and strutted in front of the mirror, eyeing her trim frame appreciatively. Man, it felt good to be young. The feeling of invincibility and power flooded her veins making her feel almost a natural high. She danced around the room, swinging on the canopy posts and jumping on the mattress until her stomach hitched with a cramp.

Sarah swept to the closet and wrenched open the double doors. Kate's closet revealed even more clothes than what had been shoved in the suitcase-mounds and piles of jeans and shirts, dresses and skirts, and shoes to match every possible outfit or occasion. Every texture and color lived in the closet, like a jungle had exploded there on the spot.

Sarah sank to the floor, resting her head against the closet wall. Her temples were damp with sweat and her cheeks felt flushed and hot. She was dizzy and ecstatic and spastic all at once.

She had hit the jackpot.

Out of the corner of her eye, Sarah spied a second door, crisp white tile peeking out from behind the door.

"No way," Sarah whispered. Sarah crawled across the plush carpet and pushed open the second door. She had her own bathroom? A gleaming white toilet, white countertops, and a fully tiled shower stood amongst the onslaught of girly essentials Kate had left behind. A furry purple robe hung on the door; hair products lined the countertop, including a hair dryer, flat iron and three types of hair spray. There were soaps and lotions, razors and nail clippers.....

Kate's phone buzzed. Wiggling and vibrating on the zebra print comforter, it lit up and jumped, signaling a text message. Sarah had learned quickly to use the little phone. By allowing Corey to answer her calls and texts, he had inadvertently shown her how to work the phone, an absolute necessity apparently. The phone hadn't stopped making noise since she left Minnesota.

Sarah flipped open the phone, excited to read the newest message. *Meet me outside after your Dad goes to sleep. We gotta catch up. Party at Sam's – Raven.*

Sarah's stomach quivered and her breath caught in her throat. So much had happened to be able to get to this point. It was really happening.

Finally. She was about to start living.

***

Sarah watched the turn of the blood red numbers on Kate's alarm clock. 11:00 pm. Dean had gone to bed almost thirty minutes ago, the usual signals of flushing toilet and running water, lights dimming, and eerie quiet giving Sarah the go ahead she needed.

The thud of her heart masked any other sounds of the night. Her palms were slick and her skin tingled with nerves. She was strung out and prickly with sweat underneath the zebra striped comforter. After all these years, she was still afraid of sneaking out. She'd done it a million times for Dave back in the day, but now she was doing it for a total stranger. Who was this Raven? With a name like that, she probably had electric blue hair and a neck tattoo and rode a Harley to school.

Sarah crept out to the patio, choosing a sliding glass door over the clicking nightmare of the front door deadbolt. She rounded the side of the house, staying close to the towering hibiscus bushes for shadow. A car was parked by the sidewalk, idling in the dark. Inside the dark interior, the clear fiery orange tip of a cigarette moved and glowed in a steady rhythm, up and down, up and down, as though the holder was talking and gesturing while smoking. Sarah took a deep breath and sprinted for the car. It had to be Raven inside. Who else would be waiting outside Kate's house at this hour?

Ignoring any feelings of apprehension, Sarah pulled open the door and bent down, sticking her head into a massive plume of smoke.

A multitude of excited squeals met her ears and Sarah saw the car was full to the brim of scantily clad high school girls, each one's make-up more startling and extreme than the other. Like sardines in a can, they were squished in, five to the backseat and two in the front, meaning Sarah had to fuse into the mixture and still manage to close the door.

"KATE!" The girls shrieked, laughing and chattering, each trying to capture her attention at once. "You won't believe what happened this summer!"

"I can't believe your Dad made you go for, like, eternity up there in that hell hole!"

"You missed the best party!"

"Dan and I broke up!"

"My mom made me quit cheer!"

"Guess who's on the pill?"

The girl in the driver's seat waved her hand at everyone to be quiet. "Hang on, hang on, hang on! Girls, let Kate get a word in. She probably hasn't had fun in weeks, so let her take it in slowly. We don't want to shock her system." The girls laughed together. The driver, Raven, Sarah concluded, had jet black hair with a lone pink stripe. She had dark eyeliner and bright red lips. Her see through shirt had a black bra beneath it lined with rhinestones. *So....not too far off in my expectations*, Sarah thought. The girl in the middle of the seat passed Sarah the lit cigarette from her mouth and lit another while she applied a layer of lip gloss.

Willing her nerves to calm, Sarah took a deep drag off the cigarette, and immediately burst into ragged, barking coughs.

The car pulled away, the girls shrieking with laughter. "Looks like you've been away too long," Raven said, clucking her tongue in mock scorn.

Sarah nodded and wiped tears from her eyes. The smoke burned in her throat and stung her eyes like she'd been standing inside a bonfire instead of inhaling a tiny cigarette; she never had gotten the hang of smoking, even in her most dire hour.

She watched the house grow smaller in the side view mirror until they turned the corner and headed toward downtown. She glanced at her worn, holey jeans and snug fitting tank top, made even tighter by the boost up bra she'd found in a dresser drawer, and wondered if she had dressed like Kate would have. Was her hair too plain? She'd barely put on any make-up.

The girls' incessant laughter sparked ire in her heart. She hated the instant return of insecurity and fear of judgment just because she was in a pack of peers as heartless and back stabbing as she remembered teen girls to be. Every trivial piece of gossip was reviewed and cackled over like a bunch of crows; Sarah fought against rolling her eyes in annoyance. The group reminded her of girls she's once known and hated. A group that had defamed her family's garage out of sheer jealousy; the same night Dave had thrown her from the bridge. Stupid Anne and her brainless followers.

Rubbing her sweaty palms against the inside of her thighs, Sarah gave herself a mental check. She had to remember where she was coming from, overloaded with responsibilities, a grown woman in every sense of the word. The group had initially rubbed her wrong, but Sarah reminded herself of the benefits that came with the obnoxious banter. Raven seemed to be the one in charge, but Sarah knew she could change that matter over time.

Instead of being annoyed by the pack of girls, Sarah realized she could take control of them. Use them to her best advantage. Wouldn't the girls be surprised at all she could teach them, things she was sure they hadn't experienced yet? All she had to do was gain their respect and following. And she had way more effective methods than a fake dye job and a nasty smoking habit on her side.

It was a whole new game.

No rules, no boundaries.

They drove for twenty minutes before turning down a long winding driveway lined with palm trees and shrubs. Sarah took in the glowing house with appreciation. It seemed every kid had a mansion of a house like Kate. Shadows moved across the open windows like faceless ghosts. Sarah waited for Raven to park before piling out with the rest of the group. The girls surrounded her like vultures to a kill, swarming her and grabbing at her arms. They led her into the pulsating house where music was playing so loud it felt like the walls were moving.

For the first hour, Sarah was swallowed up with mindless chatter, endless arms encircling her with casual welcome, and the ever protective presence of Raven, who refused to leave her side. Raven filled her in on every person that passed within ten feet of them, as they huddled together in a cove just outside the kitchen. Sarah was dizzy and exhausted, trying to keep up with the thrumming, animated group. Music blared, a few people danced, but forever there was shouting: shouting for more drinks, shouting to repeat what you'd just said, and shouting when kids too drunk to walk straight stumbled and crashed into furniture and each other.

Sarah had been away too long. She'd been a mother and a caregiver, a worker and maid for decades. She kept going over and over in her head that this was normal, that she had to relax.

No one suspected anything about her. In fact, it was just the opposite. They all figured she had been traumatized by her summer away and was still trying to adjust to being back. *If they only knew,* Sarah mused.

Sarah nursed a wine cooler while Raven slammed three beers from the kitchen keg.

When Raven stepped away to have a smoke outside, Sarah scanned the room, picking up on three different guys watching her from afar.

Two were average looking, tall, obvious jocks with their rugby polos and backwards baseball hats.

The third was stunning, lean and tan, in faded jeans and a button down dress shirt rolled at the cuffs to give off an air of casual, preppy appeal – as though he had stepped straight out of a magazine. His smirk, paired with his longer than average locks and whiter – than- rice smile sent shivers down her spine. That kind of boy definitely spelled danger. And heartbreak.

When Sarah's eyes connected with his, she made a point of turning away, heading for one of the average boys still making eyes at her. It was the kind of move to drive the preppy boy crazy and it made Sarah's smile slide into a sneer. She'd been hurt by a beautiful boy once….

She would save the flashy one for another day, when she was prepared and on her game.

For now, she could bide her time on something safer and test the waters. She chose the one with a dimpled grin and warm brown eyes. He was a little lean for her taste, and had acne scars across his forehead and cheek, but he reminded her of Travis Kochevar somehow and that made her feel safe.

She shot him her best smile and sauntered up to his side, placing a hand on his bicep. "Hey stranger," she said, "I've had one hell of a summer and I was wondering if you could show a girl how to have a good time."

The boy raised his eyebrows, pushed away from his buddies and grabbed her hand.

"Why don't we go outside?"

Sarah's heart skipped and her stomach gave a dip of anxiety. She could feel the eyes of the preppy boy following her out the door and she leaned in closer to the boy she had chosen, calling him Travis in her mind. She threw back the rest of her wine cooler and grabbed a beer out of the hands of an unsuspecting girl leaning precariously against the porch hand railing outside.

Her nerves needed some help and she wasn't about to back down now.

Chapter 11
Smoldering Fires

I woke to the smell of ashes and smoke, feeling like I'd slept inside a campfire ring. Evan had extricated himself from the bed without waking me and was hunched over the woodstove coaxing the flame to life.

His rippled backside and narrow hips sent fire to my cheeks, a much needed burst of heat as the temperature in the tiny house had plummeted to depths so chilly I could form vague, puffy white breaths in the air with my mouth.

Evan blew on the fire and waited, patient and thoughtful. He rose and moved around the kitchen stiffly, his muscles still aching from the long hours yesterday. He retrieved a single cup from the sparse set of dishes and set a silver pan on the stove. He threw a handful of what looked like ground coffee beans into the pan with a few scoops of water and waited for the water to come to a boil.

I couldn't pull myself from bed to join him. It wasn't just the frigid air that kept me snuggled down deep below the layers of quilts. I was afraid if I tried to stand up, the weight of my problems would buckle my knees and crush me like a bug. So much depended on how I handled the days between now and the next opening of the portals. Or between now and the fire.

Evan turned and caught me staring at him. A mischievous smile spread across his face sending an electric volt to jumpstart my heart.

"You slept hard last night," he commented. "You didn't get up and pace the floor for once."

Embarrassed, I recalled how I had turned and curled into Evan, using him for warmth and comfort. I had pressed up against him in the night and ran my fingers over his solid back, searching for something familiar and secure. It had seemed appropriate and necessary then, but now I was horrified. How could I shack up so easily with a total stranger?

Evan approached the bed and knelt down, bringing his face even with mine. My breath caught in my throat and the pounding of my ears blocked the newly crackling fire and songbirds outside. Evan's rugged face approached mine slowly, his eyes drifting closed as he honed in on my lips.

His hand slid beneath my head and lifted me to meet him. His lips covered mine and I found them soft and forgiving, his mouth cool and clear from a possible drink from the well. Reacting as best as I could, I kissed him back, but without any movement on my part to touch him or invite him to do more. Fireworks weren't going off inside my head and my stomach didn't flip flop with giddy theatrics, but the kiss was sweet and pleasant…and noncommittal.

Evan broke free and buried his face in my chest, stirring a pang of longing inside. Every time he touched me, it was as though my body desired it, yearned for it, without any need for my permission. But I yearned for someone else's touch. Travis Kochevar.

He pulled away, searching my face. "I'll be gone overnight taking the load to the Falls. I settled our last bill at the grocer, so take the kids to town today and stock up on essentials. Charge shoes and fabric for the kids at Schneider's. One pair of pants for the boys and a bolt of fabric for the girls' dresses." He paused and looked me in the eye. "And get yourself something nice. A new apron or something with lace." He grinned and winked at me. "With this new job and our land, we'll be able to have nice things for once, V. Finally, I can give you the life you deserve."

Gulping down a reply, I pulled him to me instead, so he couldn't see my expression. This was so wrong, living this lie. It wasn't fair to Evan or the children. Guilt scratched away at my heart, the itchy fingers making their way up my throat where I hastily swallowed them down, afraid I might start crying. It wasn't fair to me either. All of my precious "firsts" were being stolen by another's life. As attractive as Evan was, I didn't want to pretend to love him. I wanted something real and lasting.

Evan's face turned serious. "While I'm gone, V, bolt the door. I'll put the shotgun above the door and stoke the fire plenty full to keep you warm till morning. And don't go outside to the outhouse. Use a pot." His voice carried heavy warnings and lacked any sort of teasing. "We can't be too careful, V. Everyone knows about my promotion. Some people are a little jealous. And McGraw was let out of jail last night." Evan's face drew tight when I said nothing. "Will you be okay? I could see if Bertel could take the load himself, but he does struggle with the reins with that bad hand of his."

McGraw? What was he talking about?

"I'll get Vivie to stay with me," I murmured, getting more and more uncomfortable with the intimate moment. I was less concerned about McGraw and more worried about Evan's bare skin touching mine.

"We both know what he's capable of, V. No more making excuses for his behavior. I'm serious Victoria. Stay inside once it's dark." I shivered at the intensity of his warning. *Was McGraw a personal enemy, or an overall threat to everyone?*

One by one, the children began to stir, my body jumping into action by instinct, but my head still worrying about Evan's ominous words. The children dressed quickly while I fried up onions and a slice of ham Evan had brought home from the Wheeler's. Evan scarfed down a handful of apples about the size of a golf ball from a tree in the backyard. The pressure to provide for so many mouths amplified as I scorched the bottom of a pan of lumpy but hot pot of oatmeal. I poured a generous amount of honey over the gray mass and the children didn't seem to mind.

Evan gave swift kisses to cheeks and left well before the sun rose above the tops of the towering pines, his slight limp indicative of another long, arduous day. James and William still had work left to do for the neighbors. They took Ruth, Mary, and John along to play with the other children while they piled brush. William's lame hand wasn't going to stop him from working. With a healthy dose of aspirin donated from Vivie's neighbor, he marched alongside James with a heavily wrapped hand.

They each earned a penny for a half day's work, which bought them a handful of honey sticks and some peppermint candies from the local store. Totally worth it in their eyes.

Gracie toddled around the kitchen, busying herself with tin cups and metal spoons. I collapsed at the table after the whirlwind opening of the day, praying for Vivie to rescue me. I had no idea where or how to shop, or what I was supposed to do to fill my day. I was sure the list was long and endless, but I needed advice and more than a little direction. I couldn't do this alone.

Vivie showed up after my second attempt at making tea. The first time, I had grabbed the wrong leaves-using something similar to parsley or some other herb. I wanted something to warm my stomach and calm the nerves, but it looked like I was only going to be successful in producing something that might make me gag. She came in resembling something of an angel in my eyes, with a steaming mug of something creamy brown, a good two shades lighter than coffee.

Ignoring her and heading straight for the mug I peered over the edge. "Is this...is this hot chocolate?" I stammered, taking the mug from her hands like I was handling a delicate flower. I sniffed the edge of the mug and moaned in ecstasy. Sipping the scalding liquid, I flinched at initial contact and then melted as the sweet warmth went down my throat and settled in a lazy pool, calming my nerves like a shot to an alcoholic.

Vivie laughed. "I had a little saved up for emergencies. Figured you needed a spark of relief." She went straight to Gracie and picked up her squirming body. Nuzzling Gracie's cheeks until she elicited a giggle, Vivie sighed. "Kate, you have so much to learn. I'm sorry your first moments here have been rife with tragedy." Without being asked, she started scraping the breakfast dishes clean, preparing them for washing.

"How were things last night?" Her eyebrows rose in concern.

"You mean, did we?" I couldn't say the words. Just shook my head no. "He was too tired."

Vivie blew out a pent up breath of relief. "That's good, honey. I didn't even think about that part until late last night, and by then..." She placed Gracie back on the floor and joined me at the table. "The last thing you need is to be getting pregnant."

Hot chocolate spattered the table as I choked and coughed, hugely disturbed by Vivie's last words.

"It's ok, though. From what Sarah told me, not much was happening in the bedroom anymore. Her choice, of course, not Evan's." She clucked her tongue.

"Kate, I don't know how you're going to do it, now that Evan wants to move. I could help you here in town, but if you all go out to Clementson..." she trailed off, shaking her head. "Bertel won't move out of town." She left the sentence hanging in the air.

Still upset at the idea of being pregnant with Evan's child, I stood up from the table, eager to move the conversation to a new direction. "Maybe we won't have to worry about that," I said. "I don't plan on being around long enough to move. I'm taking the first chance I get and trying to go home."

Vivie watched me, fascinated. "How are you going to do that? Do you think Vickie will come back? Or Sarah?"

"Honestly? I have no idea." I looked around the barren room. "Why don't I explain everything while you show me around Spooner. Evan told me to shop for the kids' school clothes and groceries, and then I need you to show me what needs to be done around here."

She watched me drain every last drop of hot chocolate from my cup before rising from the table. "We could manage a quick trip I suppose. You have lots to learn," she reminded me.

"Right," I said, my mood brightening considerably as I realized we were about to leave the gloomy home. "Who is this McGraw guy that was let out of jail, and can you stay with me tonight while Evan's gone? Evan seems to think the guy's dangerous."

Vivie's face turned white and she clasped her throat as though suddenly she couldn't get enough air. "It looks like we both have some things to go over," she gasped. She motioned for me to wipe my mouth free of a chocolate mustache. "We'd better find a sitter for Gracie."

***

We got more than our share of looks as we walked the dusty trail toward downtown Spooner. Without full length mirrors available, I had to make due with filthy storefront windows to make sure I wasn't too much of a scandal. But then, I realized what people were staring at; identical twins were a rarity in these parts. Even though Vivie and Vickie had grown up here, it seemed to be a sensation no one had gotten used to. In my hometown, fertility treatments were like vaccines- everyone was getting them, and twins had become so common that hardly anyone turned an eye anymore.

We strolled the sidewalks of Spooner's crowded downtown square. We passed a grocer and post office, a photography studio and church. The Minnesota hotel stood tall next to a couple of dark and surly looking saloons, followed by a pristine, freshly painted bank. In the distance, a beautiful two-story brick school stood bright and polished in the afternoon sun, a surprisingly modern looking building for the times. I was shocked. Spooner was a booming twin town to Baudette, much more active and lively than a century ahead of time. I drank in the history in gulps rather than sips. Despite the trauma, living this history was amazing and I couldn't believe what I was witnessing. Books and film could never do it justice.

Vivie chose shoes for the kids, knowing their sizes like the back of her hand, although she admitted to buying them a size too big for each so they would last the entire year. She chose fabric and pants and yarn for knitting socks. According to her, the family would have to rely on the church goodwill for jackets this year. Poor Gracie's coat was so thin, Vivie'd had to sew a quilted lining inside to cover the worn fabric. I felt foolish buying something for myself, but then realized someone would appreciate the gesture, whoever came to take my place. I chose a lace trimmed flannel gown. Not exactly Victoria's Secret quality, but feminine and practical.

We charged everything to an account, and I signed the bill with an exaggerated signature. It was embarrassing how a family of six children's entire wardrobe could fit in two of my dresser drawers back home.

We moved on to the grocer and gathered the essentials: flour, sugar, oatmeal, tea, salt, and coffee. At the last moment, I added six peppermint stick candies to the total and signed the bill. I knew the kids needed some sort of reward for having to endure such a poor exchange for a mother.

One of the Wheeler girls was waiting outside the door when we finished. She had a makeshift table set up using two crates and a scrap piece of plywood. Canned potatoes, green beans, beets, carrots, sweet corn, honey and assorted jams lined the warped shelf. I bought three quarts of each and put in an order for eggs, three chickens, a side of bacon and ham hocks, and freshly churned butter and cream from the Wheeler's farm to be dropped off later that day. I had no idea what Evan could afford, but Vivie approved every purchase, and even threw in a couple pints of canned rhubarb jam. "Evan's favorite," she whispered.

Vivie and I left our purchases with the girl and walked across the narrow road to the pharmacy. Inside, a long polished bar ran the length of one wall of the store. Several sturdy wooden stools sat empty by the bar but Vivie motioned me to a small table set away from the listening ears of the help. I couldn't help but steal a longing glance at the rows of glass cases housing paper wrapped cookies, breads, and muffins. Tiny bits of fudge and caramel rolls glistened in the sunlight. *What I wouldn't do for a piece of chocolate right now*, I thought, feeling slightly desperate and horribly deprived.

Occasionally, an errant gust of grit and dirt blew through the doors and settled on the shelves and floor. It was bone dry outside; everything had a stale, baked feeling to it. The buildings had cracks throughout their coats of heavy paint and the flowers wilted heavily in their pots. My skin felt coarse and the slightest touch left white tracks across my sunburned skin. The bottoms of my feet looked like a road map, the endless criss-crossing lines dug deep into my heels. Vivie approached the counter and ordered two root beers. An older man, gray in the hair and heavy in the jowls, promptly went to work, wiping clean the insides of two glasses left to dry on the shelf. His attempt at making small talk was thwarted; Vivie took the two prepared sodas and immediately turned her back, indicating to the man she was not available for his daily dose of small town gossip.

She plopped down next to me and chugged a mouthful of the brown drink. I tipped up the green tinted glass and swallowed three large gulps, nearly draining the glass in one effort. The crisp, sweet liquid felt heavenly on my parched throat. The refreshing burst of hydration rejuvenated my drained spirit. I wondered how much the drink had cost; I had forgotten that a soda would be a luxury in these times.

Vivie was all business. "First things first. I'm staying with you tonight while Evan's gone. McGraw is nothing but trouble and has been ever since Vickie broke off her engagement with him for Evan after she left school."

"She used to be engaged?" Intrigued, my ears perked up.

"Vickie left Dan sometime after she got out of school. She met Evan and was swept off her feet. But when Sarah came around something happened between her and Dan McGraw, something I'd rather not get into. Dan never did get over Vickie leaving him and he tried exacting justice for his hurt pride. His actions led to jail time and lots of rumors." She leaned forward. "All you need to know is to stay away from Dan McGraw."

I rolled my eyes heavenward. What was it with women in this family being drawn to dramatic love triangles? It was disturbing, and just the thought of another Dave Slater in the area made the root beer spin and pop in my stomach. "Thanks, Vivie, for staying with me. I hope Bertel won't mind." I decided to forego asking for details. The less I got involved, the better.

"Bertel's going with Evan. He's happy I won't be home alone, so I'll be able to stay till midday tomorrow. Now," her face relaxed as we moved off the topic of McGraw, "let's go over your chores. There are certain things you have to do every day, and some once a week. There's wash and mending, done every Tuesday. Every morning, before the kids wake up, three loaves of bread go into the oven, one for each meal." She eyed me with amusement. "That means you have to get up *before* everyone else."

I made a move to protest in my defense, but she waved me silent. "The days Evan is here, you make him a dinner and a snack to take with him. That means you not only have to be up first but you have to start the fire and haul the water. Sometimes Sarah would get away with shirking her chores by claiming a headache or stomachache, but Evan is hard worked as it is." She paused to think. "Trips to the store are the first Monday of the month after the new shipments arrive, so you have the best selection. You'll have to stock the cellar for winter though, which reminds me, we need to get some bales of hay for insulation for around the house and cellar. Don't want the preserves to freeze up like last year."

Before I could remind her I didn't plan on being around for winter, she continued.

"You and I will start cleaning rooms at the Minnesota hotel every Friday for the Cathcarts once the kids start school which is next week. Once a week, we run out to the Wheelers' farm to help with chores around the house. That Wheeler woman is one heifer short of a herd, if you know what I mean." Vivie winked. "But she pays in food, and we need all the help we can get."

I sighed and twirled my glass. It was like I was supposed to be excited or willing to take all this information in. It only made me tired.

"Also, you have to haul two cords of wood before the end of the month and replenish the stacks behind the house. James and Will can help you. A lot of times, the mill will give you cast offs for free if you get there early enough in the morning. You'll use two cord plus more this winter and you need to be ready. Every other day, empty out the woodstove of ashes and clean the grease and lard from the stove top. It helps prevent fires. Oh!" She slapped her hand to her forehead. "We forgot to buy kerosene. You'll need a new barrel before long as the days will be getting shorter. I'll check your stock in the root cellar to see how much you have left. And you need to take out the beds and air them this week before they're shut in for the winter. I'll have to show you how to stuff the mattresses. And if you have extra fabric, you'll need to add to the quilts."

I held up my hand. "Ok, that's enough," I said. "Why don't you walk me through a normal day, starting when we get back. You can teach me to bake bread and give me ideas for simple meals. The rest will have to wait."

"But Kate," Vivie protested.

"Look, Vivie, I'm not planning on being here through the winter. I'm leaving as soon as I can."

"That's what Sarah said. For more years than I can count."

I pushed my glass away, my stomach more upset than ever. "Like I said. Let's start with the simple stuff. I still burn grilled cheese."

"What is it like? What happens to you?" Vivie asked, her voice low and conspiratorial.

"What's what like?" I said, toying with her, but glad for the change in subject.

She inclined her head and frowned at my attitude. "It's not fair how you and Vickie and Sarah can travel and hold the information over everyone else. Like you know everything and have seen everything." She pointed at me. "All I want is a little detail, and you and Sarah shut up tighter than a clam."

"Maybe we're trying to keep you safe," I said. "Maybe if you found out about it, you'd want to try. I know I wished I'd been warned. I would have stayed far away from the portals." The last part was a lie, but I didn't want to glorify the power.

Vivie shook her head. "I just want to know what it's like. What it feels like."

I nodded, understanding the curiosity. It was the stuff of fairytales. "It's pretty painful.- Your head pounds, you lose all control over your body. The portals sort of swallow you up and the next thing you know, you're in another place." *And in some cases, another body.*

"Where are the portals? When do they open?" Vivie's eyes sparkled.

"I only know of two portals- one in Gran's barn and one in the Rapid River in Clementson." I hesitated. "Well, I guess I know of three now. The root cellar is where I showed up this time. Gran said, well…my grandma, your daughter, told me the portals open up with the occurrence of the northern lights followed by an electrical storm and lots of lightning. Between the magnetic activity and electricity, the portals become active." I lacked the enthusiasm Vivie wanted, knowing all too well how devastating a trip through the portals could be.

"My daughter," Vivie echoed, her eyes tremulous. "Can she travel? Does she travel?"

I ignored her questions. How much of the future could she handle knowing? "Look, Vivie. It's not as glamorous as you'd think. The first time I went back, I was almost killed by Sarah's demented boyfriend."

"Why did you do it again?" Vivie said. *Touché*.

I looked out the large storefront windows to the dusty streets beyond, searching for the answer. "I don't know. I guess I felt like I could make a difference. Maybe bring Sarah back to Gran and live happily ever after." I took my finger and drew swirls into the dust that had settled on the table.

"Sounds amazing," Vivie filled in wistfully. "I wish I could find Vickie. I'd risk it in a heartbeat."

"But things didn't go how I planned. I traded places with Sarah, instead of traveling as myself. I messed up everything. Sarah's gone, I'm stuck here...." I paused as the pharmacist wandered closer, pretending to wipe down the already gleaming countertop. "I wasn't supposed to travel for real. I know it's hard to understand, but the first time I went, it was more like a dream than anything. I went home and nothing had changed. No one had aged. But, now I'm here for real. The chances of me finding someone to switch back with is almost impossible." A depression deep and dark filled my heart as I realized what I'd said.

"There have to be other travelers," Vivie insisted. "You said that you didn't know everything about time traveling. You're guessing half the time, and getting lucky the other half. I know you'll find your way back. Maybe Sarah's out there right now, trying to find a way to save herself and Vickie."

The pharmacist coughed. I looked up, only to be distracted by a calendar hanging next to the old fashioned till. September 1910. I jumped in my seat, knocking my knee into the table top, sending a sonic boom echoing through the empty store. I knew I had to tell someone soon; it might be the only way for me to survive.

"Vivie, I have something to tell you. Something awful."

Vivie leaned even closer, pushing her glass away so that our foreheads almost touched, our heads bent together like a pair of birds.

I rubbed my throbbing knee and lowered my voice to a conspiratorial whisper. "A fire, Vivie. A fire is coming in October."

Vivie laughed a little and leaned back. "Is that all? We have fires all the time. There's probably a hundred fires right now out in the peat. It's nothing new. Not for our time." She heaved a sigh of relief and sat back in her chair.

My hand snaked out and grabbed her arm. "I'm from the future, Vivie, remember? I know about things. I've read the articles. And this is no small logging fire, or brush fire leftover from the sparks off the train tracks." I swiveled my head around to make sure the pharmacist had moved on. "In the first weeks of October, I can't remember the date exactly, a forest fire will consume over 300,000 acres here. It will level these towns. People are going to die," I said, the urgency in my voice causing my tone to go up a notch. I wished I had paid more attention to the article when I'd read it. But who would have guessed I'd travel to this exact moment in time?

Vivie stood stock still, eyes widened in horror. "Are you sure?"

"Positive. I read the articles. Baudette and Spooner will be in ruins."

Vivie gasped, looking out the window as though the fire might be upon us that very moment.

"What are we going to do?" she hissed loudly, her head bobbing like a pigeon's as she looked from me to the window and back.

"Everything all right, Mrs. Brown, Mrs. Foxhoven?" the old man asked, sauntering over to remove our empty glasses. He peered down at me with an almost accusatory glare. Were we going to buy anything? Or just sit and gossip all day?

"Fine," I mumbled. "Thanks for the root beer." I tugged on Vivie's arm and headed for the door. "Let's finish this outside."

Vivie walked in a daze, stumbling over her feet as though we had sat down at the local bar and had a few beers instead of a simple soda. She searched the horizon with wild eyes, hardly seeing the people right in front of her.

"Snap out of it, Vivie," I scolded, pulling her into an alley between Schneiders' Clothing and Olles' Hardware.

"I don't believe it," she said, clenching and unclenching her fists in the folds of her dress. "What will happen to us? To everyone else?"

"That's the thing, Vivie. Since we know what's coming, we can prepare. The trains running to Canada will be the only way to safety. We'll board the children at the depot and wait out the disaster. We'll figure out a way to keep Evan and Bertel close to home and we'll try to warn others nearby."

Vivie shook her head. "We have to tell everyone. We need to spread the word now." Tears ran freely down her cheeks. "You're just thinking of this now? What, were you hoping to be gone before it happened, leaving the rest of us to die?" she asked.

My silence spoke volumes. Guilt licked at my conscience. That's exactly what I had been planning. But I knew who died and who didn't. Vivie was going to be fine.

"We're going to be prepared," I reminded her. "We'll pack bags and keep them hidden until it's time to run. There's no sense starting a riot in town over something neither of us can prove. The goal is to save our families, Vivie." I stopped, unsure if I should tell her what I knew.

"It's because of the drought isn't it? How dry everything is? We're practically a living matchstick, this town. There hasn't been rain for weeks. The rangers program has been eliminated by the government, so there are no patrols." Vivie was blabbering now, uncontrollably. "I'll have to warn the Wheelers and the Olsens and the–"

"Vivie!" I shook her hard and watched her eyes rattle around in her head. "I didn't tell you this to send you into a panic. We have a month before anything happens. I need you! So that means no freaking out! We will save our families. We will be ready," I emphasized. "But I need you to stay in control because if you don't," I took a huge breath to control the wavering in my voice, "Mary and I won't survive the fire."

It seemed to be the last straw for Vivie and I instantly regretted telling her. She melted into me and we collapsed against the painted walls of Schneiders' Clothing.

"You can't leave me," Vivie sobbed. "If you die, Vickie will never come back." It was a poor way of viewing the situation, from my point anyway, but I knew Vivie had mourned her sister almost as long as Gran had mourned Sarah. "And Mary…poor Mary. She's only a child," Vivie said, as though that was enough of a reason for the girl to be spared from the flames of an unbiased fire. "All this time I've been so angry at losing Vickie, and you're telling me I would lose her anyway? What about her family? Her kids? They need a mother."

People were starting to stop and stare down the narrow alley. A few called out, but I motioned them on quickly with a wave of my hand. All sorts of rumors would be flying around town as to the crazy twins having a meltdown in the alley. Vivie's sobs began to subside, but she refused to let go, afraid that I might up and vanish before her eyes, leaving her with no one.

A shadow fell across the sliver of light between the buildings adding a sinister, dark feeling to Vivie's raging emotions. I narrowed my eyes at the intruder; a man twice as wide in the shoulders as Evan, a man large enough to block the entire entrance to the alley. He was dressed in jeans and a flannel shirt and had large, menacing boots laced up to mid shin, the kind of boots that could squash a small dog beneath their wide treads. Vivie sensed my alarm and straightened herself, wiping her tears surreptitiously on the sleeve of her dress. Gone was the spineless jellyfish; Vivie had become ramrod straight, her mouth drawn in a tight line. Only I could see the nervous twitch in her hands, hands she kept hidden behind her back.

"To what do I owe this great pleasure?" the stranger growled, his words slightly slurred. "It's been a long time since I seen a pretty lady, and now I have two here, all wrapped up nicely, like a package just for me." The man took two lumbering steps forward, bracing himself against the walls of the stores with meaty hands that could easily encircle a neck, maybe even a waist. "I hear tell your *men* are gone on a trip a long ways from home," the giant man hinted, saying the word 'men' sarcastically as though Evan and Bertel were anything but. "If I had pretty wives like you, I wouldn't leave them all alone, especially at night. All sorts of bad things come out…wolves, bears, things hunting their prey." He laughed a deep, rumbling laugh that bounced off the walls and shook me to the core. The laugh didn't light up his eyes but instead provoked the fire burning inside. The threat was clear. Crystal clear.

From three feet away I could smell the booze oozing from his pores and floating on his breath. It was barely noon and the man was smashed. Not good. He worked his lips around a large wad of something vile stuck inside his lower lip. He took another step toward the two of us and spat a long, brown stream at our feet. The rank tobacco exploded by our toes and my lip curled in disgust.

Hardly anyone had taken notice of our little get-together in the alley; the busy sidewalks of before now eerily empty. It was as though I could hear the ominous music in the background, the creepy escalation that usually accompanied a villain's attack in a movie. I backed up against the solid brick wall for support, giving myself a better view of our escape options. A few garbage cans, broken crates, and a wooden ladder were all that sat in the narrow alley. We had no weapons and no escape; the back of the alleyway had been boarded up and secured, maybe as a way of keeping the stores from falling down.

The man rambled on staring directly at me, barely stringing his words together. "You thought I forgot, didn't you? Thought I'd come out of jail all nice and reformed, maybe forgiving of your," he hiccupped and stumbled over a broken crate, "transgressions." I could barely understand the words coming out of his reeking mouth, let alone the fact the colossal thug knew a word like 'transgression'.

"Get out of here, Dan," Vivie said, finally finding her voice. "You don't want to go back to the jail so soon after getting out, do you? If Evan finds out about you talking to Vickie, you're a dead man."

Dan laughed again, his whole torso shaking. "I'd like to see the day." His laughter stopped as suddenly as it had started. "Believe me. I can't wait for that day to come." His mouth turned down in a sneer and he struggled to turn around. He spat another wad of tainted saliva to the ground, barely missing the hem of my dress. Wobbling on drunken legs, Dan stumbled back out into the sunlight, squinting against the barrage of light. He seemed to be deciding which way to go, his head turning to look right and left, then right again.

Just when I thought he would turn and leave us alone, he leaned back into the alley, his whiskey polluted breath and sour, moist clothes making me gag in revulsion. "I'll be by soon enough, Victoria. Just to check up on things. I been gone a long time and I want to make sure you're safe and all." He smiled a malicious, wolf-like smile and pointed directly at me. "Don't think you're gonna get away with it 'cause you're a woman. You owe me. And I always collect on my debts."

Dan lurched away letting a slice of warm light back into the alley, but not nearly enough to melt the ice that was now working its way through my veins. The way he had looked at me stirred up visions of Dave. Dan spoke to me like he *knew* me, like he owned me. Vickie and Dan had been engaged, so there had been some history there. How much, Vivie had yet to share. It didn't make sense, how possessive and annoyed he sounded. Vickie and Evan had been married for years and had six children. The engagement had to be old news. *And what could I possibly owe him?*

"So... that was McGraw?" I asked, already knowing the answer. I shuddered and busied myself in straightening my clothes and smoothing my hair. Anything to keep my shaking hands busy.

Vivie stared at me in shock, her knees quaking beneath the thin fabric of her cotton dress. "What do you think he meant, 'collect his debts'?"

"Like I would know, Vivie?" I shot back, irritated. She had read my mind and picked up on the same bothersome words. "I've been here a handful of days remember?"

Vivie trailed me to the sidewalk, both of us eager to be back in the open, glaring sunlight and away from the shadowy alley. We eyed the streets warily, checking every shadow and corner, but Dan McGraw was gone.

"Do you think he'll try coming by tonight?" Vivie asked. "Maybe we should go to the sheriff?"

"He was drunk, Vivie. The man would be stupid to come to the house right after being released from jail. If this town is as small as I think it is, everyone knows what McGraw's like." I tried shrugging off the nagging feeling of worry. "We've got nosy neighbors, six children, and a shotgun." I picked up my step and focused on the rest of the day ahead. "It's not like we live in the middle of nowhere. What could he possibly do?" Secretly, I wondered about McGraw's intent against Vickie. Clearly, the two of them had unfinished business. But what?

Vivie followed silently.

Weaving our way back to the ramshackle homes lining the bay, we stored the purchases from the grocer in the root cellar and the new fabric and yarn in a trunk beneath the bed and went to retrieve Gracie from the neighbor. We had a few hours until the rest of the children came home and I had a fire to start, bread to bake, meals to plan, and clothes to mend. The conversations of the day hadn't been as enlightening as I'd hoped and Vivie was a mess. Between the confrontation with McGraw, news of the fire, and Bertel and Evan gone for a solid twenty- four hours, her reserve was crumbling right before my eyes. Right when I needed her most.

Chapter 12
Vulnerable

Baking bread seemed to take Vivie's mind off of McGraw. It turned out I wasn't half bad at mixing and kneading and forming the doughy lump into a loaf. In fact, I was proud of my accomplishment and couldn't wait to taste the crispy browned crust and soft white insides.

Vivie explained the few utensils in the kitchen, some I'd seen before at Gran's, and some hanging from the walls of the local Cracker Barrel in my hometown. She explained making cream and butter, how to make quick fixes for stomach fillers like fried dough and lard sandwiches. The latter had my stomach rolling, but Vivie insisted the children were used to the meager selection. They just wanted something to get them to the next meal.

Together we cleaned the house, swept the floors, hung the bed sheets outside to air out, and mended John's pants. The result was passable, maybe worth a 'C' in Home Economics class. We had worked past dinner (what I called lunch), consumed in our thoughts and efforts to forget our conversations of the day. Vivie stoked the fire in the woodstove and turned to face me. Gracie had fallen asleep in my arms after sucking on a stick of rhubarb coated in salt.

The chores had returned Vivie to her normal self. I was grateful she didn't bring up the fire again, but I knew the conversation was far from over. We both had questions nagging at the backs of our minds.

"Looks like the kids are working an extra long shift today. They will have eaten at the farm. Why don't we make some dinner for the two of us? I'll get a chicken. I can show you how to make gravy and mashed potatoes. A real crowd pleaser."

I nodded, acknowledging the persistent sharp pang of hunger that had followed me most of the day. I tucked Gracie into bed and stretched to the ceiling, my back cracking three separate times. Maybe we would both be able to talk sensibly after a solid meal.

"I'll get a pot of water boiling outside and run home and get the chicken. You grab the flour and salt, and about five potatoes. " She headed out the door, her chestnut hair glowing red in the afternoon sun. "And a couple scoops of lard, too." She scurried down the road, hugging her arms to her chest. A cool autumn wind had picked up on the bay, sending whispery reminders of the weather on the way. Any day now, the town would wake up to a solid freeze in the morning, the icy fingers of Jack Frost having dusted the ground a ghostly white. *But not before the fire*, I reminded myself. Until then, this place would remain dry as a matchbox.

Rounding the side of the house, I headed straight for the root cellar, remembering to grab a stick to wedge in the door to keep it from blowing shut and lock on me again.

I analyzed my decision on telling Vivie all the secrets of the impending future. The news had rattled her to the core, and I was afraid she would bring more trouble than was necessary. But, on the other hand, how could I not tell her? All I had wanted was to keep the family alive and safe. I didn't plan on being around when the fire came, but if I was, I knew what had to be done and I knew what to expect. It was afterwards, when the towns would be decimated, that I worried about the chances of survival. A fire in October would be followed quickly by the dropping temperatures of winter, and possible snow. Who knew where they would be able to stay?

The door to the root cellar was heavy. I wrenched it open and it banged to the ground, its hinges squealing like a stuck pig. Cobwebs hung in the corners and I ducked, flinching against the imagined spiders in my head. Squinting in the gloomy, dust filled light I made my way to the mostly barren shelves, eyeing the sack of flour and barrel of potatoes. Apparently, I had some work to do if the family was going to have food through the winter. Sarah's priorities had not been in planning.

Maybe she had known she would be leaving. I shook my head. Impossible. What kind of mother left her family unable to survive? I had to believe Sarah was out there somewhere, devastated, lost without the family she had raised herself.

I briefly contemplated learning how to can, then nixed the idea. What was the point of stocking up if it was all going to be lost in the fire? "That's going to be Vivie's worries, not mine," I murmured, feeling slightly guilty.

A hand snaked out from the shadows and pulled me into the darkness, covering my mouth before I could make the slightest of sounds. My feet scrabbled against the floor as I lost my balance, landing roughly against the chest of my assailant.

The smell gave away the intruder before I heard the deep voice.

"Do you honestly think I wouldn't come back for you after what you did?" McGraw growled into my ear.

He spun me around and pressed his body heavily against mine, digging my shoulders into the dirt walls just high enough so that my feet lifted from the floor.

"How is it that I'm good enough to sleep with for all those years, but the moment someone catches us, *I'm the bad guy*."

He had me pinned against the wall, crushing my lungs so that I could scarcely draw a breath. Like a mouse to a python, I was losing control quickly. Stars blinked in front of my eyes and McGraw's face doubled and went hazy. Dizzy, I struggled to make sense of the situation. I didn't fight back. I didn't resist. Instead, I concentrated on molding myself into the wall, hoping against hope that I could melt into the cracks of the hard packed dirt and disappear into oblivion.

It seemed like an eternity, but Dan McGraw finally backed away, letting my body slump to the floor like a wilted flower.

"Say something!" he roared. McGraw bent at the waist and squinted at my motionless form. "You sent me to jail, Vickie. You let me go to jail!" He gripped the back of my head and made me look at him, his features grim and marred in the dim cellar. A few of his teeth were chipped and missing, allowing his foul breath to escape his clenched jaw. "You can't marry me. Not good enough for your ma, but you sure as hell can sleep with me. Use me. Make me believe that you loved me." His mouth twisted in pain. "And then your *husband* comes home early one day, and you have the nerve to pretend I'm attacking you?! Raping you?" He spit out the words and yanked my head until pins and needles tingled down my spine.

Holy, sweet mother of everything that is wrong, I thought wildly, watching my life pass in front of my eyes. Sarah had been having an affair with Dan McGraw the whole time she'd been in place of Vickie! *What was Sarah thinking?*

"And your idiot husband has no idea that some of those children could be mine," Dan was rambling. I snapped to attention, grappling with the newest tidbit of information. Vickie's children might be McGraw's?

Gasping, I tried clearing my head, only too aware of Dan's massive body, his anger radiating an unseen heat that made it impossible to think.

"You let me go to jail," Dan had jumped back on track, his thoughts focused and pointed. "You ruined my name. You made my mother's life hell. No one will buy from her anymore. She lives on the other side of the tracks now. In Old Baudette." I tried inching away while he talked, hoping for a chance at the stairs, but he gripped my ankle in a wrenching twist that stopped me cold. "You ruined lives Vickie. You chewed 'em up and spit 'em out like the chaw in my lip. Tried to have your cake and eat it, too. And look where it got you." He waved his arm around indicating the property above. He snorted in derision. "And your Ma said I wasn't good enough for you. Looks like Evan didn't amount to much more than a duck fart."

My mind spun. Caught up in another scandal? How was this possible? Sarah had really been playing with fate, screwing up the limbs of the family tree without anyone being the wiser. The blood line was tainted. I fought the fear in my throat that rose steadily like bile and forced the first few words from my mouth, making them up as I went along. "Dan, I had no other choice. I never wanted Evan to know about us." My heart beat rapid fire in my ears, hoping he would buy what I had to say. "When Evan caught us, I had to act quickly. If Evan knew that what we had was real...that I had been cheating on him, he might have killed us both right there. I could never let that happen to you." My voice shook and trembled, and I hated that it made me sound weak, like I was already pleading for my life.

McGraw looked unconvinced at my forced theatrics.

"It killed me to see you have to go to jail. But it was better than seeing you dead. I thought of you every day and every night locked up in that place because of me."

I moved to a kneeling position, prepared to lunge for the stairs if he came at me again. Where was Vivie?

Dan McGraw leaned forward, hostility evident in the daggers he shot from his eyes. "You never loved me, Vickie. Not like I loved you. I was just a toy you batted at and played with like a finicky cat. I had a lot of time to think, Vickie. A lot of time. About how I would end you and the hold you have over me." He advanced slowly, cautiously. "I thought maybe I could just choke the life out of you. Throw you in the bay." He shook his head. "But that would be too quick. Too easy." He chuckled and moved over in front of the stairs, reading my mind as though the thoughts were written in the air.

My toes dug into the hardpacked dirt vying for a grip. This wasn't even close to being a fair battle; my only chance to catch him off guard and make a run for it.

McGraw kept talking, rubbing his hands together as he went over his long thought out plans. "Then I thought maybe I would take one of the kids. I don't know which one…maybe the littlest one. Just poof! She's gone. And you won't know if she's alive or dead. A long, torturous sentence to serve." His smile ran creases of age through his features, his few remaining teeth like crooked Chiclets in his mouth. Gross. *What had Sarah seen in this guy?*

"The children didn't do anything. Don't hurt the children," I argued. Then, a sudden thought out of desperation. "I'm going to leave Evan. I swear it!"

It was the wrong thing to say.

McGraw lifted his hand and whipped it out across his chest, landing it square to the side of my face. Rocketing across the floor, I skidded and slid on the dirt until I crashed into the wall.

"You been saying that for ten years, Victoria." McGraw cursed. "Those children are a living, breathing reminder of what you stole from me."

I could hardly hear him through the ringing of my ears. My face stung and immediately began a puffy swell in reaction to the attack. Tangy metallic warmth filled my mouth and I spat a dribble of blood to the ground.

"I gave up a family for you. I gave up *my life* for you." McGraw advanced, his fingers curled like the talons of a hawk.

The definitive click of a shotgun hammer being cocked echoed loudly in the tiny space. Time stopped. Breaths and heart beats and words stopped. McGraw froze and raised his hands to the sky, scraping his knuckles against the ceiling.

A scratchy but firm voice broke the stillness. "Get the hell away from my sister before I blow a hole in your back the size of this county."

I slumped against the wall. Vivie had found me.

McGraw turned on his heel and marched up the steps, one slow footstep at a time. Vivie kept the shotgun trained on his midsection, never blinking, her grip like steel.

"Figures you would protect her," McGraw drawled. "You're probably just like her," he tossed his chin in my direction. "You probably got two men on the side, what with your husband practically being a cripple." McGraw dropped his hands to his sides, seeming to size up Vivie and the depth of her courage. I heard Vivie's intake of breath and watched her eyes narrow as though the verdict of McGraw's trial had just been decided. Her finger tightened, turning white around the trigger.

Ruth and Mary, James, Will, and John came barreling around the corner. They had found the peppermint sticks I had left on the table and their smiles shone ear to ear. They stopped short at the sight of Dan McGraw, their footsteps quieted as though the lot of them had fallen in a batch of quicksand.

I ran up the steps, the side of my face numb and swollen. Vivie lowered the gun but kept a firm hold on it. I watched as McGraw approached Ruth and Mary, his large, intimidating paws reaching out to stroke their shoulder length braids. The girls watched my face for a reaction, their own bodies frozen in uncertainty. William took a courageous step forward and grabbed Mary's hands, pulling her away from McGraw's caress.

McGraw eyed William, taking in the boy's looks curiously. I could see the connections churning over and over in his mind. He sent me a look that turned my knees to water. "Yep," he drawled. "These will work out just fine," he hinted, eyeing Mary especially, his hand lingering in the space where he'd stroked her hair. "Nice seeing you, Vivian, Victoria." He bowed like a gentleman and backed away, threading his way between the neighboring houses. He was gone before I could think of anything to say. Not that my mouth would have worked.

"Get into the house, kids," Vivie ordered. The stunned five turned and immediately raced for the front door. They made it around the corner before Vivie dropped the gun and fell to her knees. "It wasn't loaded," she said, her shoulders sagging in relief.

***

After the incident with McGraw I had to laugh hysterically when Vive had the nerve to pull a beheaded chicken from the ground and hold it up high, blood still dripping from the neck; my supper, waiting to be cooked. She made quite the picture, a dead chicken in one hand and a shotgun in the other. Tears streamed down my face as I eyed the filthy feathered body.

"I'm not wasting the meat," Vivie said, apologetically. "And you need to learn how to butcher a bird and cook all the parts. Even the feet."

I was glad the children had been ordered inside because I took that moment to choke on my saliva and gag into the grass. Seriously? Hadn't I seen enough blood and trauma for a lifetime?

"I already stepped the head off for you. That's the worst part. The damn thing flopped all over the place. Got blood on Mrs. Moeller's roses." Vivie sighed. "Poor old lady. Those roses are all she has."

Shuddering, I knelt in the grass, praying repeatedly for control. "Vivie, please. It's too much."

"It isn't when you think of it as a meal for your family. Chicken is not something they have every day, Kate. They need this to survive and grow. Simple as that."

She guided me through boiling the bird, pulling the feathers, removing the innards and keeping the important edible parts. When we were finished, it looked like a pillow had exploded on the back lawn. All in all, once I ignored the queasiness of my stomach the chicken resembled something one would buy in a store back home. I wasn't sure I could forget the earlier picture of the headless body to eat any of it that night, but I knew the children would be happy. Chicken and fresh bread! I would be a hero.

Supper was a magnificent affair. The children stuffed themselves and William even forgot to complain about his sore fingers as he gnawed the marrow from a bone. Vivie and I helped the children to bed and locked the door, sitting in contemplative silence for at least an hour before we allowed ourselves to fully realize all that we had learned that day, and all that we had experienced. Exhausted, I held myself up at the table by the elbows, sweating profusely. I wished we could open the door for a bit of fresh air, even if it meant a few more mosquitoes.

Eventually, we spoke in hushed tones, clutching mugs of steaming coffee at the table. The children had been asleep for a few hours, but Vivie and I wouldn't even consider falling asleep. We had vowed to stay up all night, the shotgun perched alongside the table like a third party to our meeting. I had doused my coffee with a liberal amount of sugar and choked it down with exaggerated gulps. It did nothing to quench the constant dryness of my throat and left me feeling more tired than ever.

A screeching whine sounded just outside the window and I jumped from my chair, heart in my throat. Loosening the collar of my dress, I moved to the side of the window to peer out into the cloak of darkness. I held my breath, preparing for a face to jump up before me in the mottled glass, but it was only a cat, angry at being left outside away from the warmth of someone's kitchen.

Perspiration dotted my upper lip and collected beneath the folds of my dress. "Is it warm in here?" I asked Vivie, aching for a hint of night air. My clothes felt tight, my skin too warm...all I wanted to do was lay down and sleep. The past few days had taken their toll…

She shrugged and stretched. "I was about to put some more wood in the stove. Do you want me to hold off?"

"I've been hot all day. Like I got a sunburn at the beach." I peeled off my day dress and threw it to the foot of my bed. I had removed the required restrictive corset after McGraw's attack, allowing as much oxygen back into my lungs that had been denied.

"Your underclothes are soaked through!" Vivie said, crossing the floor to feel the damp fabric. "Are you feeling ok?"

"I don't know. Feeling kind of tired. I thought it was from the stress or effects of the traveling."

"You have a fever!" Vivie turned me to face the lone mirror above my bed. My cheeks were flushed and the hair at my temples was damp with perspiration. "What did you eat today?" she said, her brows knit together in concern.

"Not much. I guess I've been distracted. My stomach hurt this afternoon, but I just figured it was from hunger." I had eaten a few bites at supper, but had been overwhelmed with serving the voracious appetites of the children and then preparing them for bed, washing their grimy hands and legs and wiping their faces until they shone.

"You need to lie down," Vivie instructed.

"I can't. McGraw." I said the words but didn't mean them. Suddenly, I was so tired I could barely stand; the heat in the room stifling my every movement.

The coffee burned in my stomach, setting off a white hot pain that tore straight through my insides like a knife. Hunched and panting, I made my way to the bed and sat down. "What's wrong with me?" I grunted, biting my lip to keep from moaning too loud.

Vivie stoked the fire and crossed to my side. "We never really got to finish our conversation today. After you told me about the fire, I got distracted, and then McGraw," Vivie paused, searching the slanted and patched ceiling for her next words.

"What is it?" I fell back against the pillow, stunned at the speed of my decline. One minute I had been a little warm, the next, I'm helpless in bed, barely able to hold up my hand.

"You remember Martha and the baby?" Vivie said, as if I could forget that day.

I nodded, my eyes closed.

"Remember I told you Martha felt unusually warm? Turns out, she had typhoid. Has typhoid," Vivie corrected. "She and the baby are barely holding on, but the doctor made a visit last night. Kate," Vivie whispered, and I shivered, knowing she only used my real name in serious circumstances, "I think you may have been exposed to typhoid. Should I go get the doctor? I don't want to leave you and the children alone."

I struggled to answer. Typhoid? That made up, foreign sounding disease? Like dysentery or cholera- the diseases from another time; the kind you caught when you played the game Oregon Trail. I couldn't have typhoid. I got things like gastroenteritis, or tonsillitis, or bronchitis. Real sickness was supposed to end in "it is". *Vivie should know this*, I decided, *so she wouldn't worry*.

But my eyes refused to open and I couldn't remember what I wanted to say. I was so thankful for the darkness; the peaceful, numbing power of black. Easier to be nothing and nowhere instead of thinking and living and doing.

When I woke up, Vivie was there right by my bedside.

But three weeks had passed. And I didn't remember any of it.

Chapter 13
The Gift Missing Under the Tree

Sarah practically skipped home from the bus stop. It didn't matter she was grounded and forced to ride home on the bus instead of with Raven. Dean had caught her sneaking out once out of the handful of times she had done it since school started, so statistically, she was doing pretty well. Sneaking out had been worth every extra chore, every early bedtime. Taking her phone away though, had been like losing a limb. Sarah didn't realize how dependent she had become on her little portable connection to the world.

Sarah paused at the mailbox, flipped open the lid and smiled. Raven had left her a note inside, along with Ethan White's phone number. Turned out, the preppy boy from the party wanted her bad…real bad. Her choice to slight him the first night back had done exactly what Sarah thought it would. She would play the game; keep him chasing her for a while. It was intoxicating to be in control again; she could barely walk the halls without giving her hips an extra swing and her ponytail a flippant toss. There were so many options, so much power to wield. Not like her previous relationships. Not with Dave or Evan or Travis. Maybe with Dan McGraw, but he had scared her. Excited her and frightened her all at the same time.

Sarah sprawled on the front lawn, throwing her backpack into the grass for a pillow. She pictured McGraw and Kate, the poor girl who would be thrust unknowingly into the nasty love triangle. Sarah smirked and sighed, relieved to be free of the whole situation. Dan would be out of jail soon. And coming for her traitorous ass.

Once Evan had discovered their little tryst, she had chucked Dan to the dogs with barely a thought for how he would react, what it would do to him. Of course, she had expected to have traveled again before McGraw saw the light of day. But that was then.

Sarah thought back to when she and Dan had first met. How she had run into him a year after she'd arrived in 1895, saddled with husband and shack right in the middle of Spooner, Minnesota. She was out on one of her blueberry picking days on a quiet stretch of horse trail that would someday be Highway 11.

He had surprised her and himself, stumbling over her crouched form as he hunted the thick forest for bear. She had been struck by his physical presence immediately, drawn to his wide shoulders and his tanned, muscled back. His face had a chiseled, lean look, his cheek bones standing out prominent against the scruffy beard he had just begun to grow. When he saw it was her, Sarah was taken aback at his sneering glare, the tick in his jaw. He was not happy to see her and Sarah was intrigued.

Flustered with attraction and captivated by his obvious animosity towards her, Sarah had instantly claimed Dan as a personal conquest. Over time, she found ways to run into him where it would be just the two of them. A few brushes up against him, a few long glances. Sarah had no idea the forces she played with.

After coming to terms with Sarah being Vickie's replacement, Vivie had eventually revealed Vickie and Dan's troubled past, which only drove Sarah further into Dan's arms. Like the apple in the Garden of Eden, Dan became the forbidden fruit she lusted for. The ultimate game of all games.

She worked hard convincing Dan that Evan did nothing for her, that she was an unhappy bride and had made a horrible mistake in breaking their engagement.

It took time for him to trust her, but when he did, they had started the hottest, most dangerous relationship Sarah had ever known. Evan was too busy working himself to death to ever be the wiser, and Sarah had the perfect distraction to fill her lonely days. Her first son, James, was hardly walking before she was pregnant with her second child. The father? No one would know.

But over the years, Dan had grown impatient and increasingly jealous. One day he had shown up on her doorstep, indifferent to the neighbor's prying eyes. They had fought and eventually ended up in bed, tearing at each other's clothes until Evan walked through the door. Sarah had screamed in surprise, which Evan took for fear, and immediately jumped on Dan's back, beating the larger man to within an inch of his life. Dan's trial had been brief and biased from the beginning. Sarah hid inside the house until he was sentenced and jailed. She knew if he got out, he'd have murder on his mind.

Evan went back to his normal, workaholic life, intending to ignore the idol gossip and the stark evidence that Will and Ruth had the long pronounced nose and close set eyes of his wife's former flame. The rift between Sarah and Evan grew with every child. Sarah spent her days bone tired, taking care of children that she felt nothing for, dreaming of the day when she would be able to travel again. Her life became more than the lie it already was, Sarah soon forgetting where the truth ended and the lies began. Time erased everything, including her sense of who her true self was, as though the teenage farm girl never existed.

"Kate!" Dean screamed the name three times before Sarah realized he was yelling at her.

Sarah's head snapped up shocked to see Dean home from work. Sarah held in a groan. Did this mean her Chemistry teacher had called Dean to rat on her failed test? She would probably be grounded for another week.

Sarah took her time ambling to the front door where Dean stood tapping his foot impatiently, a cordless phone in hand.

"I just got off the phone with your school." Dean's voice sounded strained, and the bags under his eyes showed what Sarah had figured, he wasn't getting much sleep.

"Look," Sarah began, running a frustrated hand through her hair. Who could she blame this time? The irony of her becoming a child again after being a mother and wife was not lost on her. But the constant supervision and rules! It was enough to make anyone crazy.

Dean waved her quiet. "I had to get permission to remove you from school for an extended leave."

"*What?*" Sarah shouted. "I'm under house arrest now? I can't even go to school? That is so totally unfair! I haven't done anything…"

"Save the theatrics, Kate. Your Grandmother called."

Sarah froze in mid-tirade. A tingly feeling of apprehension went through her like an electric current. "What did she want?" Sarah tried to make her voice sound casual, only half interested.

Dean reached out and touched her shoulder, his eyes going moist and soft. "Grandpa had a heart attack, Kate."

Sarah's stomach dropped. Her dad? "Did he…?" She couldn't bring herself to say the word. He hadn't been around for most of her life, but he was still her father.

"He's alive, but Mom thinks he might not make it much longer. She wanted to know if we could come back. To say our good-byes." Dean rubbed his eyes. "I cashed in our frequent flier miles and arranged for you to get your school work."

Sarah thought desperately of an excuse for her to stay, one that wouldn't make her come off as a callous, heartless granddaughter who didn't care about her dying grandfather. Something inside her made her wary of going back to Baudette. Back to where her mother might try and convince her to rescue Kate and go through the portals.

"Dad, I just started school. I don't know that I...."

Dean cut her off. "Kate, I know you don't have a close relationship with your grandfather. But I need to do this. I'm not asking you to go. I'm telling you."

"I could stay here." Sarah offered, knowing it was a shot in the dark. "I could stay at Raven's."

Dean didn't have the energy to pretend to think over her request. "Absolutely not." He looked at her hard, seeming to try and see inside her heart and soul. "You know, Kate, I thought something had happened with us up there in Baudette. I thought you had changed. That you had grown up because of what you experienced. I thought we had gotten closer. But ever since we got back, you fell right back into the crowd you were trying to be a part of before our trip. I don't get it." He strode away before she could say anything, dialing the phone as he went. "Better start packing."

***

Sarah couldn't keep from cringing when the car stopped just outside the iron cattle gate. It was late and the darkness had swallowed up everything but what lay in the bright fluorescent head beams of the airport rental car. Snoring in the seat next to her, Corey had curled up and used her shoulder as a pillow for the hour and a half drive from Bemidji. Sarah pushed

Corey off of her, watching his tiny head resettle on the bench seat without waking, and reluctantly got out of the car to unlock the gate. The moment the chilly air touched her skin and the familiar scent of the farm floated past her nose, Sarah felt her knees wobble and her head began to pound to a sickening rhythm. Fumbling with the lock, she managed to free the rusty chain and swing wide the gate before turning to dry heave behind an old fence post.

She drew a steadying breath before making the brisk walk to the car. Sarah shook off her feelings of anxiety and panic, staring hard at the lopsided two-story farm house looming up ahead. What would her mother say? Sarah hoped she would be too distracted with her dad's health to bother about Kate. But deep down, Sarah knew this visit would more difficult than the last.

The moment the three of them swept through the screened porch, her mother was waiting with a wide smile. A smile that was as fake as a centerfold pin-up's chest.

"You won't believe it," her mother said, turning to shoot Sarah a pointed glare. "Grandpa made a full recovery." Her mother immediately began apologizing for the false alarm, making Dean fly all the way there, for the expense, the trouble. Dean waved it off with an exhausted shrug, but Sarah could tell he was slightly annoyed.

Sarah paused, her lips pursed in anger. Really, could she have expected less? She had to hand it to her mother; the woman had nerve to scam them into coming back. Sarah considered running down the driveway and hitchhiking to Canada with the first available trucker. Start up a new life. It's not like she hadn't done *that* before.

Storming past Dean, who was carrying Corey to the sofa in the living room, she ignored her mother's idle chatter and headed straight for her old bedroom upstairs. Halfway up the creaking, dangerously steep staircase, Sarah stopped and purposely stared at her portrait on the wall. The last evidence of her old life, an innocent girl who'd had her life ripped away from her without a choice, only firmed her resolve to remain where she was, using Kate's body as a means to an end, a solution to a conflict.

She refused to feel guilty. She would keep herself from traveling for another twenty years, at least. A normal teenage life was owed to her. A chance at being young and free of responsibility.

She found her old bedroom and flung herself onto the lumpy mattress. She couldn't help it. She'd had a taste of the good life and she wasn't about to give it up now.

Sarah racked her brain. If she eliminated any risky portals, then her mother would have to give up her mission in saving Kate. The rapids portal was easy enough to stay away from. The root cellar no longer existed in town; the shanty homes on Baudette Bay lost in the fire of 1910. But the barn portal, that would be an easy fix. Sarah pulled a pack of cigarettes and a book of matches from the inside pocket of her purse. Raven had slipped them to her in a sympathetic hug before leaving Florida.

Sarah fingered the matches, knowing exactly what needed to be done. The barn portal had to go. Her mother knew nothing of the other portals; she would be safe.

The third step squeaked, giving away a presence on the stairs. Sarah threw the matches and cigarettes back in her purse and tucked the purse beneath a pillow.

Her mother appeared in the doorway, looking as though she had aged ten years. At her age, ten years was a death sentence.

"Sarah," she whispered, her mouth in a shaky half smile, her chin trembling like a leaf desperate to hang on in the breeze.

Sarah stood up bracing herself for rejection, formulating hurtful words in her mind as she moved to cross the room.

"I never thought this would happen," her mother said, her voice compassionate, not judgmental or accusatory like she'd been expecting. She held open her arms. "I'm sorry, Sarah. For how I acted, for what I asked of you. You have been through so much." The tears began then, her wrinkled face puckering and shaking as she attempted to control herself. "All I have ever wanted is to have you back. I prayed forty years and when it finally happens, the first thing I did was push you away. Will you ever forgive me?"

Sarah's heart lurched but she said nothing. This wasn't quite what she had expected.

"I think I was trying to protect myself. All those years of hoping and then you are right there. I didn't want to believe it."

Sarah knew she would relent, but wanted to hear more. "Why did you trick us into coming back then, Mother? I know as well as you do that Dad wasn't sick."

"I needed you to come back. I couldn't leave things the way they were. It almost killed me, watching you drive away with Dean like that. All I want Sarah, is to hold you." She still held her arms out, her bony hands still firm and strong as a vise, so contradictory to the stooped shoulders and sagging skin on the rest of her body. "You look just like you did when you were taken from me. It's like God is giving me a second chance. Who else gets that luxury?"

A hint of smug victory sent her forward into her mother's arms. They had so much to do. So much to share. Sarah wanted to hear all about how her siblings grew up, who they married, what had happened to Dave Slater and Travis Kochevar. She wanted to walk the farm in bare feet and take a dip in the back forty creek no matter how cold the water.

Because after she healed the hole that had been there for all those years, after she answered the questions she's asked herself a thousand times: what happened while she was gone… she would be able to walk away and leave it behind forever.

Sarah hugged her mother, breathing in the familiar scent of lavender and powder that hadn't changed since she was a baby, but Sarah didn't feel the bond she had been hoping still existed.

After going through the portals, Sarah knew she'd changed. She'd thought she wanted to come back and join her old family, rekindle old friendships. But she had been alone for so long, lost in time and living lies. She'd had to raise herself, take care of herself. It had made her cynical and hard. And ruthless. She was no more a part of this family than she was with the people in 1910. She didn't belong anywhere.

Releasing her mother, Sarah stepped back. What a disappointment. It was like waking up Christmas morning and seeing the one gift you wished for missing from under the tree.

Chapter 14
Skies of Red

The reins slipped through my hands for the hundredth time. Since the bout of typhoid, I was weak and fragile, practically a walking skeleton. After watching me mope around the house for the week after Dr. Clark pronounced me cured, Vivie got the idea to visit the land Evan had received from his promotion, trying to force the acrid, smoky outside air down my throat to invigorate my body back to life. The problem was, I wasn't sure I wanted to live after the feverish weeks of pain I had endured.

Somehow, Vivie had managed to take care of it all while I wasted away in bed, leaving Bertel to himself while she sent the kids to school each day and cooked and cleaned for both homes. She never told Evan about McGraw, and McGraw had the good sense not to come back after his drunken ambush. So the secrets kept piling up, one on top of the other like a twisted, teetering game of Jenga, threatening to spill at any moment.

Cedars and pines, taller than the eye could make out and wider than two grown men could encircle with their arms, grew alongside the horse trail to Clementson. Leaves crackled beneath the hooves of the horses we rode, horses Vivie had to borrow from the Wheelers in exchange for five loaves of homemade bread.

We had ridden for an hour, covering the distance at a steady rate, just hard enough to make me feel bruised and battered on the inside as well as the outside. Homesteads were spaced far and wide. So much so, that in spite of the well-worn trail, my knees trembled at the slightest rustling of brush. The road resembled nothing of the Highway 11 I knew. All around, the wilderness closed in upon us, unsuspecting of the imminent farms and settlers that would one day take over and tame the vast growth to be ordinary fields.

"...and the northern lights were beautiful. Like a blue green shimmering lake in the sky."

I snapped to attention. "What did you say?" I looked at Vivie in earnest, not believing my ears. I had tuned her out most of the ride, irritable and cross at her for making me see the exact plot of land Evan wanted to build on. Going to see it was like accepting it. Accepting it as my future home.

"One night while you were sick and talking a streak about someone named Travis," Vivie shook her head and laughed. "It made Evan madder than a hornet's nest, I tell you."

"No, about the lights," I prodded, dreading what she had to say. My cheeks couldn't help but flush in reference to Travis, the rush of blood a welcome sign that I could feel something again.

"Right," Vivie turned and gasped, realizing what she had said. "Kate! The northern lights were out while you were sick with the typhoid!" She bit her fingernails and her face turned ashen. "I didn't even think about the portals. I was just trying to keep you alive." Crestfallen, Vivie looked like a wounded child, her mouth screwed into a pucker to keep from crying.

"Judging from the looks of things, it doesn't look like there was a storm," I said, my anxiety easing as I thought about the conditions for time traveling. I had almost jumped from my horse in panic thinking I had missed a chance to go home.

"No. No storms," Vivie confirmed, relieved she wasn't at fault. "Not a lick of rain," she muttered to herself.

"You know what that means," I said, pulling on the reins to slow my horse. We had passed Silver Creek moments before, its brackish shores prominent from the lack of rain. Clementson and Gran's land weren't far.

Vivie adjusted her skirts and turned in her saddle. "The fire is coming."

I nodded. I had gotten used to the constant smell of smoke in the air. Between logging, woodstoves, and peat burning in the forest, the smell of burnt wood and ash blew constantly on the wind. Every morning I woke up wanting to flee the area, but there was nowhere to go. Nothing would be safe for miles.

"What day is it?" I asked, knowing I had spent most of September lost in a feverish haze.

"October 4th."

I blinked, surprised at how much time had passed. What was happening at home? Gran had to have told Dad and Corey by now. Would I get the chance to explain myself face to face?

"Any day now," I said. "Are your bags packed?"

Vivie didn't answer. Her mood had darkened to match the shaded hollows of trees in the forest, the thick overlapping limbs clasped together like hands, blocking any hopes for the sun to reach the forest floor.

"I just don't understand why we can't tell others what is happening." Vivie looked at me. "Children could die, Kate."

"Who will believe us? You've said yourself how many fires pop up every day. How just last week, your friend Clara Williams stood on the roof of her house beating away flames from a wild brush fire. They won't leave, Vivie. Not until the times get desperate. The land is all they have. They have nowhere to go," I argued with her, hating the sickening swirl of guilt in my stomach. Did she actually think I wanted anyone to die?

I heard it before I could see it. The rushing roar of the Rapid River shot arrows of anxiety straight to my heart, and I tightened the grip on my reins. There were no paved roads to the popular make-out spot, no gravel drive. I strained to see through the dense forest for any hint of the root beer colored, rocky passage, but the trail opened up just short of where I imagined the bridge must be.

The white tipped nose of my horse rose into the air and snorted. The horse kicked into a bouncy trot sensing the nearby water and I blinked back surprise as the forest seemed to part and spit out a lively little town straight from its fertile earth, with stores, a hotel, and a white church with steeple. Clementson was a bustling little haven in the middle of the wilderness.

Strategically located for floating timber down the river, there was a multitude of families living in the area that had taken opportunity of the booming logging industry. I wouldn't have believed it if I hadn't seen it. Ninety years from now, Clementson had one run down store, a tiny church, and a few fishing shacks. The saw mill, the hotel, the post office and the beautiful white church and steeple wouldn't exist.

I remembered hiding out in the old cemetery when I was a girl, afraid to be put to work on the farm like the other cousins. The people I was about to meet filled the graves I had once tread upon. My shoulders gave an involuntary shudder and I shivered in my heavy overcoat.

"Let's stop and get you some tea," Vivie suggested, breaking her morose silence. "Bertel has a running tab here at the saloon."

We tied up the horses outside Fader's General Store. I walked slowly and comically, stretching out my sore limbs like a bowlegged cowboy after the long ride.

Vivie led me to the doors of the saloon, a rough looking building with a balcony upstairs. Three women, hair mussed and cigarettes dangling from their mouths, watched us approach. They were stretched out across the balcony like cats basking in the sun. Their long legs peeked out scandalously from their gauzy, lacy skirts, and their tops weren't much more than an elaborate corset.

"Are you taking me for tea in a whorehouse?" I squeaked.

Vivie frowned. "They have the best food and service. Everybody says so."

"Yeah, I bet," I smirked. I couldn't help but stare at the women as we passed beneath the balcony. I had never seen a real, working prostitute. Not that I knew of, anyway. I was shocked to see they looked nothing like the movies portrayed. They weren't ravishing beauties, with creamy skin and heaving bosoms. They were normal, everyday women. Tired of their jobs and worn down from their hard lives of making ends meet.

Averting my gaze to discourage attention we crossed the saloon floor and sat beneath the stairs to the rooms up above. I couldn't keep my eyes from wandering to the doors upstairs, silky scarves adorning their knobs.

Vivie laughed. "Relax. Even the preacher eats in here. I promise, the food will make you feel a hundred times better."

We sat at a table far away from the two other customers eating at the bar. I had to admit, the smells were delicious.

"The venison stew here is amazing. Bertel took me here once when I accompanied him on a trip to the Falls."

"Vivie," I started, "why are we really here? Why did you drag me all the way out here when you know I want nothing to do with this? I don't plan on living here. I don't want to think the thoughts much less act on them."

"I've been thinking about the portals," Vivie interrupted.

I waited for the waitress to set down a steaming mug of tea and move away before saying anything. Vivie confused me, changing the subjects we talked about faster than a sneeze. I thought she was preoccupied with fears of the fire, and now she had caught me off guard.

I hoped she wasn't going to ask to take her with me, or ask more questions of how to time travel. It hadn't taken me long to realize Gran and I knew nothing about the rules of time travel except that it wasn't consistent and it wasn't safe.

"I've been thinking about why the portals exist," Vivie said, watching a tornado like dust cloud blow in from the streets of the town square.

This should be good, I thought.

"You know, this place was inhabited long before white people. And this land has so many legends and stories and myths, it's hard to know what's real."

Stifling a giggle with my hand, I remembered Dad stopping the car on our way up to Baudette in Bemidji, Minnesota to take a picture by a giant statue of Paul Bunyan and his blue ox, Babe. I waited for her to spew out some story about Paul Bunyan carving the portals with his axe before going out to conquer the Grand Canyon.

I looked into my teacup until my smile had dissipated. Maybe the story would involve magic beans, or a leprechaun, or a bog witch. Biting my lip, I looked up to see Vivie giving me a stone-faced frown. Pretending to cough, I wiped the smirk from my face and bent forward to listen. "Sorry," I murmured.

"Like I was saying," Vivie said, straightening her back, "things happened here long ago. Scary things. All kinds of people made their way through these parts. Good and bad. My Ma told me about a war that almost happened here."

"A war?" I spat out, laughing again, forgetting my manners. "Over what? Did someone steal someone else's cow?"

"Do you want to hear this or not?" Vivie pouted.

"Sorry," I choked. "I just can't imagine a war in the middle of frigid nowhere-land. It's not like Canada's beating down the door to get over here." I clenched my jaw to keep from laughing. Visions of Canadians rushing the border wearing tuques and carrying hockey sticks flashed through my mind.

The waitress set down two bowls of venison stew without us even having ordered. I guessed the menu wasn't big on variety. But it smelled good, and the steam felt nice on my face. Large chunks of garden vegetables peeked out from the brown gravy. My stomach growled.

Vivie started back in, ignoring her stew. "My Ma said it would have been the kind of war that ended the white's settlement in Baudette. It would have been a massacre." The word massacre got my attention. It was an evil word, laced with trouble and terror. Vivie rocked back and forth, satisfied she finally had me listening.

"Did you know we are part Indian?"

"Native American," I corrected automatically, having been raised in a sensitive, politically correct world. Realizing what she'd said, I raised my brows. "Really?" Her intellect was truly dizzying. How did this relate to the portals?

I took a few bites of the steaming stew and moaned in ecstasy. Vivie was a decent cook, and I could make a passable loaf of bread, but this surpassed all expectations and bordered on magnificent. Despite the harsh, questionable atmosphere, the food was amazing. I gobbled my portion easily and swiped the bowl clean with a crusty piece of bread. I tried listening to Vivie's story but kept my eye on her bowl of stew while she chattered away.

"My Great Grandmother was one of the few survivors in a terrible plague that wiped out most of a tiny town north of Duluth. She was taken in by a tribe of Ojibwe Indians. Eventually, she married one of the tribesmen and had four children."

I nodded, secretly doing the math in my head. What percentage of Native American blood would I have? Would it qualify me for college scholarships?

"Her husband was killed." Mortified at my lack of attention and lack of respect, I shook my head clear and tried to focus.

"And she stubbornly refused to leave the settlement where he died. Eventually, the tribe left her behind, eking out her existence on the Rainy River. Eventually, she met a trapper and remarried, but the children were from her first husband. Her *Indian* husband." Vivie opened her eyes wide to emphasize her point. She seemed to finally notice her full bowl of stew and swallowed a few healthy bites.

"And?" I said, confused. Wanting more stew, I searched the empty room for the waitress.

"The Ojibwe Indians are a mystical bunch. You know they have their own beliefs and gods and such," Vivie waved her hand to skip over the sordid details. "One of the original tribes to settle in Baudette and Spooner shared the lake and all its property willingly with the oncoming of white settlers. Everything was friendly enough, until whites began destroying what the Ojibwe felt to be sacred land. Land where they buried their people."

Scraping the bottom of her bowl, she swallowed her final bite and leaned back in her chair. "The Ojibwe had massive sacred burial sites and so forth. One day, a chief of a local tribe came to warn the towns that a massacre was in the planning. Many branches of the tribes were upset that their sacred sites were being destroyed by whites. The white people were coming in droves, clearing the land, moving whatever they wanted out of the way."

Vivie hushed her voice to a whisper, "It got me to thinking. A lot of those sacred sites were close to the water. The root cellar and the Rapid River are water sites. The barn where your Gran lives is close to the water. I don't really believe in magic, but what if it's all related somehow? People said the chief leaders of the tribes had special powers. Visions and such." Vivie's eyes were wide and fearful. "What if they cursed the land somehow? What if their remains changed the land?"

"So you think the portals exist because of the Indians?" I asked, unconvinced by her story. *How many things have the Native Americans been blamed for throughout history? Too many to count*, I thought. And I didn't believe in magic either. "I don't know, Vivie. It seems more complicated than that. Lots of people claim that Indian burial grounds are haunted, but I don't buy it." I couldn't help but think of Spook

Hill in Lake Wales, Florida. Cars rolled uphill on a supposed haunted trek of land where a famous Indian chief had been buried. I had been there and seen it for myself, but I kept my mouth shut, not wanting to encourage Vivie.

"Well, one thing is for sure. The traveling power seems to run in the bloodline. And I bet if you followed the bloodline to the beginning, it would start with my Grandmother and then my mother." Vivie scrunched up her face, thinking hard. "I wish I knew what they'd looked like," she murmured.

"You don't know what your Mom looks like?" I said, feeling a twinge of sympathy for Vivie. I felt like that sometimes, after the divorce. Like at any given moment I had no idea what my mother looked like because she was never there.

"Our real mother died in childbirth. Our aunt raised us as her own. I called her Ma, but she's not. There's no picture of my real mother. Not even when she was a kid." Vivie's sigh was full of longing-longing for a mother she never knew.

Thunderous hooves beat out the rest of our words as a man on horseback rode up to the saloon's open doors. In one fluid motion he jumped from the horse, threw the reins around a hitching post, and pulled on the frayed rope of a large brass bell, hung just above the entrance to the saloon. The metal clanging sent out a shivering ring to the people in the town square.

The streets seemed to stop. Everything but the wind paused to turn toward the bell. Vivie and I left our dishes on the table and moved to the entrance. Everyone knew a ringing bell meant something important, usually something awful.

The man's horse was damp with sweat and foamy in the mouth, like it had raced many miles against an invisible foe. Upon closer examination, I noticed the stranger's face and hands were darkened with streaks of black soot and his hat and hair were flecked with pieces of burnt ash.

A shiver ran the length of my back. It was happening.

A crowd assembled in front of the saloon, whispering and murmuring in low tones. The three women from the upstairs balcony leaned far over the edge, peering at the crowd below, giving ample views of their chests to the men below.

"A wild fire has taken the towns of Cedar Spur and Graceton!" the stranger shouted. Gasps shot out across the crowd, as though each individual had been shocked with a current and then passed it to the next.

Vivie took a step forward, her intent obvious.

I grabbed her arm. "Wait!" I hissed. "Don't go shooting off your mouth."

The stranger held up his hand for quiet. "The fire is under control, but conditions are right for a flare up. The folks that lost their homes will need someplace to stay. They arrived on the train in Baudette today. Are there any volunteers who would take on a family?" The stranger waited, eyeing the crowd carefully. When no one said anything he added, "It could be any one of us next. It's our duty to take care of our own."

Finally, a man in a striped shirt and stained apron stepped forward. "There's an empty room above Fader's. We could take a family or two for a spell. They could work for their food and lodging." The man cleaned his hands on a towel hanging from his waist, seeming to wash his hands of the rest of the responsibility. Several women had their heads bent together, whispering and clucking like a bunch of noisy chickens. No one else made an offer. Times were tight. Families were large and overcrowded as it was.

Like a bubbling pot ready to spill over, the guilt built up inside. I couldn't take anyone in, not in the tiny shack I lived in. But I had the knowledge to save others, to keep them from having to resort to last minute escapes and seeking emergency refuge. Would the people listen? Would they believe?

The stranger hesitated and then turned back to his horse. "I'll take this information back to the depot and bring back anyone interested in coming out this far from the depot."

Someone cleared their throat and the crowd parted, giving way to a man in a pressed black shirt and matching pants. "The church will sponsor anyone who needs it. They can sleep in the pews if need be. Any roof is better than no roof at all." The crowd murmured approval. "Don't worry, I won't try to convert them," the man added to the crowd's amusement.

The stranger tipped his hat. "Thank you, preacher." Pulling himself astride the horse, he dug his heels into the horse's side. The horse snorted, tossing its head in protest. I was sure the last thing it wanted to do was turn around and run the long, rutted road back to town.

The stranger rode away as quickly as he had come. The people went back to their business and the manner of the square went back to its original calm, as though nothing had happened. The three prostitutes each lit another cigarette and resumed their posts. As though people twenty-five miles away hadn't just lost everything to their name.

But twenty-five miles in this time might as well be like the fire had taken place in Alaska. They didn't think it could happen to them. As far as they were concerned, it wouldn't happen to them.

I sighed. Vivie leaned against the doorframe, clutching the scarred wood until her fingers had gone ghostly white.

"Do you think they stopped it? The fire, I mean." As if I needed clarification.

She looked strained with false hope. "Maybe they changed the future."

I didn't want to tell her what I really thought, that this was only the beginning. "I don't know, Vivie. But we should go." Despite my words, I collapsed into the nearest chair, the tiredness returning. "The kids will be back from school and you know how the neighbor hates to watch them for too long."

"But you didn't even see your property!" Vivie protested.

Heat welled up inside, but I bit back my anger. "It's not my property, Vivie," I said flatly, reminding her again of my mission to leave before the move became reality. *It will never be my property.*

"We should tell people. Warn them," Vivie tried again.

Looking around at everyone going about their business as though the stranger had never come left a sense of proof to my prediction. They wouldn't listen.

I choked back the bitter taste in my mouth, the delicious memories of the stew ruined from the recent news. "Don't, Vivie," I said. "Just don't."

Chapter 15
Old Flames

Sarah's heart clenched and her nails dug into the palms of her hands. Slater's Farm Store sat in ruins, barely hanging on in the soft summer wind. She traced the perimeter of the store, one agonizing step at a time.

Dave was dead. Her mother had told her that much. For some reason, it didn't make her feel any better. She had wanted revenge; had plotted and planned for forty years how to destroy Dave Slater. He had taken everything from her. How had she let him reign over her for so many years? Knowing what she did now, about the powers a woman can wield over a man, she would never have let Dave Slater own her like she did. Beat her. Terrorize her. Guilt her into staying.

Bile rose in her throat and burned at the back of her mouth. She bent to pick up a rock and threw it through one of the windows, hitting one of the few whole panes left. The glass shattered and the remnants burst and fell like mini jewels, glinting in the sun.

Who would she have become if she hadn't traveled? Would she have chosen a different path? Would Travis have helped her? Their relationship had shown so much promise. But her heart had been heavy as lead. Dave would have found a way to get her back- would have scared Travis away despite Travis's pledge of loyalty. It had been that way every time she'd tried to leave him.

The traveling had been a blessing and a curse. She had found a way of escape...of pleasant detachment from any sort of commitment or feeling. She'd learned to use people for her own needs, and not to depend on anyone else. When she got bored of one life… she traded it for another. Knowing it was temporary had gotten her through some of the tough times. But now what?

Her insides felt like a deflated balloon. She had wanted revenge and justice, and she had wanted it to be on her terms. She had hoped to find restitution in being with her family and had pictured them begging her forgiveness, but they would never know the truth. And her own mother, plotting her demise seconds after she had arrived? It was like the world was trying to bury her so it could move on and ignore the ripple of discomfort it felt at her revival.

"Dave got what he deserved."

The voice startled her, and Sarah spun around to find her mother emerge from behind the shelter of overgrown hedges that clung to and enveloped the corner of the store.

"Somehow, I doubt that," Sarah muttered.

"You didn't want to hear the whole story. About what Kate did for you? How she risked her life for you. She exposed him to the whole town for the liar and murderer he was. She tried to give your soul peace." Her mother took a few hesitant steps forward. "Kate knew all about it…she lived it through you. She even tried to get Travis Kochevar to help capture Dave, but in the end, she did it herself."

"Yeah, I get it. Your precious Kate captured the big bad villain." Sarah could not keep the envy from her voice. All her mother could talk about was Kate. "Travis still lives here?" She regretted the question as soon as she said it. She didn't want to know what happened to him anymore.

"Married three times with one son. Folks say he wasn't the same after your death. Said he blamed himself for letting you go back to get your sweater alone. I never knew you two were that serious."

Even as her heart twisted with grief over the news of Travis, Sarah sneered, "You didn't know anything! You couldn't possibly notice a thing with eleven children at your feet. But I was dying inside, Mama! I was counting the days until I could leave Baudette forever!" Sarah laughed . "Who knew how true that wish would turn out to be?"

"Sarah, oh Sarah, I wish I could erase your pain." Her mother's hands clenched at her sides.

"Oh, I know you do, Mother. You want to erase me all together. "

"It's not true! I want to figure out how to save both of you."

"It's not possible!" Sarah screeched. "Don't you see it's either her or me?"

"No...no...I can't accept that. There has to be a way. The lights were out last night," her mother reminded her. "The northern lights, followed by a storm...it's our only chance."

Sarah stepped away from her mother and kicked the uneven siding of the farm store until a few of the loose boards gave way and fell to the ground.

The pain in her foot made her feel alive, like a fighter. "You're something, you know that?" A laugh of pure incredulity bubbled to the surface, bursting forth from her mouth like a streaming fountain.

A logging truck roared by on the highway, silencing the feud. The backdraft scattered dandelion seeds through the air in miniature puffs of white.

Sarah watched the truck disappear down the road, letting a firm resolve take root in her chest. She would not be guilted into finding Kate. Nobody ran her life...not anymore.

"I'm not going back, Mother. Go find yourself another lackey. Hell...why don't you throw one of your other children in the river. You know, as a trial and error kind of thing. After a while, you won't miss them."

She was glad to hear her mother gasp. She wished her words could wound as easily as an actual weapon wielded in her hand.

Sarah picked up another rock and chucked it at the ramshackle trailer house that used to be Dave's childhood home. It couldn't really be called a home anymore. It was missing half the roof and the front door, and it sagged on one side where the foundation had given way. Dave had cracked one of her ribs in a back bedroom while his father was passed out on the living room couch. The cracked rib was the only thing that had stopped Dave from taking her virginity. Not that it mattered much in the end.... it had been stolen by someone else.

She kept her back to her mother long enough to hear a loud sigh of defeat and the quiet whisper of brush as her mother cut through the waist high weeds to head back to the farm. She considered taking a trip to the rapids just to see it once more; the place that had ended life as she knew it. But her stomach had soured and she couldn't risk an accident, even if there were no chances for the portals to be open.

The portals.

The idea of the portals snapped her back into focus. Back to the original plan. Which was to get rid of any known portals, beginning with the barn. She would head into the town library and research any stories of accidents, outlandish claims of time travel, or the appearance of strangers coinciding with the disappearance of locals. She could start with all major Minnesota newspapers and narrow it down. It would take time... but she had time now.

But the barn had to be first. To prevent any last heroic acts or sacrifices. Tonight, after everyone was asleep, she would start her trail of vengeance.

Chapter 16
When Fate Catches Up

I woke to the sound of the door being blown off its hinges. Gusts of cool, smoky air invaded the tiny space, sending the ashes inside the woodstove into a gray, pasty cloud, coating the floor and cabinet with a filthy dust. Jumping from bed, I struggled to pull the door closed, sliding the latch into place in a blind free for all, my hair plastered to my face and my nightgown blown half way over my head before I was done. Evan was gone. The children stirred in their sleep, James the only one to fully open his eyes before falling back against his pillow to catch the last precious minutes of sleep before school.

My nerves were wired tight and the base of my neck had an ache like someone had placed a vise between my two shoulder blades and clamped down hard. I hadn't been able to sleep. The visit to Clementson had rattled me more than I had let on and last night, the northern lights had returned.

I checked out the window periodically as I readied the woodstove for breakfast, hoping for a sign of gray clouds or a possible thunderstorm. Anything that would bring some lightning and spur the portals to life. But the only sign of life outside were the strong gusts of wind, howling past the window, trying desperately to breach every crack and crevice of the crooked home. Days before, Evan had packed the outside walls with bales of hay, a sort of insulation for the winter months ahead. I only saw it as fuel for the upcoming fire that would eat this home and every other one on the bay like it as an appetizer, insatiable and merciless. Fortunately, the fiasco in Cedar Spur and

Graceton had been a mild setback. I knew the fire coming would be worse, but at least we still had time.

Unsure of what to do, I sent the oldest children to school with their lunches and headed to Vivie's home, pulling Gracie along on her chubby toddler legs. In a matter of weeks, I had become a natural at cooking, bandaging wounds, tutoring, bathing, and cleaning for six children. Though the work tired me to an almost comatose state by nightfall, the days had passed quickly and no major emergencies had happened on my watch. It also left me too tired to wait up for Evan.

Vivie was waiting for me at her table, a cup of hot tea cooling at the open chair as though she knew when I would arrive to the second.

She spoke before I could take a sip. "I'm going out to Graceton. They need help salvaging whatever's left of the homes. And they're still fighting fires left smoldering beneath the brush." Her eyes were flat and her shoulders slumped. She hadn't been over to see me since the ride to Clementson and I knew it had to do with my unwillingness to tell anyone about the fire.

"I'll come," I jumped in. "I'd rather do anything than wash the bed sheets one more time." I took a long sip of tea and examined my hands. They were dry and white and rough around the edges from too many frigid wash days. "Do you think it looks like rain?" I asked, hopeful.

"I don't know. Feels like it though. My knee started to ache last night." Vivie drained her cup and stood, the swell of her skirt stirring up a cloud of dust as it settled to the floor.

I bit the inside of my cheek, instantly sorry I had brought up the rain. Vivie had to have seen the lights last night. She knew why I had asked about the rain and she knew I was intent on getting myself out of there, especially before the fire. Would the guilt never cease? Was I supposed to feel bad about leaving them all behind when I wasn't supposed to be there in the first place?

"I'll leave Gracie with Mrs. Wheeler and we can ride out together. I'm sure she wouldn't mind watching her for a few jars of your strawberry rhubarb preserves," I hinted, hoping to show I was still there for the time being. I was still her friend.

"Whatever," Vivie said, walking out the front door, leaving me all alone.

***

We arrived at the lumberyard in Graceton to a picture of utter chaos. From a few miles away, we had spotted smoke, but rode on anyway. By the time we reached Bertel, Evan, and the rest of the volunteer crew, they were beaten and ragged, sweat pouring down their hollow blackened cheeks like tiny streams.

Evan noticed our arrival and stepped away from the huddled group of men, their voices raised and clashing, each trying to shout their opinion over another.

"What are you doing here, V?" His words sounded harsh and bitter and tired. He hadn't slept much and he definitely hadn't eaten enough. His pants were held tight to his waste by a length of raw twine. "You should be taking care of the children. It's not safe out here."

"We came to help," I said defensively. "The kids are busy at school."

"You need to get yourself back home," he ordered, pointing a sharp finger back toward Baudette. "This wind is fueling the fire from a few days ago and they're expecting it to start up again…worse than before." Evan spoke the words I was too frightened to say. "This fire could reach Baudette if the wind is right."

My stomach dropped. Today was the day; it had to be. The conditions were right to send the sparks and flaming embers all the way to Canada.

Beside me, Vivie screamed. I followed her gaze to see a sky of red, swirling balls of flame dancing and roaring across the scarred and blackened tree line, the wind carrying the fire ahead of us faster than we could process what was happening. In minutes, a wall of fire had erupted on the horizon, eating its way across the smoking landscape, eager to find more fuel.

The men of the lumberyard took off in every direction; some toward their homes, some heading for the train depot, some to Peppermint Creek in search of safety. Evan threw me up onto my horse and swatted its hind quarters. "Get home!" he yelled.

I pulled the reins taut and the horse reared up, uncertain and flustered by the sudden panic. "Evan! You have to leave, too! I need you. We need to get the children to Canada. To the depot."

Evan shook his head. "I need to stay and help. The fire won't make it to Spooner. Keep the kids at home and I'll get there as soon as I can."

Frightened, I looked around, searching for Vivie. She was tugging on Bertel's arm, pleading with him to return with her.

"Vivie!" I screamed over the commotion. The fire had brought with it a deafening roar, like a hideous monster searching for its prey. "We have to get back! We have to get the bags and the children!"

I yanked back on the reins and turned the horse toward Baudette. We rode hard and fast, the fire on our heels. Ash and bark rained down on us from the sky. Twice, my horse jumped and reared not understanding the source of the stinging barbs to its flesh.

"How could we be so stupid?" I yelled aloud to the vast wilderness. *Leaving the safety of our homes to come toward the fire?* One mistake could mean death. Hadn't I learned that the hard way with Dave and the rapids?

The main street of Baudette came into view, its white clapboard storefronts looking ironically fresh and bright against the darkening, bloody sky. Vivie did her best to shout to any onlookers that the fire was coming, to run to the depot...but I didn't stick around to see if they would listen. Though the fire was miles behind us, I felt the heat on my back as if it were threatening to consume me on the spot. There would never be enough time, enough distance between me and that fire.

Vivie and I rode straight to the school to deliver the devastating news and to remove the children from class. We ignored questions and complaints until we arrived at the doorstep to Vivie's home.

"Get your things, Vivie and go to the bridge. I have to ride out to Wheeler's to get Gracie. You and the children wait for me by the wooden wagon bridge into Baudette, and then we will cross together and go to the train depot."

James and William sensed the urgency in my tone and pressed the children to hurry the short distance home. The air already felt thicker, and the six of us coughed and wheezed in our efforts to breathe. The insides of my nose felt coated with soot and my eyes burned and itched.

The six of us crowded into Vickie and Evan's shack, the children nervous but quiet, watching me as I pulled out the bags I had packed ahead of time and set them on the backs of James and William. They reminded me of a picture of two hobos with the ragtag bundles bulging with clothes, preserves, and pans. I grabbed two of the quilts from the beds and rolled them up like sleeping bags. I tied them closed with the strings of my apron and handed them to Ruth.

"Everyone put on your coats," I ordered, "and pick one thing to take with you. Only one!" Though the tiny home had been a thorn in my side and a trial to endure, it was all the children had ever known. Soon, they would be homeless and the little one room house didn't seem so shabby after all, in light of what was to come. Like the preacher had said, any roof was better than none. I swallowed the knot in my throat and turned my back to keep the children from seeing the truth on my face.

Ruth grabbed her doll that had been fashioned out of an old flour sack. John carried his sole wooden truck Evan had carved for him when he was born. James and William grabbed the shotgun above the door, and the pocketknives they'd received last Christmas. Mary scrambled beneath the bed and pulled out a worn and patched version of a homemade rabbit. One eye was missing and the whiskers had been diminished to stubs, but Mary slept with it every night.

"James, Will, you're in charge. Take everyone and wait for your Aunt Vivie by the bridge," I ordered. "If the fire gets too close, don't wait for me, cross and go straight to the depot." This sent Ruth and Mary into hysterics, the idea of leaving Gracie and me behind.

James and William nodded solemnly. To them, this was another step in proving their manhood. With Evan gone so much, they'd had to face reality and grow up quickly. In reality, I was only two years older than James and the contrast to our upbringing wasn't lost on me. It made me long for my old life like never before. The harsh life of early settlers was not the whimsical, picturesque idea I had made it out to be. This life was raw. Raw and hard.

"Is it a big fire, Momma?" Mary piped up, wiping her tears on the soft ears of her rabbit.

"Everything will be alright," I whispered, patting each one of the children on the shoulder. "But it is so important that you get to the trains. Do you all understand? Aunt Vivie will take care of you."

Tearing John's hands from my skirt, I left the small huddle, not daring to look back. Seconds ticked away in my mind. Would there be enough time to get back?

The Wheeler's horse was at the school where I'd left him. Someone had been kind enough to tie him up, and I found him stomping and snuffing the air with impatience. I rode past the limits of Spooner, dead south on a trail that would one day be the site of Baudette's courthouse. Every breath felt thick and smoky. Was it my imagination? Couldn't everyone see what was about to happen?

I reached the Wheeler farm in record time. Tying the horse to a fence post, I sprinted a very unladylike sprint across the yard. Mrs. Wheeler watched my harried arrival from her front porch, a glass of lemonade in her hand. She made a motion for me to join her, but upon closer examination of my sweat soaked clothes and frazzled appearance she bit back her offer, handing Gracie to me with a slight huff of indignation.

"Victoria, you must take better care of yourself," she chided. "It's not proper for a lady to go about looking so tired and unkempt. Whatever are you doing with your time?" she pried, eyeing me as though my looks were contagious.

"I'm so sorry, Mrs. Wheeler," I gasped, feeling as though I had run a marathon, though truly the horse had done all the work. "But I need to warn you and your family. A wildfire has taken hold out in Graceton and is moving its way here rapidly. It could be in Baudette as we speak."

Mrs. Wheeler tensed, set her jaw, and nodded. "Well, then Victoria, I suspect I will go get my husband from the field and get the hired hands to start bringing up some water from the well. Thank you for the warning."

"No, ma'am," I interrupted. "I mean you need to leave. Get your family heirlooms and pictures and leave. Get to Canada as quickly as you can." I had already stayed too long. Sweeping Gracie over my shoulders like a sack of potatoes, I started out across their front lawn to make the two mile trek to town.

"Wait!" Mrs. Wheeler called out, her voice carrying on the breeze.

I couldn't risk an ounce of energy turning to hear what she had to say. I needed to be at the bridge, and I needed to be there fifteen minutes ago.

***

Vivie was pacing the entrance to the wagon bridge, her arms crossed over her stomach as though she were suffering from a cramp.

Spotting us through the town square, she waved furiously to get my attention. "Kate! Thank goodness you're here. I almost left without you." She hadn't even realized she used my real name in front of the children.

Weary and gasping like an asthmatic, I coughed and choked on the oppressive air. It took several precious minutes before I could speak.

Sensing my fatigue, Vivie ripped Gracie from my arms and started across the bridge. I trailed behind, winded and sore, pushing the children ahead of me with weak gestures. Halfway over the bridge, I paused to retch over the side. A stitch of pain in my side burnt through my reserve. The depot was still a trek away.

Lifting my eyes, I searched the fiery skies ahead. The flames had reached the outskirts of Baudette; the sky was red and roiling with heavy, black clouds of smoke, and the bits of smoldering bark were now raining down on the heads of panicked crowds in the streets. The wind showed no signs of slowing. The fire would be upon us in no time. Jolts of adrenaline rushed through my weary limbs, giving me renewed strength. There was nothing like the threat of the grim reaper to motivate you to move.

The children were waiting on the other side, their faces hidden inside their clothing, filtering the heavy, hazy air from burning their tender throats. Townspeople rushed in all directions, the bridge pounding and echoing with hurried footsteps. A lone train whistle sounded through the panicked crowd, spurring me into action. Trains were already running across the border.

"What do we do?" Vivie asked, hysteria creeping into her voice as men and women rushed the streets, brushing past us without another glance.

"Get to the depot. We will squeeze our way onto the train." I broke into a bout of wretched coughs, the smoky air clogging my parched throat.

I turned to the children, surprised at their calm obedience and trusting nature. I scanned each face, testing their understanding, making sure they understood the importance of the moment. Of listening. Of being ready to see things they weren't accustomed to seeing. Their lives depended on their inner strength more than their sturdy build.

I felt the exact moment my heart stopped beating in my chest.

"Where's Mary?" I said, trying to keep the alarm from rising in my voice. The group looked around, stunned.

Vivie handed Gracie to James. "She was just here. I swear it."

Frantic, we strained to see across the wagon bridge into Spooner. The brilliant blond tresses of Mary's head were nowhere to be seen.

Ruth spoke up. "That man took her to the depot."

I stared hard at Ruth, trying to process the words, but not understanding. "What man?" I said, confused. There were dozens of people crossing the bridge rushing in all directions. Like ants on a collapsing anthill, the twin towns were alive with chaos, the people coming and going with what looked like little purpose. "What man?" I said again, the panic seizing my voice and pushing it another octave higher. I grasped Ruth's arms in a painful, panicked grip.

Ruth shrank away, afraid I might lash out. "I don't know. I was watching John. Aunt Vivie told me to watch John." Her eyes welled with tears. "I had John," she insisted again, afraid of taking the blame.

"What did the man look like? What was he doing?" I demanded.

"He was that man from the backyard. The big man who touched Mary's hair. I heard him say he could help her run faster. For her to take his hand."

Sickness heaved inside and I clenched my jaw.

"You were getting sick over the bridge," Ruth accused. "You weren't helping at all! Mary couldn't keep up and she was crying!"

Vivie reached out and gripped my shoulders. Without saying a word, we stared hard into each other's eyes, the truth of the situation passing between us as though we were speaking aloud. McGraw had bided his time, watched us from afar and waited for a weak moment. He couldn't possibly know the danger he faced. Was it a ploy? Would he really take Mary?

Or was he just trying to get me alone to give chase and play his twisted game of revenge?

"I'll go," Vivie said, the sacrifice evident in the firm line of her mouth. "You can't fall for his trap, Kate. He won't do anything to me."

"No," I argued. "Too dangerous. If something happens to you, then Gran will never be born, and then, neither will I." I was past caring if anyone heard my secrets. They wouldn't understand anyway. I hugged Vivie, holding on for a second longer than necessary. "I will find her and meet you across the border. Take the children to safety and don't come back." I grabbed the shotgun from Will, the steel heavy and warm in my hand.

Tears leaked from her eyes and Vivie turned away. "It's happening, isn't it?" she said, referring to the secret only the two of us knew. The fate of Mary and Vickie.

"Not if I can help it," I whispered. Sprinting across the bridge, I dodged the fiery rain, my eyes focused on one thing only- Vickie's rickety house on the bay. I didn't dare look back for the fear of the nearness of the fire turning my guts to jelly. For a brief instant, a flash of selfish survival mode kicked in and I contemplated turning back, leaving Mary behind. Just as quickly, I shook the negative thoughts from my head and pushed forward. If I was going to survive, so would Mary.

I could still do this. I could beat the system.

Above me, partially hidden by waves of rolling black, a flash of lightning zigzagged through the sky.

Chapter 17
Flames of Fate

Sarah crept along the farmyard perimeter, slipping Rex pieces of bacon to keep him quiet. It was strange; the clouds in the sky had developed overhead so quickly, it was as though they had been conjured in a spell. Sarah could have sworn that after dinner the sky had been a cloudless blue, not a hint of a storm.

A flash of lightning lit up the darkening sky and Sarah jumped. Her nerves were taut, every muscle singing inside her body as she went forward with her plan. Hopefully, she would be able to start the fire before the rain came…then it wouldn't matter, no rain would stop the barn from going up once the hay caught.

Sarah didn't feel an ounce of guilt for what she was about to do. She knew her mother struggled with the fact Kate had been taken in exchange for her, but she wasn't going to give her the chance to remedy the situation. She was taking out one of the portals to keep Kate from coming back. Sarah had no idea how many portals there were, but the less options, the better.

Thunder rumbled in the distance and Sarah picked up the pace, hopping the poles to the barn entrance with ease and skipping to the loft ladder. She patted her pocket once more, triple checking to make sure she had the matches. One match in four corners should be plenty; the hay was dry as the desert sand.

Sarah scaled the ladder, stopping once half-way up to listen. Something had rattled the chains hanging by the entrance. Sarah scanned the darkness, blaming her paranoia on the wind. Everyone was asleep, and had been for hours.

Making her way across the loft floor, Sarah closed the hatch, securing the latch for extra measure. There was no way she was going anywhere near the portal tonight.

Heading to the back two corners, Sarah lit first one match and then another, the eerie flash of orange making her face take on a brief demonic glow. She threw them onto the piles of loose hay and watched as a thin thread of smoke rose from where the matches fell, snuffed out before singeing the smallest blade.

"What do you think you're doing?"

Sarah froze, a newly lit match in her fingertips. The orange flame slowly diminished in size, the heat stinging her fingertips before she blew it out. She turned and stared hard at her mother who wheezed and puffed from the exertion of climbing the loft ladder, her gray hair loose from its usual bun, making her look wild and strung out.

"I'm taking the decision out of your hands," Sarah said simply. "You think I don't know why you made us come back here? You think I don't know who you chose?" she spat out, hoping her words dug deep within her mother's heart.

Her mother took a step back as though physically struck. "Sarah, you know how I feel. This has been the best and worst time of my life- knowing you are alive, seeing you as though nothing has ever happened. I have longed to see you for as long as you dreamed of coming back. But I can't leave Kate in the past, Sarah. It was foolish of me to mess with fate. It's not right."

Fury boiled up within Sarah, steeling her nerve and igniting the flame of jealousy that burned within. "How could you choose her over your own daughter!" Sarah screeched. "I'm your own flesh and blood! How can you stand there and talk about fate when my own life was taken from me without a choice! I died the night Dave threw me in the river!" She took a step back and lit another match, this time turning it to catch the entire book on fire.

Heat burst from the matchbook, engulfing her hand in a ball of flame. Taking her time, Sarah knelt and held the fire to the ends of a pile of hay, blowing softly to build the intensity.

"Stop it, Sarah! Don't do this!" From the shadows her mother grabbed a pitchfork and rushed her, pushing Sarah aside to beat the spreading fire.

"Don't do this?" Sarah echoed, outraged at her mother's lack of loyalty. "I was cheated, Mama! Cheated! I never had the life Kate had. I deserve this!" She paused a moment. "Kate can figure out how to get back on her own."

Flames licked the sides of the barn walls, creeping higher and higher to begin their feast of the rafters. Sarah felt the heat press against her skin; the smoke curled and filled the open ceiling, descending on the two of them like a heavy woolen blanket. Sarah coughed and covered her mouth with her shirt. They had to get out soon, or they would be trapped.

"That's where you're wrong, Sarah." Her mother's eyes filled with tears. "Kate won't find a way back. She's going to die in the fire."

Sarah squinted through the black haze. The smoke seemed to seep through every orifice, scorching her retinas and searing her nose. "Fire? What fire?" Sarah took a step away from her mother, sickened with hate. "You know what? It doesn't matter what fire. You just confirmed what I already knew. You want to rescue Kate from some fire, but you have no problem sending *me* back to die." Sarah threw her hands in the air. "I don't believe this."

"No, Sarah. I came out here tonight to try going back myself. I thought maybe we could go back together."

Stung, Sarah stood motionless, frozen by the boldness of her mother's statement.

"You need your family, Sarah. I need to find Kate."

Outside, thunder rolled ominously overhead. Large, heavy drops of rain pelted the tin roof above, countering the inferno inside.

"You don't know what I need, Mother. I will never go back there! Never!" Sarah ducked and made a dash for the loft ladder, her Keds slipping on the loose hay, making it more of a scramble instead of a sprint. She paused by the ladder. "We could have had everything we'd missed. We could have made up for lost time. You're a hypocrite! You accuse me of leaving my family behind, but what you did was worse. I'm making up for your mistakes, Dave's mistakes, everyone's selfish mistakes. I'm going to use our powers to keep myself young and alive forever. While you and everyone else withers away and dies, I will live a hundred lives! Starting with Kate's body." Sarah spun away. "See you at your funeral."

Like a viper striking its prey, the pitchfork swung through the air and took Sarah out at the feet. Sarah collapsed on the wooden floor, gripping her ankles in agony.

Her mother stood above her, a look of pure horror on her face. "I never wanted to hurt you, Sarah. I love you." Tears poured down, mixing with the sweat that shone on her face, a face masked with grim determination. "The life you lived maybe wasn't what you chose, but you have lived a long life. You have experienced more than you know. It wasn't a choice…but there is a choice now. Let Kate have her life back. Don't let the same thing happen to her," she said, shouting above the roar of the fire. A wave of smoke covered her face, and she doubled over coughing into her nightgown. "Go back to your family." She gasped again and fell to her knees. "Help me find Kate before it's too late," she managed to croak.

"You're crazy," Sarah whispered. How dare her mother ask her to sacrifice herself to try and bring back Kate. Sarah knew from her multiple travels that it was nearly impossible to control what happened, who you became. The fact she had succeeded in getting a second chance at life was only a small percentage of her ingenious findings. Truthfully, it was mostly a matter of luck.

The fire had brought the temperature to a skin searing high. The smoke gave Sarah the edge she needed to get away. While her mother fought for breath, Sarah snuck down the ladder. Let the crazy old bat find her own way to safety....if she could.

The walls of the barn creaked and groaned, the century old beams blackened and bowing from the fire; the rain hadn't penetrated the tin roof yet. Above her, she heard a thud, the loft floor trembling with the impact. Sarah paused in her descent. It was one thing to wish harm upon Kate, but her mother? Despite all her mother's faults, Sarah knew that invisible tie linking her to the flesh and blood of her mother was unbreakable. She couldn't leave her to burn alive.

Sarah struggled up the ladder, wincing with each step to her swollen ankles. She squinted through the roiling black to see her mother collapsed on the floor, the smoke too much for her fragile lungs.

Sarah swore under her breath. She was risking her life for someone who so casually was trying to end hers.

Sarah crept to her mother's side. "Mama!" she yelled, hoping she wouldn't have to carry her mother from the loft.

Nothing.

Spying the hatch, Sarah unlocked the latch and threw the door open with haste. She would push her mother down the hole and hope for a safe fall. The hard part would be dragging her from the barn before the walls gave way and collapsed on them both.

Sarah grabbed her mother's ankles and pulled her in a jerking motion over to the hatch. She set the body on the edge, never noticing the hazy, swirling blackness below. Sweat poured down Sarah's body, running in rivulets and dropping into tiny puddles on the floor that immediately evaporated in the intense heat. Dizzy, Sarah gasped for breath. Smoke immediately filled her insides, contaminating her lungs. Sarah hacked and heaved in blind, spastic movements. She could no longer see or make sense of her surroundings.

Lightning flashed outside, sending a brilliant light over the terrifying scene inside. The fire had almost consumed the entire loft, and the path to the ladder had been swallowed in flames. The two of them would have to go together. Grasping her mother behind the waist, Sarah scooted up behind her, ready to push them through the hole.

Moaning, her mother rolled her head to the side, her voice barely a whisper. "Do it, Sarah. I am ready."

Sarah looked at her mother, unsure of what she meant. Did her mother think she was trying to kill her? "Don't worry, Mama, I'm going to get you out of here!" Sarah yelled. She gave one mighty push and dropped through the hatch, clinging to her mother tightly, her face buried in the ancient gray tresses of her mother's hair.

Sarah held on throughout the fall, clutching her mother as though she were a child again. She breathed in the tainted lavender and powder, picturing her mother as she'd once known. As she wanted to remember her.

She didn't have to worry about how the two of them would survive the fall. The bales below never caught their bundled bodies.

Though she was sure she had held on as tightly as she could, Sarah felt nothing in her arms. Her entire body went dull and limp, floating in a strange sort of dance that neither went down or up. In all the confusion, Sarah had missed the tell-tale signs the portal was open. But her mother had known.

Somehow, Sarah was certain she had been tricked. Deceived into going back for Kate. Everything, everyone….her entire life had been one gigantic lie. Fury seethed hot and molten through her veins.

Sarah knew she had mere seconds before the portal would decide her fate. She directed her thoughts and energy to the only person that could save her. She closed her eyes and tried to remember everything from the picture, exactly as it had been.

She still had a chance. A one-in-a-million chance.

Chapter 18
Where there's Smoke, There's Fire

"Mary!" I croaked hoarsely, the smoke infiltrating my throat and burning an ashy path to my lungs. "Mary!"

Smoke billowed across the sky forming an enormous black blanket ready to suffocate the tiny twin towns. In the distance, the orange and red flames of the wildfire popped and danced gleefully across the parched land, scoring their way through hundreds of acres in what felt like a heartbeat.

Screams could be heard coming from across the river as panicked families crowded into the river, flooded the train depot, and ran for safety across the narrow wagon bridge leading from Baudette to Spooner. It would do them no good, I knew. The fire would take everything- including Mary and me, the last of the travelers on Vickie's side of the family.

Hitching up my skirt, I raced up and down the street calling again for Mary. Letting loose with a sob, I collapsed on the front steps of Vickie's rickety clapboard house and tried to think. It had to have been McGraw that took Mary. But where? And where was Evan? I needed him more than I'd ever needed anyone. I wouldn't survive the day if he couldn't get us to Canada. But first, I had to find Mary.

Then it hit me.

Racing to the back of the house, I saw the root cellar doors flat against the ground, the lock slid into place. Mary was in there. McGraw was drawing me back to finish me off. Maybe Mary, too. I laid down the shotgun for a moment to lift the heavy wooden latch and open the doors.

A loud crack sounded above and I ducked instinctively, throwing my hands over my head. My skin began to tingle and sing with a burning sensation. I looked to the sky and saw flashes of heat lightning streaking from cloud to cloud, their brilliant flashes a contrast to the darkening clouds of smoke. A surge of hope lifted my heart. What if I hadn't missed it? What if there was still time?

"Mama!" a thin voice called out, weak and frightened.

I jumped, forgetting for a moment why I was there in the first place. "Mary! I'm right here, sweetie. Mama's here," I yelled back, searching for her slight frame in the shadows.

I grabbed the shotgun and descended the stairs. I had no idea if the gun was loaded, but worst case scenario, it would make a solid bat. Scanning the shadows for McGraw, I desperately fought off a shiver of fear. The place reeked of his disgusting presence but I had yet to see him. Like Dave Slater, he had the manner of appearing from thin air.

Beneath the shelves of canned fruits and vegetables, Mary lay curled in a ball, her head hidden in the folds of her dress. I dropped the gun and hurried to her side, scooping her up like an armful of wood.

Mary sobbed and shook. "I was trapped, Mama. The bad man let the doors close behind me and I was trapped. The fire is gonna get us," she wailed, bordering on hysterical. Her chest heaved and hitched as she tried to breathe. Her tear stained face was streaked with grime and dust.

Pulling her dress up over her mouth and nose, I carried Mary up the steps and looked to the river. In no time at all, the fire had reached the center of Baudette and consumed several of the buildings on Main Street. Next it would turn toward the stretch of rickety riverside homes, sustained by powerful winds. The flames would reach and cross the wooden wagon bridge before we could cross to the train depot. Mary and I were trapped. We had to find another way.

A coughing spasm shook my body as I choked on what felt like soot in my throat. My eyes teared and stung, raw and itchy from the smoky assault. I turned for the shores of the bay intent on stealing one of the neighbor's canoes tied up to shore.

Mary's screams reached my ears, startling me from my frantic thoughts.

"The bad man, Mama! Over there," she wailed, completely distraught and continuing to unravel. She was pointing to a nest of trees, pines and tamarack that peppered the neighbor's yard like rustic skyscrapers. I spun around, frazzled and on edge. Was this McGraw's game? To send me to the brink of insanity? Didn't he know I was already there?

Swearing under my breath, I walked backwards to the house. The sky rained down the first of many burning cinders, hissing as they greedily lit the dry grass in polka-dot patterns of fire. The streaks of lightning continued across the angry sky- a reminder to the dry and unstable conditions that only fueled the insatiable blaze.

I dropped Mary at the top of the root cellar, her sobs wrenching the nerves in my skin so tight I could barely think straight. Where should we go? Would the flames catch us before we could make the trek to Clementson?

McGraw appeared from around the corner of the house, toting the shotgun I had left in the root cellar. His face held a grim, resigned determination. He didn't want to kill me any more than I wanted to die, but for now, revenge was the only answer to his aching pride and heart.

"Dan," I said, holding up my hand to slow his steps, "the fire is going to take both towns. We need to leave immediately or all three of us will die."

McGraw stared at the spreading patches of fire that had sprung up from the raining cinders. He seemed mesmerized by their tiny glow. "No," he corrected. "*We* won't be going anywhere."

"But-"

"You're going to get down in that cellar and take the little brat with you. And then I'm going to make my way over to Canada in Ole's rowboat."

"You can't be serious. You could live with the death of a child on your conscience?" I said, choking on indignation and fear. "She's just a child."

"She's going to die sometime," McGraw said simply, throwing his hands up. "We all die sometime." He took a step forward and Mary whimpered. "I told you not to play me, Vickie. I told you to quit your lying and cheating or it would all come back to get you. Sending me to jail was the last straw."

I shoved Mary behind my skirt and swallowed hard. I had nowhere to go.

McGraw raised the gun and pointed it at my chest. "Either walk down those stairs by yourself, or do it with a bullet in your back."

Going into the cellar was a death sentence. I knew that and so did he. I tried one more time to appeal to whatever was left of his conscience. "Dan."

"Get in that cellar!" he roared.

Mary let go of my skirt and scampered down the cellar stairs.

"Mary, No!"

McGraw motioned with the gun for me to follow. He knew I wouldn't leave Mary there alone.

"You're going to hell for this," I muttered. There was no one to save us. Vivie wouldn't return and Evan wouldn't be able to cross.

McGraw laughed at my threat. "I've been living in hell my whole life," he said.

"Well, you're at least going to jail," I shot back. "Vivie knows where we are. She knows you took Mary. Our deaths will be on your head."

"If you think I'll be around when the dust settles, you're mistaken. I'm taking the first train out of here and the cops won't even bother to come looking. Not after this mess."

The conversation was over. My brain couldn't come up with another distraction, another plea.

He watched me march down the stairs. Mary and I stood rigid at the base of the stairs, staring up at him as he bent to close the doors. The only thing I had left were the daggers of hate I shot from my eyes, wishing their metaphorical points could pierce his skin and stab his hardened heart.

The wind dropped bits of fiery wood onto our heads like rain. I tried shielding Mary from the burns, pushing her further into the cellar closer to the shelves and preserves. An eerie howl came down the steps, circled the tiny space and left, just as the second door to the root cellar shut, the wooden latch sliding ominously into place.

"Guess I'll see you in hell," McGraw said through the cracks. He ground his feet into the door when he turned to leave, sending a shower of grit into my upturned face.

I waited a good, long five torturous minutes before going to check the doors. Maybe McGraw had been playing with us. Maybe he had only pretended to slide the latch. Heart hammering, I lifted Mary into my arms, feeling my way along the dirt walls as I climbed the lopsided stairs.

Please let the doors be open. Please let the doors be open, I begged, fighting for control of my weakening reserve. Silent tears oozed from the corners of my eyes and my throat grew tight with dread. When the doors refused to budge, I collapsed on the top step in a heap and bit my lip to keep from screaming hysterically. The chaos could be heard from miles away, the shrieks and sirens chilling me to the bone. No one would be looking for us. No one would be able to hear our cries.

Mary had quieted in my arms, comforted by the darkness and the nearness of my body holding hers. I flopped against the wall in defeat, unsure of what to do. Maybe if I could coax Mary to sleep, she would never know what was coming. She could die peacefully, without fear or pain. I took comfort in the thought that the smoke would probably get to us before the fire. Small comfort that it was. Suffocation couldn't be much better than burning, but what did I know?

I thought of Gran...miserable and disappointed, missing a daughter and a granddaughter that she would never get back. I pictured Dad and Corey receiving the news that Gran would have to share -the disbelief, the rage, the sorrow. Dad would never forgive her or me, for that matter.

I hugged Mary tighter, squeezing my eyes against the onslaught of emotions, reigning in every desire to come unglued for Mary's sake.

It wasn't fair. I would never be married. Never have children of my own. I would miss out on trivial things like Prom and my first car. And worse yet, I was still a virgin. I had come close with Travis, but never all the way. Why that mattered the most at this point in time, I didn't know, but it mattered.

Mary's breath evened out and I realized she had fallen asleep in my arms, her warm body stuck to mine with a layer of slick sweat. I breathed in the smoky scent of her hair and traced the hem of her dress with my fingertips.

A tiny shiver of electricity jolted me from my anguish and into peak awareness. I knew that feeling.

My skin popped with goose bumps and the hair on my neck stood on end. A slow, rhythmic throb began in my head and pulsed its way through my body, numbing the fear and confusion. The cellar became blurred, seeming to shift in a circular, swirling pattern. The walls turned from a solid dirt foundation to a seemingly infinite hole of darkness blacker than night, humming with an energy that was almost tangible.

The portal.

My heart surged and a wave of relief overtook me, weakening my knees and flooding my eyes with fresh tears. I had forgotten about the northern lights from last night and the heat lightning in the sky. Did that make it possible?

No matter where the portal would lead, it would have to mean living....right? I shook my head. Did it matter? Anything was better than facing the fire. I knew without a doubt that the entire town would be reduced to rubble. I couldn't believe for a second that Mary and I would survive through it.

Mary stirred against my shoulder, her fingers digging into the cloth of my dress, clenching the fabric with the grip of desperation. She deserved to live as much as I did.

Outside, loud resounding cracks sounded as one tree after another fell along the bank of the bay. Stray dogs barked and yipped, confused by the onset of pandemonium. Fortunately, most everyone would have made it to safety by now. It would be a matter of minutes before the first homes along the Spooner side of the bay would spark and light up, crumbling to the ground in ash.

Smoke had finally settled over Spooner, creeping its way between the cracks and crevices of homes, and seeping through the wooden pores of the root cellar doors above. I longed for a breath of fresh air; I couldn't remember the last time I'd taken a breath that wasn't laced with smoke.

I had only moments to think- how long would the portal stay open? It was obvious that Mary had the birthmark, but could she travel? If I left her behind she would die; it said so in the papers, and Gran had confirmed it with the family tree history. The choices were slim and dangerous no matter what I decided. Could two people travel at the same time? Would there by anyone out there to trade places with?

I swallowed hard, clutching Mary to my chest. I had the chance to keep her alive, even if it meant destroying myself in the process. One of us might make it through….Mary was younger, stronger. She deserved to live longer than eight years.

I closed my eyes. Conjuring up pictures of Gran and Dad, Corey and the farm, I held my breath as though plunging into a pool of water. Entwining Mary's arms with mine, I gripped her like a vise and whispered a prayer of total faith. It was out of my hands.

Together, we stepped into the vast emptiness.

Chapter 19
Scattered Pieces

Smoke filled my lungs, burning its way down my throat and coating my mouth with a thick, smoldering heat. Fire raged all around me, the heat curling the hairs on my head and scorching the bare skin on my arms and feet.

I rolled to a crawling position, spreading my arms in a vast arc and sweeping my hands across the floor. Like a blind man, I searched with my eyes closed-the heat so intense my eyes refused to open against the attack. Where was Mary? I thought I'd had a good grip on her when I stepped through the portal, but I must have dropped her in the confusion.

Screaming against the pain, I buried my head into the soft cotton of my shirt and tried to gain an ounce of fresh air. The portal hadn't worked. The fire was upon us... and now Mary and I weren't even going to die together. They might never find our bones in the remains of the root cellar.

Focusing on my hands, the skin red hot and blistering, I froze in shock as I realized that I was searching through *hay*. There was no hay in the root cellar. But there was hay in Gran's barn.

Arms surrounded my waist, hauling me high into the air and over a wide pair of oxen-like shoulders. I hung on in silence, petrified and on the verge of collapsing from exhaustion. Before I could register the unsung hero's deed, I was discarded upon the grass just outside the wall of flames, far enough away where I could breathe without choking. Black columns of smoke curled into one massive cloud above the burning building.

Voices and sirens sounded around me. I hacked and choked, retching a few times into the grass. From my limited view, I could make out the familiar buildings of the family farm. I had gone through the portal. Had I brought the fire of 1910 with me? The portal somehow sucking the treacherous fire through to the present time, setting the barn on fire?

And what about Mary?

Remembering the girl's warm body tucked into mine, the way she had quieted at my presence and trusted me to make everything better clenched my heart to a standstill. What had happened? Had she died in the portal? Did she go to another time? Clambering to my feet, I searched the barn's doors for clues. Where had my rescuer gone? I needed to know…to make sure, that Mary wasn't in the barn. No matter how painful and dangerous it would be to go back inside.

Just as I lunged to enter the glowing mouth of the barn doors, arms hugged me around the waist and lifted me off of my feet.

"Kate! What are you..? How did this..? Are you ok? Where's Gran and Grandpa?" Questions fired next to my ear as I struggled to get free.

"Mary!" I shrieked, hoarse and unclear. My mind was on fire itself, my head throbbing with fear. I couldn't fail. I had to save Mary.

"Kate!" someone shouted, sounding blurry and far away. "Katydid!"

Dad's face was in front of mine, inches from my nose. His eyes were large and round, terror screaming from their depths. He was shaking my shoulders and talking so fast, spittle flew onto my cheeks.

Flashing lights approached from the driveway; a fire engine accompanied by an ambulance raced across the grassy trail to where I stood, weak kneed and delirious with aches far beyond the physical.

Paramedics leapt from the ambulance in slow motion, like modern day super heroes, armed with their special weapons of morphine and oxygen, bandages and saline. They swarmed me like a hoard of bees, pushing Dad into the shadows while ushering me to the back of the waiting vehicle. I tried protesting, tried fighting back. They strapped me down, plugged me into a bunch of wires and covered my face with a mask. They wouldn't even let me try and speak. My eyes traveled the length of the gurney, checking my body for signs of extreme burns. Shocked, I noticed for the first time, my body was no longer horribly curved and thick. The heavy swell of my chest had flattened to the width of a pancake. My hands weren't spotted and my skin wasn't jiggling or loose, that I could tell anyway. Not only had I gone through the portal, but I had come back as me. I had my body back...sorry, burned, wreck that it was.

I could feel the motion of the ambulance as it began to move, the IV drip swinging as the driver made the quick turn down the gravel drive. The two paramedics in the back rushed back and forth, taking shears to cut away the damaged fabric of my clothing, passing instruments without a word of instruction. Like they could read each other's minds.

My lips, cracked and dry, moved to form words against the oxygen mask covering my face. I had to tell them...tell somebody, to look for Mary. But no sound came from my abused throat. Instead, the surge of adrenaline that had carried me through the portal started to fade, my insides coming to grips with what had happened on the outside of my body.

A wave of hurt overwhelmed me, sweeping me off my feet and into a massive undertow of pain that wouldn't release its hold. Suddenly, every nerve ending, every hair, every inch of skin on my body began singing in agony. My eyes rolled back in my head and an uncontrollable trembling shot down to the tips of my limbs, making me seize and twitch like bacon in hot oil. I jerked against my restraints, wanting to claw the paramedics in delirious panic.

What usually took minutes to make the trek to town to the local hospital felt like hours....days. As they wheeled me in, the fluorescent lights flashing past my eyes at a hypnotic rate, the pain began to subside, the heat in my skin going from searing to tingling to nothing at all. A peaceful velvety darkness descended on my smoke and fire ravaged body. The hospital vanished....and I was alone.

***

I can't remember how many times I tried opening my eyes before I actually succeeded. It was as though the doctors had sewn my eyelids shut, unwilling to let me face reality. Was it that bad? Would I be disfigured for life?

The hazy view of my room came slowly into focus. Dad sat hunched over in the sole chair, the heels of his hands dug deep into his eyes, his shoulders slumped with fatigue. His shoulders gave a jump and then a shiver. A soft sob tore through his throat and I saw the faintest trek of tears squeeze past his hands, down his cheeks and drop to the floor. The past two months had been insane. I could only guess how flabbergasted he felt being in the hospital for the second time that summer.

"Dad," I croaked, but it sounded more like a garbled moan.

Immediately, his head shot up, the obvious red rims of his eyes the least of his haggard and drawn look. Approaching the bedside warily, Dad rubbed the length of his scruffy face looking as though he had aged a decade since I had last seen him. How long had I been gone?

Pain held me captive; I wanted to reach out and touch his arm reassuringly, but underneath the mask of morphine was the threat of an instant surge of agony if I moved too quickly.

Dad's eyes traced over my face, the weight of worry drawing his mouth down in a frown. "Kate? Honey? Don't try to talk. Just blink or something. If you are ok, blink once." He leaned down to examine my reaction closely.

I blinked once, squinting against the light that seemed to get brighter by the minute. A fierce headache was beginning its tight knot in the back of my neck and working its claws up into my head.

A ventilator pumped fresh oxygen into my blackened, damaged lungs. I closed my eyes, still unable to communicate what I needed to say. It was frustrating being so helpless.

Dad cried openly. He talked to my still form, unable to quell his emotions. "What happened out there, Kate? What happened in the barn?" His breath caught and I heard him sniff and wipe his arm across his face. "What were you doing out there?" he said, the sadness in his voice so heavy and troubled I was afraid it would settle upon me and crush my soul.

How could I tell him? I didn't even know what had truly happened, or what the outcome had been. And where was Gran? Surely she'd had to explain my disappearance by now....my quest. Why did it feel as though I was being accused? Was he upset that I had abused my powers without telling him? Or....did he think I started the fire? The thought hit me like a ton of bricks. *What did he think I had done?*

A nurse entered the room, businesslike and in a sour mood. She checked my machines, my chart, and wrote her name on the whiteboard hanging on the wall. Sue. She barely glanced at me and Dad, wallowing in our apparent misery.

"Sir," she said, her voice firm and hard. "Why don't you take a break? I have to change the bandages and it will be awhile."

I flinched, feeling the little blood I had leave my face at a rapid rate. Apparently, the pain wasn't going to be over any time soon.

"How's my dad, Louis Christenson?" Dad asked, his puppy dog eyes looking almost pathetic in their desperate hopefulness.

Grandpa? Why would he be asking about grandpa? My heart lurched again. The mysterious hero, pulling me from the fire on shoulders wide as an ox. Grandpa had pulled me from the fire and gotten injured as well. But that didn't answer why there was a fire in the first place. I had a hard time believing that fire could travel through time, but the timing was too coincidental not to consider it. Lightning? The portals had been open and they needed lightning to work. Another possibility.

I sneaked a glance at the nurse to see her response, but she kept her head down, not meeting Dad's gaze. Not good.

Did that mean Gran might be hurt, too? What about Corey?

Gasping through my raspy throat, straining to make words that wouldn't come, I tried calling to Dad as he started to leave the room. I needed to know what had happened. Couldn't wait another minute.

And Mary. Poor little Mary who I'd pulled into the unpredictable realms of the portal. Dad hadn't asked about a little girl. Was that why he was so sad?

They'd found her body in the ashy remains? Did he know about Sarah? Had Gran told him anything? What was going on?

Dad disappeared down the hall, his shoulders hunched and curved like an elderly man. He shuffled and moped and lacked any of his usual cheerful, 'glass-half-full' attitude. Which only added to my dread. The nurse approached the bed without a word. The dead calm in her eyes led me to believe she lacked any sort of human emotion. Maybe she was a robot. Weren't nurses supposed to have some sort of pleasant bedside manner to combat the stale depressing environment?

The moment she peeled back the first bandage and air touched the red, blistered mess that was my skin, I didn't care about Nurse Sue's bedside manner anymore. I breathed rapidly in and out for a few seconds, fighting the surge of unbelievable pain until, thankfully, I blacked out.

Chapter 20
The Line Unbroken

"I just don't understand why you would be out in the barn in the middle of the night," Dad said again, dragging the subject up at an awkward moment- right when I was changing into my clothes to be discharged from the hospital.

"We can't talk about it here," I said, my voice scratchy and raw from the ventilator. Irritable from the struggle to pull up my sweatpants with heavily bandaged hands, I did not want to attempt this conversation yet. I could tell by the tone in his voice that the blame was resting primarily on me.

"Can't talk about it here, or can't talk about it at all?" Dad fired back.

Ignoring his questions, I limped to the wheelchair in the doorway and sat down, waiting for Sue to escort me to the parking lot.

I understood why Dad would need answers. He was in a lot of pain, not physical, but mental and emotional. So was I.

He was trying to piece together the night I returned from 1910 and deal with the fact that both his parents were gone. Grandpa had died from the fire-smoke inhalation. Gran had....well, I wasn't sure where Gran had gone.

Dad confirmed no other body had been found in the barn's ashes which left the mystery of Mary. Had I managed to kill her as well?

One of the most baffling parts of the puzzle was that Dad acted like I had been with him the entire time I had traveled to 1910, even when he had gone back to Florida at the end of the summer. Apparently, I had started school, gotten grounded, and missed tryouts for cheer. If Sarah and I had traded places in the beginning, did that mean she had been living out my life? And pretty awfully, too. Was it her life's goal to ruin people's lives once she inhabited their body? If so, where was she now? Back in 1910?

I wanted to scream in frustration. I wanted answers.

How could I prove any of what I had to say without Gran? She had not shared any of my adventure with Dad, and I couldn't figure out why. Was she never aware that the exchange had taken place? All this time I had been searching for Sarah, she had been in my place. Had she told Gran who she was when she made it through the portal? Did either of them plan on getting me back?

My throat felt clogged with sadness, as though sadness were an actual edible thing that sat lodged in my windpipe. Overwhelmed with guilt and horror and helplessness and still suffering from the physical aches of the burns, I didn't know where to turn. I didn't know if I would ever be normal again. I knew I had to make things right with Dad, but where to begin? I needed him as an ally, and it didn't look like he was going to be won over too easily. Again, I wondered why Gran had left the explaining up to me.

On the drive home, we sat silent and pensive, Dad swimming in a sea of grief so deep I wasn't sure he'd ever find shore. We passed Silver Creek Bridge, the water level low enough to have the boats wedged into the brackish, muddy shoreline. Apparently it hadn't rained enough lately…just like the drought of 1910, but not nearly as devastating.

The farm's mailbox came into sight, its overly large, metal barn shape standing out against the traditional narrow, square boxes beside it. I glanced away. I couldn't bear to look at the farmhouse knowing

Gran and Grandpa wouldn't be there. Everything would change. Had changed.

A flutter of movement off to left of the road caught my eye. A flapping of dirty white, like a flag making a peace offering, wavered for a second inside the ditch and disappeared.

"Wait a second," I said, pawing at Dad's arm with my bandaged hand. Straining to see past the steep drop by the side of the road, I leaned over onto Dad's shoulder and propped myself up to see out his window.

"What is it?" Dad asked sounding exhausted just forming the words that came from his mouth.

I waited a second, caught the glimpse of a tractor approaching in the rearview mirror, and shook my head. "Nothing," I mumbled, unsure if I was seeing things or wanting to see things.

Dad pulled to the side and let the tractor pass before resuming our trek to the driveway. Again, a flash of white caught my eye as we turned past the mailbox. A blip of movement and then nothing. Somehow, I managed to pry the door open with my thick, bandaged hand and hop to the ground before Dad had come to a complete stop in front of the iron cattle gate.

I crossed the road heart in my throat, not sure what I was thinking; only I had to see what that white flash was. It beckoned me to come closer…

"Kate?" I heard Dad say, blowing out a sigh of frustration. "What in the world are you doing?"

I crept to the side of the road, not realizing I held my breath. Peering into the overgrown weeds I searched for the flash of muted white and found it, full and beautiful in the dry, sunburned grass.

Mary's dress.

Stumbling down the steep slope, I collapsed next to the ball of fabric, pulling the crumpled form to my chest in a frantic burst of energy. Ignoring the stabs of pain in my hands, I pulled back the rolls of faded fabric to find her face. Her beautiful, angelic, porcelain face.

She stared back at me, startled and frozen in sheer panic. Mute with fear, she let me pull her to my chest, rocking her back and forth as I cried wracking bursts of tears into her hair. Mary had survived. Physically she looked the same. But behind the icy terror in her eyes was a broken, traumatized girl inside.

I realized then, she didn't know who I was. I didn't look like Vickie anymore. I was a fifteen year old stranger, grabbing and hugging her like she was my long lost relative. Which she was…only she didn't know that.

"Mary," I said, "Mary, are you okay?" I didn't understand it. How could she have traveled here and survived? How had she kept her same body and age?

Shaking, she shook her head. No, of course not. She was not okay.

"Mary," I whispered, "I know something really bad has happened. You don't know who I am, but I know who you are. I promise I will tell you everything and I will help you if you come with me." I looked her over from head to toe. She looked thin and battered, her dress torn and stained. She had to be weak and hungry, the dark purple beneath her eyes indicative of little sleep. Where had she been?

Mary didn't respond.

"My house is right over this hill. I have food and clothes. And you can have a nice warm bath," I offered, trying to think of ways to win her over. "I'm a friend of your mom, Vickie and Aunt Vivie," I said, hoping she would connect the names.

Dad appeared at the roadside above, scratching his head as he looked down upon the two of us. "Kate? What are you doing? Who is that?"

Mary shriveled against me, terrified of yet another stranger.

"Dad, this is Mary. We need to help her. She's part of the puzzle."

"What?" Dad looked doubtful, rubbing his hands over his face in that same tired gesture of before. "What does that mean? We need to call her parents?" By the tone of his voice, I knew he could tell it was more than just calling her parents. He looked around nervously, as though he worried we were being watched, or that cops would spring forth from the bushes and cart him off to jail.

Urging Mary to stand, I helped her up the steep embankment to stand by Dad's side. She hid behind my legs, holding tightly to the tail of my shirt.

"I don't know, Kate. This is an awful lot to take in," Dad complained, eyeing Mary warily.

"You don't even know the half of it," I said.

"I wouldn't mind knowing the half of it. Or more like all of it."

Dad's voice held a tremor of anger. I guessed he was still holding all the blame on me. Which it was sort of my fault. Mine and Gran's. But not the fire. I had no idea why I had gone from one fire to the next.

"Look, I told you I would explain everything, but not here and not now." I looked at Mary. "Mary needs us, Dad. She's been through something beyond scary."

***

It took a while before Mary would eat. Her nerves were taut as a stretched rubber band. She was afraid of everything. the running water in the sink, the car outside, the flash of electricity when the lights were turned on...Good grief. She would be damaged for life.

The kitchen was lined with casseroles and cakes, preserves and homemade loaves of bread. All in response to Grandpa's death. His funeral would be on Wednesday and I knew Dad was wondering what we were going to say about Gran. The heavy weight of sorrow filled the empty house, squeezing into every corner and squelching the afternoon sunlight.

Who would take care of the farm?

Corey came through the door moments after we arrived. He had stayed with Dad's brother and his family while Dad took care of me in the hospital. Mary took a shine to him right away. Once her plate had been cleared, she followed his nonstop chatter out the door and all the way to the old tire swing hanging from the oak in the front yard. To Corey, she wasn't a stranger or a nuisance, or a genetic time traveling freak. She was just another kid, which was exactly how she needed to be treated.

Dad slid out two chairs from the table. "Kate, I'm not moving another step until you tell me what's going on. I can't take it anymore."

"I know, Dad. I know." Sidestepping the chairs, I headed straight for Gran's bedroom. The box was there next to her nightstand along with an envelope with my name on it, written in her perfect slanted script. If anything would support the bomb I was about to drop, Gran's notes and letter were like the secret decoder ring to the mystery message on the back of a cereal box.

I didn't beat around the bush. I didn't try to explain the unexplainable. I laid it all out as best I could. From Gran's request and theories, to the pictures of Vivie and Vickie and the fire of 1910. I explained how I had switched places with someone, most likely Sarah, and how she had been lost to the past ever since Dave had thrown her from the bridge. I heard Dad curse beneath his breath when I mentioned Dave.

I hesitated to show him the letter. "Gran left this behind." I set the letter on the table but kept my hand on it possessively.

"I don't get it, Kate. You were with me the whole time. It wasn't like when you dreamed Dave threw Sarah from the bridge. Weeks have passed. You went to school." He drained a glass of iced tea. I had a feeling he wished it was a glass of Jack Daniels. "And what about the link you claim to have? All the generations of women who supposedly have this power pass it down from mother to daughter. You don't fit that piece either."

"I didn't dream Dave throwing Sarah from the bridge, I lived it. It wasn't a dream," I corrected him. Frustrated, I banged my head against the wall behind me. I knew what I was saying was far-fetched, but there was so much evidence. We had a living, breathing child from the past in the front yard!

"Dad, listen, please!"

"And what about the barn, Kate? What about Grandpa?" His voice grew thick and he turned away. "What about the fire? And Gran? What about those answers?"

"I don't know, Dad. I wasn't there. I went from the root cellar to the barn and that's all I know. I never started a fire. I think it may have been an accident. Or lightning! Or what if Sarah started it? It would explain why I had someone to switch with and how I was able to come back." I had a sudden thought, one that took my breath away. Why had Sarah gone back with Dad to Florida? Why had she started to live my life instead of trying to get me back? A sickening swirl began in my head and I grabbed the table for strength. *Sarah didn't want to come back. She was going to leave her children and her husband and live out my life. The fire wasn't an accident. She was getting rid of one of the portals.*

"Stop dragging Sarah into this!" Dad yelled. His eyes darted around the room, as though he was searching for something stable and real. Something that couldn't change before his eyes. "I just can't wrap my head around this, Kate. It's too bizarre." He looked hard at me. "Just be honest. Are you doing drugs?"

There. The accusation was out and on the table. The underlying thoughts Dad had been thinking the whole time.

"What the frig, Dad? Are you kidding me?" I yelled, struggling to keep my composure.

"Watch your mouth, young lady," Dad warned, the vein in his neck pulsing and pushing against his skin.

"Really, Dad? You're going to worry about my mouth right now?" I snarled. "Quit being a parent for a minute and listen to what's going on."

"I will never stop being your parent!" he thundered back, a new flush of red coloring his face almost purple. "I will always be your Dad! I will never stop being your Dad!" The anger left him as quickly as it had come and he sagged in defeat.

"That's not what I meant." The room seemed to be spinning out of control along with the situation.

"I can't bear to think about what you're saying happened, Kate. I can't think about all this craziness. It would mean I could have lost you." His eyes pleaded with me to see his side. "I could have lost you." "His head dropped and tears poured from his eyes like I'd never seen. "You're all I have. You and Corey."

Desperate to gain some sort of stability, I reached for Gran's envelope. Ripping open the letter, I unfolded the stationary. I started to read the words aloud, throwing out Gran's last words like ammunition. *He wasn't hearing me.*

Dearest Kate,

A lot has happened, and I fear we have messed with Fate to the point of disaster. I pray you find your way back to your father. I am leaving this letter for you in hopes my plan will work. Tonight, the Northern Lights were out again, and I must make an attempt to find you. To trade places with you. I have no idea if I can still travel, but I must try. I hope you are doing everything you can to watch the lights and be prepared.

I must confess something terrible. The unthinkable has happened. You and Sarah have switched places. She has taken your body and will not give it back. As much as I do not want to condemn my own daughter, her selfish acts have led me to believe she is a cold, heartless woman, captivated by the powers of traveling. Sarah is consumed with it, and I believe she aims to keep herself immortal by living the lives of others. Sarah has been through more than we can imagine. I am not asking you to sympathize, but to understand her motives. She was lost as a child and forced to grow up too soon. This is no excuse for her to use you, but I don't know what to do to convince her to help.

For some reason, you did not travel in the suspended form as we had hoped. From what little information I got from Sarah, I fear you have been sent to 1910, the year of the fire that claimed my Aunt Vickie and her daughter, Mary. I cannot live with myself knowing you may be left there to die. So tonight, if the conditions are right, I will try to travel. You may

have to come back as an eighty-year-old woman, but at least I will have saved you from the fire. There are no words to express my sorrow and regret. I hope you will find a way to fix what has been broken. Please tell your father everything. I cannot find it in myself to tell him, for I am afraid of what he may do to Sarah. And I don't want to see his eyes when I tell him it was my fault I lost his only daughter. I love you, Kate with all my heart. I know I will see you again someday...in heaven.
  Gran

The last words I spoke were muffled and garbled behind the onset of tears and a new onslaught of emotions.

"I don't believe this," Dad muttered, rising from the table to pace the kitchen floor. "What the hell do you think you were doing, Kate?" He slammed his hands onto the counter, rattling several casserole dishes. "Why on earth would you ever attempt such an outlandish, unsafe, unpredictable, foolish thing?" He ran his hands through his hair, pulling the ends until they tugged at the tender scalp beneath. "Do you understand what you've done? Lives have ended. People are missing. Jesus!"

I flinched. Dad never swore against God.

"You can't throw this all on me!" I screamed back, wiping the tears that stubbornly continued to fall. "Gran asked me to do this! She was obsessed with Sarah and getting her back! I thought we could do it!"

"Your ego is way inflated then, missy. Your first incident was a fluke. A lucky mistake that led us to the truth about Dave. But what you and Gran have done..." he trailed off, speechless for once.

"What we've done?" I stood up to face him, almost eye to eye. "We saved a life, Dad. In case you haven't noticed, Mary is outside running alongside Corey. She was supposed to die in the fire, Dad."

"As much as it hurts to say it, Kate, those things happen. They happened in the past, and that's the way it's supposed to be. You don't travel back and try to change things. Tragedy happens. Look what's happened because of it."

"You might try to pin the blame on me because I'm standing here. But that's not fair. Sarah started this whole mess. She's purposely been traveling, taking people's lives and turning them upside down. She's evil, Dad."

Dad raised his hand against any more attacks on Sarah. "Enough," he warned.

"You don't want to hear anything bad about your precious dead sister," I growled, "but because of her I would have died in that fire. She was going to leave me there. Look at the evidence, Dad. She's been playing me this whole time, leaving her family and life behind for something better. She had six kids, Dad. Six!"

Dad turned as though he'd been slapped. His body caved in on itself and he hunched over the counter for support. Time passed slowly, painfully. Eventually, the vein in his neck receded and his posture began to relax. "I don't want to fight, Kate." He reached out for me and I ran to him, burying my face in his shoulder, desperate for some sort of support. "What are we going to do? What about Gran? Where is Sarah?"

"I don't know for sure," I said.

He rubbed my back for several minutes, staring into space. He seemed to be mulling over everything he had heard and learned, letting it sink in the old fashioned way. With time.

"I need some water," he said finally, his voice trembling slightly. Dad strode to the sink and grabbed a glass from the cupboard. He paused, his gaze suddenly caught on something just outside the dusty glass of the kitchen window. I thought maybe he had spotted Corey or Mary, but he stood frozen, his mouth held in a perfect 'O'.

I was too dazed and numb for Dad's actions to trouble me. I was caught up on something else. *Sarah had left me. Left me to die.* The hateful bitch.

I couldn't breathe. If I had gotten my own body back, that could only mean Sarah and I had switched places. What about Gran? Had she finally convinced Sarah to go in the portal? Or did she arrange an elaborate trick? And Mary? She had been able to travel and keep her own body because, for some reason, Gran had still tried to travel. But she had to have died in the portal, leaving Mary no body to inhabit, but a space to fill in the opposite world.

I felt a multitude of emotions, mixing and separating like oil and water. Gran had done the best she could. It wasn't what we had planned, but in the end, Mary and I had survived. Did that mean Sarah was lost in 1910? Had she appeared in the root cellar just in time to die? How would I ever find out what happened in the barn the night I returned?

Suddenly, Dad's glass dropped into the stainless steel basin, shattering into a thousand tiny shards. Dad didn't seem to notice, but he turned to look at me, his face ashy white. "Oh, no," he said. "The birthmark."

Chapter 21
A Bad Link in the Chain

"You're telling me Mom has the same birthmark?" I asked, incredulous. "No way. I would remember something like that."

It bothered me that he had ignored most of the implications against Sarah and pretty much shrugged off the entire time traveling events that had caused Gran's death.

"That's the thing," Dad insisted. "Your Mom had that water skiing accident when you were about four years old. Sliced her eye right where she had the birthmark. The stitches and scarring kind of ruined the shape and coloring. When you were little, before the accident, you used to try and wipe her birthmark off all the time. Like you thought it was dirt."

I smiled for a second, remembering the intimate moments with my Mom that had long been buried.

"Don't you see, Kate?"

"See what?"

"You thought your powers came from Gran and Sarah, but it doesn't fit. You're not directly in the line. But your mother has the same mark, and if your theory is right, then she's a traveler, too!"

"Dad," I said in a lecturing sort of tone. "That's throwing a wrench into everything. Even I find that hard to believe. What are the chances you would marry a traveler, too? And why would I change places with Sarah and not someone in Mom's family?"

"You said yourself Gran didn't have it all figured out. In fact, it looks like the only thing she got right is how the portals open." Dad began to clean up the broken glass. "Maybe all travelers are interchangeable. Like Legos." He threw the glass into the trashcan. "Am I going crazy?" he muttered to himself. "I'm offering instruction on time traveling." He moved across the kitchen to the pantry. He searched the shelves but walked away with nothing in his hands.

"What, no liquor?" I teased, knowing I had guessed his mission correctly.

"Why didn't Gran say something to me?" He sank down in his chair. He massaged the back of his neck and looked to the ceiling. He was quiet for a long time. "That's why she called us back. Why she faked Dad's heart attack."

He shook his head. "But Sarah didn't want to come..." He let his words die out as he realized how Sarah's actions showed her true intent.

"It was pure luck, Dad, that I'm sitting here today. Gran and I made some huge mistakes. We thought we controlled the power but we don't. And I think..."

I held my breath and then let the next words flow from my mouth as quickly as possible. "I think Gran's dead. I think she went through the portals to try and save me but died. That's why Mary and I were able to both come back. Sarah and Gran were who we traded places with."

"But how is Mary still a child?"

I relaxed a bit, knowing Dad had figured all along Gran was gone. I didn't want to be the one to drop the bombshell after losing Grandpa, too. "I think Gran died in transit. Mary didn't have to change bodies because once we were all in the portal there wasn't an actual body to inhabit, but a space to fill."

I knew the sorrow of facing Gran's death would hit me soon; I had other things to worry about that kept my heart hardened and safe for the moment.

Mary and Corey raced through the door. I noticed Dad unable to keep his eyes from Mary, following her every move with fascination as though she were a ghost.

"Dad, this girl says she lives in Spooner. Where's that? What's she doing here?" Corey snagged his hand beneath a plate of cookies wrapped heavily with Saran Wrap. He dug out four, handing two to Mary. "Where's Gran?" he asked innocently, his mouth shoved half full with cookie.

Though I couldn't believe it possible, Dad's shoulders took another hit and he slouched low into his seat. He smacked his hand over his forehead and leaned back in the chair to stare at the ceiling. Talking was one thing. But living it was an entirely different and complex problem.

I could see the questions tumbling through his mind, the mature, practical adult side taking over, contemplating the real difficulties he was about to endure. Dad was in the real hot seat, not me. He would have to face all sorts of people, some of them family, who would be nosy and unsatisfied with simple, vague answers.

What were we going to do with Mary? What would we tell her? How would we explain Gran? How would Corey handle the deaths of both his grandparents? How would Mary adapt to life in the future? Could there be any sort of repercussions? Jail time? Investigations?

"I think we need to call your mother," Dad said, frowning at the thought. "Maybe she knows more than we do and never got the chance to tell you." Dad gave me a crooked, half-hearted attempt at a grin. "Maybe it would explain a lot of problems in our marriage."

Somehow, I doubted that. "Sure, I'll call her. She'll need to know about Grandpa and Gran."

I left the kitchen before the tears began. I picked up the receiver to the phone on the wall, its long, winding cord twisted round like a braid. I contemplated the conversation I was about to have. How would I begin? Was there an appropriate segue to time travel after delivering devastating news of two deaths? I hated to do this over the phone, but what choice did I have?

Suddenly, I had the absurd thought that there was no way Hallmark would have a card for such a situation. "Sorry your in-laws died, but hey, you can travel through time!"

Dialing carefully with the tips of my bandaged fingers, I stretched the cord into Gran's bedroom to achieve some sort of privacy. I didn't need Dad hanging on my every word, just in case I chickened out and couldn't go through with telling Mom everything.

The phone rang once before a deep, male voice answered.

"Hey, Phil. It's Kate. Is Mom around?" I rolled my eyes. Mom's latest boy toy was my least favorite by far; his intellect equivalent to a goldfish.

"Sure, Kate. She just got back last night from her environmental studies tour at the Boundary Waters up there by Duluth. Weird, huh? She was up there in your neck of the woods for the past two weeks."

I shook my head at this latest bit of news. Typical. She'd told me once she would never set foot in Minnesota again, right after the divorce. But then again, she'd told me a lot of things that hadn't been exactly truthful.

A few seconds later I heard feet pattering down the hall followed by the noisy transfer between hands.

Another few seconds of silence; I could hear Phil's voice fade in the background.

"Well, you never cease to surprise me, Kate. How did you figure it out so quickly?"

Taken aback, I stuttered, "You...you know?" How could she know?

A harsh laugh barked through the connection. "Of course I know. I invented this game."

I scanned the room, my brow furrowing in confusion. Something wasn't adding up. "Mom?" I whispered, my body tensing as though preparing for a sucker punch.

Another laugh. "You wish, sweetie. Maybe you're not as smart as I thought."

"Who is this?" I said. The room began a lazy tilt and spin, as though I'd just stepped off a carnival ride.

"Oh, come off it, Kate! Don't you think our relationship is beyond these games?"

I could see the sinister smile forming behind the lips that would look just like mine. Coming from a face that had once looked like mine. *I invented this game.*

"Sarah?" I said, in utter disbelief. "How did you? Where did you? What are you doing in my mother's house? Where's my mom? What did you do to Gran?"

There was a sharp intake of breath and then a sigh of impatience. "It didn't take long to figure out, but it always takes a little luck. Where they ended up? Your guess is as good as mine, kiddo." There was a lengthy pause. "But if I had to guess, I'd say their remains are somewhere buried in a root cellar right along Baudette Bay."

A scream tore from my lips, shattering the silence of the house. My fingers and toes curled in fury, the plastic handle of the phone digging into my aching hands. "NO! It's not possible!"

Flustered and upset I kicked the side of Gran's dresser, splintering the ancient wood. I followed the kick with another, sending a coatrack flying into the dresser mirror, shattering the glass into a cobweb of lines.

"How could you do this?" I yelled, my voice reverberating through the house. *How had she known about my mother?*

"Really, Kate? You're going to ask me how I could do such a thing?" I fully expected the bitterness and pain from Sarah to ooze through the pores of the receiver. "I expected you to understand. You saw what happened to me first hand. I figured you would be on my side."

I snorted in derision. "I *was* on your side. Even risked my life to come find you. And then I find out you were going to leave me there. Take over my life and leave your family and me to die in the fire!"

The phone was silent for so long I thought she had hung up. I still couldn't believe I was talking to her. After all this time living as her, chasing her, believing in her…I learn she's evil and selfish and manipulative, lower than the scummiest refuse on the bottom of the ocean.

"How did you get to my mom? How did you know she could travel?"

Dad appeared in the doorway and saw the destruction of the room. He took two steps forward but I held him back with a raised hand.

"You're not going to get away with this, Sarah. I know what kind of person you are. You expect me to feel sorry for you? An adulterous, thieving, manipulative, selfish woman who would leave her own children to grow up without a mother."

The familiar buzzing dial tone signaled she had hung up. I knew she would be gone before I could get a chance to find her. She would leave Phil in the dust; take his money and his car and probably hide out plotting her next conquest.

"What happened, Kate?" Dad said. "Did I hear you say Sarah?"

I threw the phone against the wall, its plastic receiver exploding into pieces. "She's got her Dad. Sarah has Mom. Somehow, she went through the portals and switched places with her. She knows there are other travelers." Helpless and furious, and feeling more than destructive, I clumsily palmed a ceramic vase and moved to throw it against the wall.

Grabbing my wrist, Dad pried the vase from my hand and set it back down on the dresser. "I don't understand," Dad said. "Are you saying your Mom went back in time?"

"Not by choice. Sarah channeled her energy to find her and they've switched places. Mom was up in the boundary waters while I recovered in the hospital. There have to be more portals there." My voice rose, hysterical. "We're not going to be able to save her! She'll die in the fire!"

Dad caught me mid-fall, grabbing my shoulders before I could slump to the ground. "Kate! Kate!"

What was I going to do now? I was alone. There was no one that would understand and no one to tell me what to do next. I cried heaving sobs of helplessness that never produced tears. I'd had to be strong for everyone else... now who would be strong for me?

"Kate," Dad whispered as he stroked my hair, "you did everything you could. None of us knew what was happening. How could we possibly have known?"

Neither of us spoke as we digested the latest tragic news. I began picking up the room, my anger spent and the fury drained.

"Kate, let's go home. We'll pack up the kids and we can go back to the life you remember. Before this summer."

I was surprised he wanted to bury the whole thing. To walk away and act like our lives hadn't been permanently altered.

I sighed. "I can't. How can I forget what happened? How can we move on? This isn't some teenage phase we all have to just get through. What about Mom? And Gran? What will we tell Corey?"

"I don't know what to say, Kate. There's no rulebook for something like this. But Gran was right when she said you'd messed with fate too much. I think we need to get far away from here. I couldn't stand it if I lost you. And we have to protect Mary now. This is more than just being about you!"

"This isn't about me!" I fired back. "I can't stop until I find Sarah. She's ruined enough lives."

Before Dad could protest, a flash of movement outside caught my eye.

Like marionettes on strings, we both turned to see Corey and Mary running through the yard, Mary's blonde hair loose from its braids forming a wild halo around her head.

I stared at her, wondering how many more travelers were out there. Would Sarah try to keep herself immortal, jumping from one life to the next? What if she found a way to get to Mary?

I shivered and pulled Dad close, trying to melt the ball of ice that had become my heart. He wrapped his arms around me and the two of us became the mechanism that held the other up.

So much pain. So much loss. And I was sure more would follow. Unless...

The answer came to me like a bullet from a gun, swift and sudden.

I had spent so much time trying to save Sarah, but the reality was... what I really had to do was end her.

Acknowledgments

Thank you to those who pushed the sequel and championed my efforts. I want to thank family and friends for spreading the word and getting the *Linked Through Time* trilogy noticed. Specifically, thank you to Linda for reviewing the sequel before submission and for being the support I needed to get through the down days, and to my brothers, Jon and Joe for their input and push on marketing. Thank you to my Aunt Judy and my mom for providing me with the details on the fire of 1910 and for guiding me on the paths to my first book signings. And of course, thanks to Dad. Without him, there would be no story.

Thank you to Solstice Publishing, especially Kate Collins for her editing and insight to help make the sequel great.

And lastly, I would like to thank Nik Morton for giving my sequel the go ahead, and believing in my story.

About the author

Jessica Tornese's debut novel *Linked Through Time* was inspired by her home town Baudette, MN. She graduated from high school there and continued her education at Minnesota State University-Moorhead where she earned a degree in education. She spent several years coaching in the Junior Olympic volleyball program for Lake of the Woods and taught fifth and sixth grade for two years before becoming a stay-at-home mother in 2003.

Jessica is married and has three children. Her family recently relocated to the town of Jensen Beach, FL, where Jessica hopes to continue her career in writing. To find out more about the author and books she has written, visit

www.jessicatornese.com

Jessica has been voted Solstice Author of 2012.

LINKED THROUGH TIME

Jessica Tornese

Fifteen-year-old Kate Christenson is pretty sure she's about to experience the worst possible summer at her grandparents' rural farm in Baudette, Minnesota. Without cable, cell phones, or computers, Kate is headed for total isolation and six tedious weeks of boredom.

Until the storm.

A freak lightning accident has Kate waking up in 1960. But she is not herself. She's the aunt she never met but has eerily resembled her entire life.

Thrust into living a dirt poor, rural farm existence, Kate struggles to make sense of her situation - a boyfriend with a dark side, a "townie" who steals her heart, and the knowledge that 1960 is the very summer her aunt drowns in the local river.

But was the drowning an accident or a suicide… or something much worse?

"*Linked Through Time* is a wonderfully written book that will have you hooked and unable to put it down… plan on reading from cover to cover in one sitting! Tornese's inventive plot and richly descriptive scenes from rural northern Minnesota are awesome. Highly recommend." –Amanda M.

Other Young Adult adventures from Solstice Publishing

INVISIBLE

Jeanne Bannon

Lola's not pretty. Lola's not popular. Lola wishes she could disappear… and then one day she does just that...

For seventeen-year-old Lola Savullo, life is a struggle. Born to funky parents who are more *in* than she could ever be, Lola's dream of becoming a writer makes her an outsider even in her own home. Bullied and despised, Lola still has the support of her best pal Charlie and Grandma Rose.

Not only is she freakishly tall, Lola's a *big* girl and when forced to wear a bathing suit at her summer job as a camp counselor, Lola's only escape from deep embarrassment seems to be to literally vanish. Soon after, she discovers the roots of her new "ability".

Slowly, with Charlie's help, Lola learns to control the new super power. The possibilities are endless. Yet power can be abused, too…

Then, when tragedy strikes, Lola must summon her inner strength, both at home and at school. She has to stand up for herself, despite the temptations and possibilities of her newfound super power.

A coming-of-age story that will warm the heart.

THE ART OF MAGIC

Ann Harth

Devastated and confused by his father's death, Andrew, almost thirteen and dubbed 'a gifted artist, abandons his painting and turns his back on those who care. He trudges through school and his job delivering newspapers, mainly expending his energy to stay one step ahead of the Thickwit Twits, a group of bullies.

A gift from his dying father sits abandoned in the corner of the kitchen in the tiny flat he now shares with his mom. That is, until Andrew meets Max, an aging and eccentric artist, at the local markets in their coastal Australia town.

Max's stall is filled with dozens of paintings, but they portray only one thing – a specific 19th century cottage. Through his friendship with Max, Andrew embarks on a quest to discover the importance of his father's gift and whether Max's obsession with the cottage is touched with magic – or madness.

Review

As someone who practically grew up with a pencil in his hand, "The Art of Magic" reminded me why I first fell in love with drawing and painting. Great art inspires and sparks the imagination. *The Art of Magic* is more than just the story of two artists who must overcome obstacles. It's also a story filled with hope and along the way, surprises that I didn't see coming.
- Jeffrey Koterba, Syndicated cartoonist and author of "Inklings," a memoir

HIKE UP DEVIL'S MOUNTAIN
Penny Estelle

Ten-year old Andy Thompson disobeys his mother and sneaks into the basement of an old abandoned house that's due for demolition. He stumbles upon a mysterious box under an old cabinet.

And his troubles begin when he looks inside.

The Crew brothers, twelve-year old Jason, and ten-year old Danny, also find their way to the basement. New to town, Jason has established himself as the school bully.

A struggle ensues between Andy and Jason and the bully ends up as a toad.

Somehow, the boys must reverse the magical spell. And that means hiking up the dread mountain: fast pace, fast action and just a few scares and surprises on the way!

The lives of all three boys seem destined to change forever, *if* they survive...

THE WORKHOUSE BOY
James J Deeney

Ireland, 1870s. Times were hard and life was grim in those days. If you had no work, you lost your home. If you had nowhere to live, you went into the workhouse – or emigrated.

This is the story about the brothers Jake and Eamon Miller and their family, buffeted about in those times of hardship...

An early version of this novel was read to schoolchildren in Londonderry and the teacher told the author that she'd never had such a good strong reaction from her children over a story.

James J Deeney lives in Northern Ireland and has won awards for his writing under other pennames.

A COW NAMED JOHN

Gail Picado

Why did you name your cow John? After all, John is a boy's name.

Twelve-year-old Mike Elsasser lives on a farm in 1950s Nebraska. John is his favorite cow – she lets him go cow skiing with her in the mud. He constantly gets asked about her name, but he doesn't feel like explaining. "Just because," he tells them.

Then one day, John gets lost…
…And even worse, Mike finds himself saddled with his younger cousin, Gaylyn, a girl who smiles all the time and doesn't know anything.
While John gets up to odd adventures, the two children have adventures of their own. They fight mosquitoes, make their own ice cream, find a secret passage and risk electrocution in irrigation trenches. They get involved in the trickery of fishing and the hunting of snipe. They learn horse tricks, escape an angry sheep, keep their silly uncle at bay, and even survive a tornado!

A Cow Named John is a nostalgic and humorous story about children on a farm, their antics, and how work can feel like play – and how the search for John can be just as much fun as actually finding her.

MONARCH

Capt. H. C. Loetzerich

Chris Young makes a living as a trapper in the Rocky Mountains of Montana. He finds a bear cub cuddled to the dead body of its mother and takes it into his care and gives him the name Jack. However, not long afterwards, his canoe capsizes in the rapids of a river and he loses all his possessions, and the bear cub.

Abandoned, the little bear must learn to survive in a violent wilderness. Using his wit and lots of luck, over the years the bear grows into a powerful monarch of the forest...

To survive, Jack attacks ranchers' cattle. But he always escapes the hunters. Eventually, the ranchers hire an experienced hunter and tracker, Chris Young.

Yet, even Chris finds it difficult to outsmart the Monarch.

Then, one fateful day, rifle in hand, Chris faces the Monarch, the bear he once called Jack...

A moving parable about the relationship between man and beast. A cry from the heart.

THE LEGEND OF KOOLURA

Michael Thal

Koolura isn't an ordinary girl. She has what every child dreams. She has the *COOL*.

Koolura has doubts about herself. She and her father have relocated so often she has few community ties. Here, at her new school, for the first time in her life she feels right at home.

Koolura is a sixth grade Armenian girl and this story tells how she obtained the *cool powers* and gradually learns to use them. She has the ability to dematerialize at will and reappear where she chooses. She can move objects with her mind and she can even defy gravity!

But will these powers be of any use in stopping a stalker intent on the destruction of Koolura and her friends? He's determined to retrieve Koolura's unrealized *cool* powers with the mysterious decoolerizer.

The hour approaches for her final confrontation with her nemesis, the stalker believed to be responsible for her mother's death.

The second Koolura adventure is due out soon from Solstice!

Made in the USA
Charleston, SC
06 May 2013